A magnificent achievement. A literary tour de force of the first magnitude.
>   --*The Christian Science Monitor Lizard*

Lymore's novel makes *War and Peace* seem like the mad jottings of an illiterate toilet cleaner.
>   --*The Harvard Pornography Review*

Offensive and disgusting from the opening sentence to the final period.
>   --*Mrs. Anita Boning*

The stupidest detective in the history of *noir* fiction.
>   --*Investigation Monthly*

The great American novel has been written. Lymore's erotic masterpiece makes all further attempts at writing fiction as useless as tits on a lawn mower.
>   --*The Greater Southern Literary Quarterly*

Made me want to touch myself.
>   --*Janice M. Wetfinger*

Lymore's work is an excellent argument for repeal of the First Amendment.
>   --*The Smelly Bottom Journal*

Whatever you do, don't let anybody who matters in your life see you reading this book.
>   --*The Mississippi Tribune Review*

William James: Private Dick
The Case of the Missing Pantz

A Blind Otter Publication

Blind Otter Press
otter@blindotterpress.com
ISBN-978-0-9845466-0-2
ISBN-0-9845466-0-X
www.blindotterpress.com

William James: Private Dick

The Case of the Missing Pantz

By
Myron Lymore

A BLIND OTTER PUBLICATION

To Frank Harris

Chapter 1

My name is William Brockforth James. I am a private detective. I work out of a run down office in a run down building in a run down neighborhood of a crap hole city that could be anywhere U.S.A. My office is two rooms above a biker bar called Otto's. Otto's is the kind of place where the barkeeps, the women, and the eggs are hard boiled. It is the kind of place where you can drink hard, buy a stolen derailleur, or borrow a pair of crotchless riding pants for those kinky midnight rides. On Friday nights the twenty-speed mountain bikes line up on the sidewalk outside, and when it gets loud and late you might find some blond Sierra Club slut naked and bent over the pinball machine with the regulars lined up for a go at her. It is a nasty place in a nasty neighborhood, but the rents are cheap and the landlords absentee. That's the way I like it.

I walk through Otto's to get to the wooden stairs that lead to the William James Detective Agency. I named the business after myself.

It was a cold Monday morning. I came in from the rain and shook the water off my overcoat. Otto was behind the bar washing glasses. Old Biker Jim was drinking away the shakes with a whiskey and protein powder breakfast.

"G'morning, Bill," Otto said. A lot of people called me 'Bill.' Otto was one of them. I didn't understand why, but when you live in the naked city you don't rock the boat. Otto had a baseball bat and a forty-five on the shelf underneath the cash register. He could call me whatever he wanted.

When I got to the office Teena was at her desk.

Teena Tigbits was my secretary and receptionist. She was my Della Street, my Dr. Watson, and my Captain Hastings all wrapped into one—an employee, a sidekick, and sometimes a friend. She was a thickset woman of twenty-eight with heavy breasts and hair died red—not red like on Irish women, but red like on fire engines. She looked flushed when I arrived and was sniffing her fingers.

"Teena," I said, "give it a break. It's nine o'clock in the morning for Christ's sake."

"I wasn't doing anything," she protested.

"Any calls?" I asked.

"No. But Mr. Milpy is coming in at ten?"

"Again?"

"Again," she said. Teena took out her cosmetic case to repair her makeup, something she did several times a day, usually after one of the episodes that involved a flushed face and fingers that needed sniffing. I went into my office sanctuary. The office was more a home to me than the sparse one room apartment I kept two bus stops down Seventh Avenue. Home was a place to sleep and heat up a can of Nalley's on my hot plate. Private investigation was my religion and the office was my shrine. My license was framed in knotty pine veneer by the best frame man on Seventh Avenue. I kept it on the wall across from my desk where I could keep an eye on it. My old buddies said the license was no substitute for the badge I once wore. Yeah, I wore a badge—centuries ago. A badge, a radio, a Siamese cat. I had it all. Then one day I couldn't take the corruption any more. I learned things that kept me awake at night. So I got up. And when I was up I took on the uptown boys with their fancy cars and their trophy wives. They didn't like it, and they hit back. They hit back hard. My brothers in blue took it wrong—like I had turned on them—when all I wanted to do was clean out the corruption so honest cops could do the jobs they had been hired to do. It was a bad time and a dangerous time. A lot of innocent people got thrown into outhouse pits on the edge of town. And then Mrs. Ledspregs was impaled on a parking meter. When it was all said and done, the radio was gone. So was the cat, and finally the badge. But that was a long time ago, and I don't like to think about it, or talk about it, or wake up sobbing in the middle of the night over what might have been.

So now it's me, the license, and the Plinker. I told you about the license. The Plinker is a Ruger twenty-two caliber automatic with a nine shell clip that I keep in the top drawer of my desk for the tough jobs. Teena answers the phone, keeps the books, and lends a sympathetic ear when the clients don't pay and I have to sell blood to make the rent. Behind me on the bookshelves I keep my colleagues: Sam Spade, Phillip Marlow, Mike Hammer, Matthew Scudder and a hundred others. They are to me what law books are to the lawyer, what DNA is to the coroner, what KY jelly is to the hooker.

"Mr. Milpy is here," Teena said through the intercom.

"Send him in."

Gerald Milpy came in and took a seat in the client chair in front of my desk. He held a brown briefcase across his knees. Milpy was a small balding man of about fifty. He wore a green sweater vest over a plaid shirt. He waited for me to speak.

"What is it now, Milpy?" I asked.

"I think that my wife is cheating on me."

"Mr. Milpy," I said, "your wife is cheating on you.

You have hired me six times. Your wife has sex with almost everyone she meets during the day. She has sex with men and women, and if she went to the zoo she would probably have sex with the animals. I have provided you with pictures on six different occasions. She knows when I am taking pictures of her and she likes it."

"We are all human, Mr. James," he said. "Things are not always as they seem and I will not take any action that will endanger my marriage unless I am absolutely certain. I would like you to investigate one more time." There was nothing I could say to dissuade him.

"A hundred dollars a day plus expenses," I said.

"I know the cost, Mr. James, and I appreciate your patience with me. I will leave a five hundred dollar retainer with Miss Tigbits."

"You do that," I said.

A lot of my cases were divorce cases. Go out and prove the spouse is cheating. Believe me, they are all cheating. Now and then the local insurance agent would toss me a missing car case or sic me on someone trying to scam the disability board, but for the most part it was cheating spouses. Then Patricia Pantz walked into my office.

Milpy was gone. I was studying the techniques used by Mike Hammer while Teena cleaned my office. She was wearing some sort of peasant dress with a flowered top that was having a hard time containing her breasts as she moved. She found some a stain on my desk that I had never noticed and was leaned over the desk rubbing it—a position that gave me straight-line view down the top of her dress.

"Don't you ever wear a bra?" I asked.

"Are you telling me how to dress?"

"This is a place of business," I pointed out.

"Bra's are not healthy. They constrict. This is a Romanian sheep herder dress. It allows the blood to flow. A person can breathe. And quit looking at my tits anyway."

"How can I help it when they are hanging out in front of me?" I said.

"Go ahead then, work on a filthy desk." She stood up and was rearranging her body inside the dress when we heard the bell. Teena finished adjusting herself and went to see who it was. A few minutes later she returned and handed me an intake sheet. "It's a new client. Her name is Patricia Pantz."

Teena escorted the woman into my office and directed her to one of the client chairs. Miss Pantz was a pleasant looking woman of average weight and height. About thirty years old, she had dark brown hair that fell across and obscured one side of her face. She was dressed in gray jacket and skirt with a white blouse beneath. It was the outfit of a secretary or maybe an accountant.

"You may go now, Teena," I said. Teena stuck out her tongue at me and left the room. I turned to Miss Pantz and said, "My name is William James."

"Like the philosopher?"

"Philosopher?"

"William James. Psychologist, philosopher—radical empiricism. Had a brother, Henry."

"Miss Pantz," I said in my sternest voice, "this is the William James Detective Agency. I am William James, the owner. I do not have a brother. If you want to hire a philosopher or a person with a brother named Henry you have come to the wrong place."

"Never mind, Mr. James," she said. "I am looking for a detective. You came highly recommended."

"May I ask, Miss Pantz, who made that recommendation?"

"A girl named Betty," she said. "She comes to the library. She may not actually be a girl, but she does come to the library." Betty was an old memory from my early days in the city. It was so long ago I thought she would have forgotten me, and here she was sending me clients. Miss Pantz flushed. "She said you had a very large, ah . . . imagination. Yes, she said your . . . firm steady imaginative approach to investigation could bring even the most resistant cases to a very intense conclusion."

"You can see," I said, "from that license on the wall behind you that you have come to the right place." Miss Pantz glanced behind her. "So what kind of detective work do you need?" I continued.

"My sister, Candace, is missing. I want you to find her."

"Excellent," I said, "missing persons are my specialty, especially if it leads to a murder. Do you think that your sister's disappearance will lead to murder? Maybe she herself was murdered."

"Oh, Mister James, don't even say that. I am sure she is alive."

"I take that back then. Pretend I didn't say it. I am sure she is fine. Tell me about her."

"Candace is an exotic dancer. You could call her a stripper, I suppose, but I have seen her work and it is always very tasteful. She worked at a gentleman's club called Totally Naked Women Here. The club is over on Fourth Avenue next to the longshoreman's union hall. She worked most nights until 2:00 A.M., after which she would go out with gentlemen friends to relax. I am a librarian at the public library over on Mulberry Street. I used to work in the stacks, but now I work at the reference desk. I go to work in the morning and most mornings I would meet Candace over breakfast. She would be coming home and I would be leaving."

"The two of you lived together?"

"Oh, yes. I should have said that. We share an apartment a few blocks from here. The address is on the form your assistant had me fill out. Saturday night she did not come home and no one has seen her since. I went down to Totally Naked Women Here, and they hadn't heard from her. They were very helpful and several of the patrons seemed generally concerned that she might not be coming back. But no one knew where she was."

"Did she have a boyfriend, or maybe a girlfriend who she might be staying with?"

"No. Candace was very predictable. She didn't have a boyfriend and none of the girls she worked with know where she might have gone."

"What do you think happened?"

"I think she was kidnapped. The men at that club all seemed very nice, but I have heard things. I worry that she has been kidnapped and is being held by several large muscular men with big pecs and large penises who are having sex with her, one after another, against her will. They could be making her assume unusual positions so that they can take pictures of her vagina to sell to the publishers of dirty magazines, or they could be putting their penises in her mouth, and doing things I can't even say in mixed company. I am so afraid for her that I can hardly sleep at night from thinking about those things."

"Kidnapping, and sexual slavery," I said. "That is quite possible. Do you have a picture of her?"

"Yes, of course," she said. "I knew you would want one, but this is the only one I could find." She handed me a picture. Candace was a pretty blond of average height and weight. In the picture she was sitting on a couch naked. Her legs were spread and she had one hand in her crotch holding her shaved labia apart with her fingers. "That was taken at a party we threw at the apartment last Christmas," she said. "It was a very successful party. The men at the library have all encouraged me to hold another one this year, but it wouldn't be the same without Candace. She still wears her hair like it is in the picture."

"I'll get some fliers made to post around the neighborhood," I said.

"You mean you will take the case?" Patricia said.

"Yes, Miss Pantz," I said.

"Call me Patty, please."

"Patty, it is," I said. "Now, about the fee. I charge a hundred dollars a day plus expenses."

"I have very little money," she said. "I was hoping to be able to pay my initial retainer with this." She stood up in front of my desk, unhooked a clasp at her waist, and let the skirt fall to her ankles. She was wearing nothing beneath except a black garter belt and stockings. Her vagina was shaved, and my dick jumped to attention.

"We should be able to work something out," I said keeping a close eye on her crotch in case it tried anything funny.

"Oh, that is wonderful, Mr. James," she said. "Would you like me up on desk? Or maybe bent over the desk? Or I could get on my knees and suck you and lick your testicles. That is always nice."

"Patty," I said, "I am a normal man and you are a beautiful woman. I want all of those things, but the detective code requires that I make a breakthrough in your case before I have sex with you. I will go down to

Totally Naked Women Here, find out what I can, and stay in touch with you by phone."

"But Mr. James," she said, "after hearing Betty speak of your skills, I really want to pay some of my fee in advance." She pulled her blouse open, and thrust a pair of smooth round breasts toward me. Both nipples were rock hard.

"No, Patty," I said. "You are beautiful, but I am bound by the code." She saw that I was serious about my work and began buttoning up.

"So when *do* I get to pay my fee?"

"Soon, Patty, soon." She picked her skirt off the floor and left the office holding it in her hand. Outside the office door I could hear the sounds of Patty and Teena talking. I leaned back in my chair and pondered the case of the missing Candace Pantz. *Where was she? Was she being held a sexual slave as her sister suspected, or was that just Patty's imagination?* Nothing but questions. Once I heard the outside door slam, I grabbed my jacket and went to the outer office. I was immediately assaulted by Teena.

"Why did that woman come out of your office with no underwear on?" Teena demanded.

"She is a librarian?" I said.

Teena puzzled over my answer for minute and then had a flash of understanding. "Oh," she said, "I get it." She sat back down at her desk and looked up at me.

"What kind of librarian?"

"Reference desk," I told her.

"Oh my God," Teena said, putting her hand over her mouth. "Those women know things—secret things that can drive a man insane. Tell me, Mr. James, what did she do to you in there?"

"I can't say, Teena. Client confidentiality."

Teena pouted. "So are we representing librarians

now. It may be nice for your penis, but are you sure you want to take our reputation down that road?"

"Librarians have missing sisters who might have been kidnapped and forced into sexual slavery too," I said.

"I guess they do," Teena conceded. "But I don't like it when I have to look at bare-assed women coming out of your office."

"I will advise Miss Pantz of your concerns, Teena," I said. "It won't happen again."

I left the office to walk the streets of the city. Otto's had started to fill up with the brunch crowd. Otto motioned me over, and I took a seat at the end of the bar away from the bikers. The spandex wrapped patrons were pouring the free granola into their whiskey. Riding shoes clicked on the cement floors when they walked. It was a good place to speak softly and make your stays brief.

"That secretary of yours," Otto said. He was a large bearded man hanging on to the biker life despite his advanced age and weight. No longer safe on the racing bikes, or even the mountain bikes, he pedaled a titanium three wheeler with riser handlebars.

"Miss Tigbits?" I said.

"Yeah, her. Is she a sport?"

"I don't think she knows much about sports, Otto. I have never heard her mention any kind of sport."

"I mean does she like to show it. We are planning a wet t-shirt thing here on Friday for the regulars. As you may have noticed biker chicks don't normally have much in the boob department. I thought we could ask your secretary to come down and add a little meat to the party for a grand finale." He looked down the bar. "Think about it while I pour a couple of drinks." I did what he said and thought about it, but it didn't make sense. *Was Otto on the up and up? What was he really planning? Did these people really want to look at Teena's breasts?* The questions were going round and round in my head when a muscular woman shrink-wrapped in bright yellow racing spandex sat down next to me.

"The name's Brett," she said to me. "I'm a woman. Brett can be a name for a man or a woman but I'm a woman."

"Good morning, Brett," I said. She had short brown hair and intense eyes that seemed too wide open as if she was stuck in a perpetual state of alarm.

"Feel that bicep," Brett said, clinching her fist on the bar. I reached out poked her bicep with my index finger. "Hard as a man's, but I'm a woman. I'm in perfect physical shape. You think I'm not a woman because I don't have tits. That's because of the exercise. Not every woman tits hanging down her chest."

"I know that," I told her.

"I got nipples though, women's nipples. You can see the bumps through the spandex."

"Yes, I can see them," I said. It seemed best just to go along.

"Go ahead. Pinch one. You know you want to."

"I'd rather not," I said.

"I'll do it." She took one of her nipples and twisted it hard in between her thumb and forefinger. "Doesn't hurt at all. I rode over here on Monroe Street. Do you know what that means?"

"No I don't," I admitted.

"You don't ride, do you?"

"No," I said, "I never took it up."

"Monroe is the bumpiest street around. Do you know what riding a racing bike with a hundred and twenty pound tire pressure over a bumpy street with a skinny little hard-as-a-rock seat between your legs does to a woman?"

"Not really," I admitted again.

"Well, it ain't pretty," she said, "and it ain't dry. Gets you fucking wet down there."

"I suppose it does."

"You can touch me there," she said. "I don't mind. You'll be sure I am a woman then. Won't find no cock down there. All pussy, even if I don't have no tits."

"I'm sure you are all woman."

"You are Williams James aren't you?"

"Right," I said.

"The detective?"

"Right again."

"I saw that woman going up to your place."

"What woman?"

"The woman in a gray suit. I know her. She's a librarian, a reference librarian, over on Mulberry Street. No wonder you don't want to touch a biker woman who looks like a man when you got librarians bringing their stuff to you right in your own office. I can't compete with that, can I?"

Otto returned and saved me. He said, "Take a hike Brett. Bill here does not want to feel your nasty snatch." Otto had called me 'Bill' again. It was now a pattern and I made a note of it in my clue book.

"Fuck you, Otto," Brett said, sliding off the stool and moving on to the next guy down the bar.

"This thing Friday," Otto said to me, "is a fund raiser for cyclists hurt in collisions with parking meters." My mind flew back to the bad old days. Mrs. Ledspregs died when she hit a parking meter. The meter was supposed to break away on impact and prevent that kind of death, but the new meter poles never made it onto the streets. I was there when they pulled her body off the pole. That was when the night-mares started.

"We get drunk," Otto said. "We do a few wheelies on the sidewalk in front of the place, and yell 'show us your tits' at the ladies. All in good fun. I'd be willing to slip your girl Teena a fifty if she were to top off the night with an innocent little jump-and-jiggle on the pool table."

"I will send her down to talk to you," I said.

I walked down Seventh Avenue to the rented garage where I kept my refurbished '78 Gremlin GT with glass packs. A turn of the key and it roared to life. Out on the streets the gray clouds had fallen on city like a wet mop. The pimps were waking up their ladies to get them stoned and dressed for the evening trade. Businessmen were grabbing their secretaries for nooners at cheap motels. Junkies were starting the never ending search for another score, and William James, the private eye, was on the prowl. I stopped at Mings deli for a hoagie, a quart of bad coffee, and a carton of Marlboro's. Stakeouts are ugly business.

I drove down the tree-lined streets in a quiet resi-dential neighborhood and parked across from the op-ulent Milpy house. Nothing was moving. I unwrapped the hoagie and slopped down some coffee. After ten minutes I saw someone peeking out through a cur-tain. A couple minutes later Mrs. Milpy appeared on the front step. She was a tall black woman about forty years old. She was not fat but had large breasts and the kind of protruding round butt common in the race. I reached in my glove compartment for the cam-era. We were old hands at this. Mrs. Milpy was wear-ing a loose white sun dress with spaghetti straps and white pantyhose. She spotted me and lifted her skirt. Her black vagina was framed by the crotchless panty hose. With the hand that wasn't holding her skirt up she pointed at her vagina and made kissing motions in my direction. I dutifully took a picture. She grabbed her crotch like a baseball player adjusting himself and thrust her hips in my direction. I took another picture. She turned and walked down the sidewalk with me following slowly in the Gremlin. Every twenty steps or so she would flip up the back of her dress to expose her ass Each time I took a picture.

Coming to a small community park Mrs. Milpy approached three teen boys smoking cigarettes on a bench. She started talking to them and pointing to some nearby bushes. As she spoke she lifted her black breasts out of her dress for the boys to see. It scared them, and the three ran away. I followed her to a convenience store and parked at the farthest end of the parking lot. She hadn't been inside for more than a couple of minutes when she came running out, breasts bare, chased by a small Asian woman swinging a broom. "No fuckee suckee in here," screamed the broom-wielding store owner. "You no come back." Mrs. Milpy stood at the edge of the property and gave the Asian woman the finger. She put her breasts back inside the dress, straightened the rest of her clothes, and proceeded to a small tavern a hundred yards down the road. I stayed outside finishing my hoagie. When done with the sandwich I went inside. Mrs. Milpy was in the back of the tavern where I could hear two men explaining to her forcefully that despite her willingness to spread her legs on the pool table, she would have to put up a quarter and wait her turn like anybody else who wanted to use it. She came out of the pool area pulling down her dress in disgust. After she took a stool at the bar and ordered a beer, I slipped onto the seat next to her.

"Tough day," I said. She looked at me with tears in her eyes.

"The worst, William," she sobbed. "Nobody wants me any more."

"They are crazy. You are a beautiful woman."

"Do you really think so?" she said, drying the tears. "I wish Jerry thought so."

"Mr. Milpy loves you. He would do anything for you."

"All he loves is the pictures you take. It breaks my heart." She started to cry again. "Mr. Williams, could you do me a great favor and fondle my pussy. It would make a bad day a lot better." I slipped a hand beneath the bar. She spread her legs enough that I could cup her labia in my hand. My dick snapped to attention. "That feels so good," she said. "I am feeling better already. Slide a finger inside down there." I did. "Can I touch your cock?" she asked. I couldn't say no. She reached over and grasped my erection. "Damn, Mr. James," she said, "that's the biggest cock I ever felt on a white man."

As the words escaped her lips memories came rushing back. "Don't say that," I screamed.

"But why?" she asked. "It was meant as a compliment."

"That is what *she* said."

She squeezed my cock. "Who was *she*, William? Tell me."

"It is a sad story," I told her.

"They all are. Let me get you another drink." She looked at me with her big brown Negro eyes and squeezed my hand between her legs. With my hand on her wet snatch, I told her my story.

"I was born and raised in a small farming town in

northern South Virginia called Cuckold Falls. It was bucolic place nestled in rolling hills along the Misty River. I lived on a shady street near the edge of town where I spent my summers playing with friends in the fields and orchards that surrounded the town. It was a place where nobody locked their doors. We played baseball and drank lemonade in the summers. We raked leaves and carved pumpkins in the fall. I was fifteen and deeply in love with skinny freckled Amanda Tiddyliddle who lived down the street. We were learning about the birds and bees the country way, in the fields and haylofts. She and I would pull down our pants and curiously inspect each other behind old man Jensen's barn. She had tiny budding breasts and a wisp of fine blond hair on her pussy. For us, sex meant sneaking upstairs and listening at the door as Henry Whittle, the running back on the high school football team, boned Amanda's older sister. It meant her giving me hand jobs up in her bedroom and me shooting semen across the room so that it hit her poster of Doris Day and the both of us giggling together at the sight of Doris with cum dripping down her face.

"I have always been small in stature except down there in my pants. Amanda and I were innocent. We had no idea that I was unusual because we had nothing for comparison. In Cuckold Falls, I made up for my small stature with guts and determination. During football season I couldn't compete in blocking and tackling with the big farm boys like Henry Whittle, but I could kick a football a country mile, so I made the team as a freshman kicking field goals. I did my paper route in the early morning, practiced with the team after school, and then walked the country roads with Amanda.

"Then *she* happened. I was having a burger down at the drug store when my Aunt Salome came in to pick up a prescription. She saw me eating in the booth and said, 'William, how are you?' I told her I was fine and she slid into the booth next to me. She was my mother's sister and lived across town. Her husband owned the local hardware store and was the chairman of the Cuckold Falls town counsel. She was a big woman who liked to wear dresses that displayed her ample cleavage. She was wearing one of those dresses that day. I was at that age where I had an erection every morning, at random times during the day, and definitely any time I got near a woman's breast. There I as looking down Aunt Salome's cleavage and my young cock jumped to attention. She must have caught me looking, because the next thing I know I feel her hand on my dick. I was terrified. A grown woman, my mother's sister, was touching my penis. She was surprised too. She turned to me and said, 'William, that's the biggest cock I ever felt on a white man.' And with that comment my whole life turned upside down.

"She said I should come home with her and in those days when an adult told me to do something I did it. At her house she took me up to her bedroom and made me stand in front of her while she sat on the bed and pulled down my pants. She held my thing and told me that God had blessed me with something very special. She then pulled her dress over her head and took off her bra. Her giant tits tumbled out into the open air. 'Touch them,' she said. I held them in my hands and pinched her huge brown nipples. She pulled off her slip, wriggled out her girdle, and spread her legs on the bed in front of me. She had black pubic hair that started above her knees and ended just below her belly button. At her pussy the hair was thick and oily. She spread her labia with her fingers, exposing the pink insides. 'Kneel between my legs,' she ordered, and despite my fear, I did as I was told. She pulled me onto her, directing my cock inside her pussy and hugging my face between her giant tits. She smelled of sweat and cheap perfume, but all of a sudden, that didn't matter any more because my cock had gotten its first taste of a woman. Inside her warm wet hole, feminine muscles clamped around me. I liked it and I wanted to stay there.

"She taught me to fuck. I was young and inexhaustible. I fucked her until I came, rested a few minutes, then, trying not to look at her, I would climb on again. When I opened my eyes I saw her writhing like a obese pink salamander stuck in shallow water, and I realized that it was my cock that was making her do that. I learned what my cock could do to a woman.

"I left her room that day, ashamed and confused. 'Come back tomorrow,' she ordered, 'after football practice.' I told her that I couldn't. I had to meet Amanda, but she just stared at me as she wiped her hairy crotch with a towel. 'Tomorrow,' she ordered. 'After practice.'

"I showed up the next day, and the day after that and the day after that. She would not let me go. She had me do her in the living room and the kitchen and the garage and in the back yard. She sucked on me and put my cock in her anus. She told me over and over that she had never seen such a wonderful thing on a white man and called me her 'little Mandingo.' Amanda wondered why I never came to see her any more. I wanted to, but Aunt Salome demanded me, and, to tell the truth, I liked it.

"Then one day after practice I arrived at Aunt Salome's house and there was another woman. Aunt Salome introduced me saying that the other woman was a member of her Wednesday night Woman's Philosophy Club and that I should go with her. The woman was Mrs. Dimplick the wife of the Chief Dimplick, the head of the Cuckold Falls police department. She was a thin woman about fifty years old. She took me to her house, and she pulled down my pants. It was like she'd never seen a man before. She fell to her knees and stated kissing my balls and my cock. Then we went out on the veranda where she made me fuck her several times. A couple days later Aunt Salome handed me over to Mrs. Coffsock, the husband of Judge Coffsock. Mrs. Coffsock had hooks and straps in the basement of her home where she made me tie her to the wall, put clothespins on her nipples, and then fuck her. They handed me from one to another until every member of the Wednesday night Woman's Philosophy Club had a go at me. I was exhausted every day. My school work suffered. My coach was constantly asking what was wrong, and my beloved Amanda, feeling abandoned, ran off with a traveling circus.

"It all came to a head the one afternoon in Mrs. Wallsmang's potting shed. She was on top of me in the froggie position bouncing up and down on my dick. In walked Mr. Wallsmang looking for a crescent wrench. 'What the hell is going on here,' he yells. He drags Mrs. Wallsmang to the house by her hair and I end up running bare assed across a fallow field toward the old Henderson place. Under pressure, Mrs. Wallsmang admitted everything and turned over Mrs. Coffsock. Mrs. Coffsock ratted out Mrs. Dimplick and within a few days the whole thing had come unraveled. There were secret meetings at city hall. Although

I had helped get our high school football team to the
regional championships, I became a pariah at school
and on the team. The locker room was an icy hell after
it became clear that I had fucked most of my team-
mates' mothers. I dropped out of school and hid out
in my room at home.

"The women who had used me then turned on me.
They claimed that I had used secret powers to over-
come their resistance, that they had been hypnotized,
drugged, and blackmailed. There were more town
meetings. Our house was vandalized. Then one Saturday night the mob came. They carried torches and
had worked themselves into a frenzy. Mother, father,
and I could hear them outside the house. 'Hang him
by the balls,' 'Cut off his tallywacker.' My father took
me aside and told me that I would have to make a run
for it. The law would not help me in view of the fact
that I had fucked the wife of both the chief of police
and the local judge. The crowd was demanding that
my parents turn me over. We devised a plan. My father went out and told the mob that I couldn't come
out because I was in the bathroom taking a dump and
that I wasn't trying to escape out the back door. He
went on to say that as soon as I was done, he would
bring me out so they could cut off my tallywacker.
The crowd was satisfied for the moment and I, with
just the clothes on my back, a sack lunch of a tuna
sandwich and an RC Cola, headed out the back door
and into the cold cruel world. I learned later that the
crowd eventually got tired of waiting and went home
grumbling about people who take forever in the bathroom.

"That night I huddled in the cold beside a farm
house listening to the big game on the radio through
an open window. With five seconds left, the score

tied, and only ten yards from the goal line the team had no one to kick the field goal. They went for the touchdown and failed. I could have made that field goal. They lost because of me."

Mrs. Milpy was sobbing openly on the bar. "That is the saddest story I have ever heard," she said. "I will never say that again, about your having such a big pecker for a white man."

"Let the past be the past," I said. "Let's finish these drinks and I'll give you a ride home." On the way back Mrs. Milpy came up with an elaborate ruse whereby we would use a tripod and timer for my camera to fake the pictures that her husband wanted. We would make sure that my face did not actually appear in any of them. When we got back to the house she had me pretend to have sex with her by putting my penis inside her black vagina and moving it in and out with my hips. Then she had me put it in her mouth and she simulated fellatio. Her simulation was so convincing that I ejaculated in her mouth twice. We pretended to have sex with my cock between her breasts and then in her anus. When I had my thing in her butt I learned that Mrs. Milby was a closet racist. She was going up and down on my cock with her anus when she started panting and saying the 'N' word in conjunction with what a slut she was. I found it mildly offensive but didn't say anything. We got so involved with the simulated butt-fucking that we completely forgot to take pictures.

When we were both exhausted from all the pretending she brought me beer and chips. "How many days of surveillance did my husband pay you for?" she asked as we sat there naked in her living room.

"Five days," I said.

"Tomorrow we can use the patio. I can set up some better lighting. How early can you be here?"

"Not tomorrow," I said. "I'm on a big case. It may be a while, but the pictures we took today will satisfy your husband."

"Oh they won't be near enough, Mr. James. You get back here as soon as you can."

I dressed and left. Mrs. Milpy was a great looking woman and all that pretending to have sex with her had made me horny. I called Teena.

"William James Detective Agency," she answered, "Teena Tigbits here. How can I help you?"

"Teena," I said, "it's me. Any calls?"

"Nothing."

"I am going over to Totally Naked Women Here to snoop around for Candace Pantz. You can leave, but stop off and see Otto. He wants you to expose your breasts at some sort of benefit event he is having."

"That is disgusting," Teena said. "What makes you think I would ever do that?"

"Okay then, don't talk to him."

"Well, I might talk to him. Is it for a good cause?"

"Yeah, to help people killed in parking meter accidents."

"That sounds like a good cause. If my breasts could help . . ."

"Sure Teena, it's a great cause. I will see you tomorrow."

I fired up the Gremlin and headed for the industrial district. The sun was going down, and the dark side of the city was coming alive. Down by the docks the longshoreman were putting down their loads and heading to home or to the bars or to places like Totally Naked Women Here. I pulled into the parking lot of the club and killed the engine. The club was a squat gray building with a single door. At one time the building had been a gas station. Someone had torn out the pumps, painted over the windows to the mechanic bays, and called it a tittie bar. On top of the building was an enormous lit sign designed to be seen from a nearby elevated freeway. The signed blazed, "Totally Naked Women Here." I climbed out of the Gremlin and headed for the door with the picture of Candace Pantz folded in my jacket pocket. Outside, a couple of black men smoked cigarettes waiting for people who wanted to buy weed. I took a mental picture of both of them and filed it away for further reference. Walking through the door I found myself face to chest with a large young black man wearing a tuxedo two sizes too small.

"Five dollars," the black man said. "Cover charge."

"I am not here to look at naked women." I handed him the laminated wallet version of my investigator's license.

"*Totally* naked women," he said.

"What?"

"You said, 'naked women.' We have *totally* naked women."

"What's the difference?" I asked.

"Ours are completely naked. That's what 'totally' means in this context."

"Well, I am not here to look at totally naked women."

He stared at my license for a long time and looked look up. "Private dick?" he asked.

"As private as any other man's," I said. "Why? Have you heard something?"

"I mean are you a gumshoe, a PI, a shamus."

"That's right," I said. "You got me figured. That gives you the advantage and I don't like that. Who are you?"

"Bjorn Frow," he said, "bouncer and stripper security. Are you here you on a case?"

"You got me figured again, Bjorn. You're a pretty smart guy. I can always use a smart guy on my side."

"Honest?" Bjorn said. "I thought maybe if I ever gave up the stripper security gig I could take up being a dick. A lot of bouncers in strip clubs become dicks."

"Right Bjorn," I said. I handed him my card. "Call me some time. If I'm in a good mood I might let you ride shotgun while I work. We'll see if you got what it takes." I handed him the picture of Candace. "Do you know this woman?"

He looked at the photo. "That's Candy Pantz," he said.

"Wrong," I said. "Her name is Candace. She is missing."

"This is Candy Pantz. Candy is a nickname. Like your name is William James. People call you Bill. People called her Candy, Candy Pantz." I don't know how he knew about the 'Bill' thing, so I made a note of it in my book.

"Don't play with me, Bjorn," I said. "You say this woman was going under an alias?

"I don't know anything about going under an alias. What the girls go under in their spare time is their own business. I just know that picture is of Candy Pantz. She works here. Or at least she did."

I looked the place over. It was the kind of crap hole tittie bar that gave crap holes a bad name. The owner had stripped out the car lifts and put a couple of Swiss travel posters on the wall, but it still looked like the inside of a gas station. The centerpiece of the action was a small stage with a brass stripper pole. At one end of the room a guy was beating on a pinball machine. At the other, a bearded bartender drew draft beer for a couple of blue collar types getting a cold one after work. The tables around the stage were empty except for one skinny fellow sitting at the stage wearing a red plaid hunter's hat with ear flaps. A young Asian woman in a Kimono shuffled onto the stage. The bartender leaned into a microphone by the cash register and a bored voice came through the sound system. "Straight from the steamy streets of Tokyo, give a big hand to Finger Mi." His voice was replaced with some pseudo Japanese music. The woman began to gyrate to the rhythm while the man at the rail with the hunter's hat applauded manically. The men at the bar glanced over their shoulders and returned to their beers.

"You should talk to the girls," Bjorn said, pointing me to a small group of scantily clad woman gathered at the far end of the bar. He glanced over his shoulder at the gyrating Asian woman. "Hey Finger," he yelled, "this place is called Totally Naked Women Here, not Women Wearing Traditional Japanese Costumes Here. Take it off. These people want to see your tits."

"I'm trying to develop some mystery, Bjorn. I am building anticipation," she yelled back.

"Show your pussy. Show your tits," he ordered, "or at least what you little Asian women try and pass off as tits." She began angrily pulling off the Kimono and slamming the pieces of clothing on the stage.

"Don't talk to me about size, Mr. Bjorn Tiny . . . Mr. Bjorn with the smallest cock ever seen on a black man." I winced at the comment as images of hairy Aunt Salome flashed before my eyes. The little Asian woman held up her thumb and index fingers a quarter of an inch apart in front of her face. She had extricated herself from the Kimono and stood naked on the stage next to the stripper pole. She grabbed her shaved crotch and yelled, "Oh, Bjorn. Are you done already? I didn't even know you were in." She walked to the edge of the stage in front of the lone spectator, spread her legs, and pointed at her vagina. "Make Little-dick Bjorn happy, Fred. Look at my Asian cunt." The man started clapping vigorously again.

I left Bjorn arguing with Finger and took a seat at the bar close to where the off-duty strippers lounged. I asked the barkeep for an RC. One of the strippers, a healthy looking blond wearing a tiny bikini top and a red thong, heard me order the cola and took a seat next to me.

"On the wagon, big boy," she said.

"On the job, sweetheart." I slid my license across the bar.

"A private dick," she said.

"That again. Yeah, it's private, but that's a long sad story." I handed her the picture of Candace Pantz. "Do you know this woman?"

"Sure," she said, "Candy Pantz. Worked here until last Saturday night. Have you been hired to find her?" It was becoming clear to me that Candace and this Candy Pantz were the same woman.

"Were you here Saturday night?" I asked.

"Sure, all of us were?" I took my detective's note pad out of my breast pocket.

"Who do you mean when you say 'All of us?'"

"Well there was Finger Mi." She nodded toward the stage where Bjorn and Finger were still arguing. I wrote down the name. "But, don't write that down. Finger is her stage name. Her real name is Judy Yab-romowitz." I made a note of that. It looked like there were going to be a lot of people with secret identities in this case. "She strips as a way of working her through medical school so she can help disabled children."

"A heart of gold," I take it.

"You got that right," she said. "You don't find 'em any golder. Chesty Tits-a-lot, was here too." She pointed at a large Swedish looking woman at the end of the bar who had a Totally Naked Women Here souvenir t-shirt pulled over her ample breasts.

"Real name?"

"Ann Feebe." I jotted both names in my book.

"And she is studying to become a . . .?"

"Veterinarian."

"So she can help . . .?"

"Abused dogs and cats."

"Heart of . . .?"

"Gold, of course."

"Got it," I said, "Anything else I need to know about her?"

"That about covers it."

"How about the black woman in the corner?"

"That's Iwanna Blackcock. She is new. She took Candy's place."

"Real name?"

"Anita Whitecock."

"Studying . . . ?"

"Women's Afro-American Studies."

"So she can . . . ?"

"Help the oppressed."

"And with a heart of . . . ?"

"Gold"

I wrote it all down in the book.

"And what about you?" I said, looking into sad blue eyes, eyes that made me think of skinny little Amanda Tiddyliddle back in Cuckold Falls.

"Vagina Smooth," she said. I wrote it down.

"Real name?"

"No," she said, "Vagina Smooth is my real name. My stage name if Jane Madison."

"Your parents named you Vagina?" I asked.

"Yeah, that is my cross to bear. They meant well, though. They named my twin brother, Penis. We grew up on a commune in Oregon where clothes were optional and we lived off the bounty of the land. My parents wanted to give us names that would always remind us where we came from. We grew up as free as birds and spent out days running in the fields while our parents tended to the crops. Penis and I were inseparable. He was completely into me and I wrapped myself around him with all the love of a sister can give. We would play all day until mother would call us back to dinner with her beautiful voice, 'Oh, Penis. Oh, Vagina, come now, come quickly. It is time for dinner.' At night Penis and I would sleep in the same bed and hold each other the whole night through. It was the perfect childhood. But then the police came, piled our crops in huge mounds, and burned them. Mother and father were taken away to federal prison. As they dragged my parents and the others away, mother cried that she and father could no longer be there for us. She said we would have to take care of each other and we promised we would. Penis and I were separated, placed in foster homes, and sent to a regular school. School was the only place we could see each other and we spent every free minute together. The other children were vicious. When Penis and I were together they would jeer and sing, 'Penis and Vagina, sitting in a tree.' You know how it goes from there. We did our best to keep our hope up, a hope that we could be together again in harmony like before, but as we grew older the cruelty of the world was too much. Penis turned hard. I closed up. As soon as he was old enough Penis joined the army where his life was no easier. I dropped out of school and took to the road. Mother wrote me from prison that her brother, Mort, would give me job in the city. I arrived at his house one rainy winter night about three years ago and knocked timidly on the door. My hair was soaked and I was chilled to the bone. Mort answered and recognized me immediately. 'Well, fuck me,' he said 'There's a little wet Vagina on my back porch.' He took me in, warmed me up and gave me a job here in his club. I haven't looked back since."

"Thank you for trusting me with your story," I said.

"For some reason, I feel comfortable talking to you, Mr. James."

The voice of the bartender boomed again over the sound system, "And now, from the cold rain forests of Western Oregon we are pleased to present Miss Jane Madison."

"I have to go on now, Mr. James. I would be very honored if you would come over to the stage and look at my genitals while I dance." After being trusted with the story of little Penis and Vagina I couldn't turn her down. I followed her to the stage where she stripped naked and danced to sad Kingston Trio folk songs. The man who clapped so hard for Finger Mi had gone to the bar where he was nursing a drink and whispering to Finger. That left me the only one at the stage. Vagina was happy to have a friend in the audience. I silently mouthed the words "you are beautiful" and put folded dollar bills in front of me so that she could pick them up with her buttocks.

Vagina danced three sets and then, panties and bra in hand, led me to the back of the building and into the dressing room. "You can finish your questions in here," she said to me. "It will be more private." As we walked in she yelled, "Man, on board. Cover up." Chesty Tits-a-lot, who was now in the dressing room reading a magazine with her feet up on one of the make-up tables, threw a wash cloth over her crotch and went back to reading. "Sit here," Vagina said, pointing to a chair next to her make-up table. "And don't look at my genitals while I get dressed. It's not allowed unless I am on stage." I looked away as she put on the top and thong.

"So what are you studying?" I asked.

"Pre-law. I want to protect people with unusual names."

"How about Candace?"

"Candy Pantz was religious. She was studying to be a nun so she could inspire people to find God."

"Her sister didn't mention that they were Catholic."

"I don't think she was Catholic. She was becoming a non-sectarian nun or something like that. But whatever it was, it included skimpy underwear. The underwear thing caused some sort of problem with the real ordained Catholic nuns which never really got resolved. There were restraining orders."

"Where did she dress?"

"Right here. We shared this table." I looked through the items on the table for clues.

"What do you think happened to her?" I asked.

"I think she was kidnapped. She is probably somewhere strapped to a bed being repeatedly raped by large Irish men with red hair and curved cocks."

"And made to suck their crooked dicks," piped up Chesty Tits-a-lot from across the room.

"That's what her sister Patricia said."

"You mean Patty Pantz?" Vagina said. "She was in here looking for Candy. There is a rumor going around that she is a librarian. If that is true, that's where you should be looking for suspects. I don't want to say anything bad about libraries or the kind of people who frequent them, but where there's smoke there's usually fire, and where there's fire there's usually kidnapping and sexual slavery. That's why I think the library has something to do with it."

I considered Vagina's theory and reached for a business card that was stuck in the corner of the mirror frame where Candace put on her make-up. It said, "Reverend Sister Diana Babylon, Holy Dereamer Pentacostal Gnostic Church of the Tribulation, 1700 Pine Street. Services 9:00 P.M. Nightly. Child Care Provided."

"What's this?" I asked.

Vagina looked at the card. "I have never seen this before."

"But you are sure that Candace was on a spiritual search?"

"Oh yes, Mr. James. Very sure." I put the card in my pocket.

"Thank you, Vagina. I have seen enough here tonight."

"Thank *you*," she said. "Let me walk you to the door." She led me back into the stage area. A few more patrons had wandered in. Finger Mi was back on stage and the man in the hunters cap was back in the front row.

Iwanna Blackcock was standing topless arguing with Bjorn. "You don't have to worry," she was saying. "The women in my class are all very modern and progressive."

"I am not dropping my pants in front of your Diversity Awareness group," he said.

"But you will be standing up for all black men by

shattering that demeaning stereotype about big cocks."

"So my tiny dick is going to help other black men?"

"Rosa Parks refused to move to the back of the bus. Martin Luther King had a dream. You have a little tiny dick. Destiny is knocking at your door. Don't be too dumb to answer, you stupid nigger. Besides, our group has fried chicken and ribs after every meeting."

"Corn bread?" Bjorn asked.

"All you can eat."

"Let me think about it," he said. He saw me leaving and called out, "Wait, Mr. James. Are you leaving already?"

"I've done all I can do here," I said.

"Can I call you about becoming a dick?"

"Any time," I said.

Vagina accompanied me to the door and as I was leaving gave me a peck of a kiss on the cheek. "Are you sure you wouldn't like to stay until closing time, come back with me to my apartment, and look at my genitals again?"

"I can't do that, Vagina. I have a case to solve."

"There is something special about you, William. It's like we knew each other in another time and place, a better time long ago, and we were lovers, and I went out at night and had sex with other men and brought you the money. And we were happy."

"It's been a long time since I've been happy," I told her, "Goodbye, Vagina."

I drove back to my apartment and heated a can of chili. I turned on my little black and white television and tried to watch an old Don Knots movie, but couldn't keep my mind on the plot. *What had happened to Candace Pantz? Where had she gone that Saturday night and where was she now?* The questions swirled in my head until I fell asleep. That night I dreamed about Aunt Salome, the women of the Philosophy Club, and the field goal I wasn't there to make.

Chapter 2

The morning comes early to city streets. I woke to the sound of garbage men throwing cans in the back alley. I'd hit the RC Cola hard the night before, and my head was pounding like a boy pounding on the basement door trying to escape from his hairy naked Aunt Salome. I crawled out of the sack and made my way in the early morning darkness to Mohammad's Pig and Pancake for some food. I laid the picture of Candace on the table. Pretty and blond, she stared back at me from the photo, still spread legged and holding her labia apart with her fingers. *Where is she? What would she say to me if she could speak from the page? Would she tell me where she was or would she want to stay hidden?* The burka-clad Arab waitress brought me my sausage and pancakes. I directed her attention to the photograph on the table and asked, "Have you seen this woman?"

On seeing the picture the Arab waitress threw the hot coffee in my face and landed a right cross to my temple. Holding me by the collar and the belt she threw me out of the diner and into the street. My face hit the pavement with a crunch. "Pervert," she screamed through the veil of her burka. I struggled to my feet as she continued her attack. I was aiming a Venezuelan karate chop at her throat—a secret blow capable of disabling any assailant—when she caught me with three sucker punches to the solar plexus. Then an uppercut to the chin sent me to la-la land. When I came to I was on my belly in the street, and two cops were putting handcuffs on me. The waitress in the burka was leaning against the restaurant wall smoking a cigarette.

"He's waking up from his little nap," one of the cops said and rolled me over. My head started to clear.

"Take it easy," I said. "I used to be one of you guys." The bigger of the two cops put his face a few inches from mine. I could smell booze coming from his pores. I remembered his face from my days in blue.

"Well well," he said. He had breath like a whiskey scented fart. "If it ain't Mr. William James?"

"That's right, Bruno," I said. "Long time, no see."

"Not long enough, James. We're taking you down town."

"You got nothing on me," I said. "What's the charge?"

"Disorderly conduct, disseminating pornography, and one count of three thirty-eight."

"What's three thirty-eight?"

"Public sex with a goat," Bruno said. The woman in the burka let out a high-pitched screech of a laugh.

"That wasn't pornography," I told him. "That is a picture of a woman who is missing. I have been hired to find her."

"Tell it to the judge," Bruno said. He and the other cop pulled me to my feet. "Looked like porn to me."

"And for the goat thing," I said "This is the city. There isn't a goat within a hundred miles of here." The Arab woman in the burka let forth with another staccato laugh as they dragged me toward the cop car.

"I love that that law," Bruno said. "The charge will get dismissed. I like to leave it on a person's arrest record as a souvenir of our meeting. Then whenever you get in a little trouble in the future they run your record and see public sex with a goat; charges

dismissed. And you get to explain it all over again."
They shoved me in the back of the cop car and headed
for the station.

"Bruno," I said from the back seat of the cop car,
"why the attitude? We are both on the same side. I
was one of you. Now I do it on the private side
without all the bureaucratic bullshit, without the
paperwork, without the paycheck or the health
benefits, without the car or the respect, but it is still
one man standing against evil, one man trying to
make the streets safe again for the little children who
are about to be molested by the perverted members of
a women's philosophy club."

Bruno turned to face me in a rage. "James," he
yelled, "you are not a cop. You never were a cop. You
worked parking enforcement. You were a fucking
meter maid."

"I know there were interdepartmental rivalries," I
said, "but we all wore the blue. We all swore to serve
and protect."

"James," he said, "the car you are riding in has four
wheels and can go a hundred and forty miles an hour.
The one they let you drive had three wheels and
topped out at twenty-seven miles an hours. They issue
me a forty-five caliber handgun and a twelve gauge
shotgun. They gave you a ticket book and a spray
bottle of mace for vicious dogs."

"We both enforced the law," I told him.

"You were a fucking token. There had never been a
male meter maid before you. Parking division was the
designated pussy farm for us regular cops. When
things were slow we could stop down there for poon
or a quick blow job. Then damn woman's liberation
comes along. All of a sudden dykes we used to knock
around for jollies are being hired as cops. We get

damn diversity training. You can't call a nigger a nigger any more. Memos tell us not to cum in the meter maids' mouths. Then, don't fuck them in the ass. And finally, don't fuck them at all because now it isn't a pussy farm, it's law enforcement and they've actually hired a male meter maid. That man was you. As far as I and a lot of other cops are concerned you are what is wrong with this world, and if we have to stick you with a fucking-a-goat-in-public beef to get even, then that's what we will do."

Bruno's ignorant comments about parking enforcement made me see red, and I would have kicked his ugly cop ass right there if it hadn't been for the fact that I was handcuffed in the back of the car and there was a bullet proof screen between us. "Your day is coming Bruno," I told him. "I fought rot in the department before. I can do it again and you are as rotten as they come."

"Yeah, James," he said, "I know your story. But it seems to me like Commissioner Filopad is still a commissioner and you are no longer a meter maid. What does that tell you?" He showed me the finger and turned around to face the street.

Through the pain from the beating all the memories flooded back.

I was just out of the service with nothing to show for it but my last paycheck and my uniform. I wasn't welcome back in Cuckold Falls so I headed for the city. Any city. I got myself an apartment, a job slinging hash in a hash joint, and a girl named Betty to take to the movies on Saturday night. But things weren't good. The apartment had no bathroom, the job was greasy, and Betty turned out to be a guy. Civilian life just wasn't sitting well on me. I missed the gun, but most of all I missed the uniform. I was walking down the street one day and saw two cops beating a homeless guy, and I realized that they were getting paid good money for doing it. I went down to the city and applied for a job on the force.

I learned the ways of the city fast. You don't become a cop unless your daddy was a cop and maybe not even then unless your granddaddy was also a cop. All my applications got rejected and it looked like I would spend the rest of my days slinging hash and dating cross-dressers. But fate stepped in. I put one of my applications in the wrong pile and it went to parking enforcement just at the time the department was fighting sex discrimination charges. Fearing I was some sort of spy for the ACLU, they called me in for an interview and put me through the selection process. I didn't have the high school diploma they normally required, didn't actually pass the civil service exam for the position, and failed the physical, but I had a dick between my legs and they needed someone who had something other than a pussy. Thirty days later I was in uniform.

With my uniform, my ticket book, and my three wheeled cart, I hit the streets. There is some ugly parking out in the city and I saw cars in places where there shouldn't have been places. The city is brutal, and no small part of that brutality gets aimed at those who fight the good fight against illegal parking. I admit that I took my lumps out there, but I am a survivor, and I survived. When the going got rough the only thing that kept me sane, the only thing that could chase away the thoughts of ending it all, was the support of my sisters in blue.

When I first got to the Division they didn't know what to do with me. Parking Division had to be dressed and on the streets at eight in the morning. Our locker rooms were down by the docks. They had never had a man in the division before. The captain hung towels around one of the end lockers to give me some privacy. It wasn't great but I kept my eyes to myself and so did they. That was until one of the towels fell when Helga Hansen was looking my way. Suddenly I hear this loud Swedish voice bellowing, "Jesus Christ almighty, William James. You are swinging some mighty lumber under those pants. That's the biggest damn cock I ever seen on a—."

"Stop," I shouted. "Don't say it." I covered myself with a towel, but Helga's yelling had attracted a crowd.

"Please William," one of the girls begged, "Helga's seen it. We want to see it too. It's not like we've never seen one before." Others chimed in. Under their repeated urgings I relented and showed them my penis. The girls were kind and supportive. They lined up to touch it and whatever hesitancy they had felt about having a male in their midst was gone. After that we had no more use for the towels. The girls became comfortable around my cock, treating it like an adopted cat that they could pet and fuss over when they had a few spare minutes. They sought out my advice about their own anatomies. *Do my tits hang down too far? Should I shave my pussy? Is it sexier to swallow or let the cum run down my face?* I did my best with these questions using what I had learned from the Cuckold Falls Women's Philosophy Club and my travels, but the girls were less interested in answers than they were just being able to talk to somebody.

A week or so after the incident with the towels, Helga's boyfriend left her. We had just finished showering after a hard day on the carts when Helga sat down next to me in the locker room with her big Swedish tits hanging to her lap. "William," she said, "I was wondering if you could help me through this dry spell I'm having with men. If you could just lay some of that good wood of yours on me two or three, or maybe five times a week or so, it would really ease the tension. It shouldn't be too much bother for you. I cum really easy. Barely touch my snatch with cock and I get my nut."

What could I say? I started doing Helga after work in one of the bathroom stalls. It was supposed to be private but the girls could hear what was going on. They would hoot and whistle while we were doing it. The stall itself was stinky and cramped, so one day Helga, who was never the most modest person anyway, said screw the bathroom stall. She bent over the bench in front of the lockers and I gave it too her doggie style out in the open. The sound of my hips slapping against her big pink Swedish ass brought the whole department running to get a look. While they cheered me on, I slammed her from the back and her big white titties bounced in the humid locker room air. The girls yelled encouragement and when we both orgasmed they gave us a round of applause. After that day we abandoned the bathroom altogether and let them look. And look they did. Every time I did her, whether doggie style, missionary style on the locker room floor, or with the big Swede on top, we drew a crowd.

Then Minnie Crolesmack came to me one morning. She said that her husband had become impotent and that as a result she was so tense during the work day that she was becoming a danger to herself and others on the streets. Minnie Crolesmack was a small bullet shaped woman with no tits to speak of and a flat butt. She had short brown hair and when not in uniform always wore jeans and a t-shirt. This morning she was wearing only cotton panties. "I know I'm not attractive like Helga," she said pointing to one of her nipples. "But look." She pulled off her panties and spread her legs. "I shaved it. And the men tell me it is plenty tight. If you could do me in the morning before we leave, I know I could be the officer that I always imagined I would be."

"You are very small," I said. "Are you sure I won't hurt you?"

"Oh absolutely not," she said. "I've been shoving things inside my snatch bigger than you ever since I reached puberty. You can do me as hard as you want, even in the ass, without having to worry about anything except how grateful I will be when you are done. I know you probably want the prettier girls—."

"Stop that," I said. "We are officers of the law. Comrades in blue. If I can help you be a better officer, I will."

"Thank you, William. Thank you so much." She lay back on the locker room bench and spread her legs. Although a plain woman with no tits, she had a nice looking cunt. I put my cock inside her. It was warm, wet and tight. As I moved in and out she started moaning with the motion. The sounds brought onlookers from other parts of the locker room.

"Minnie, you lucky bitch," Helga bellowed and slapped me on the ass. Minnie smiled and made rapid yelping sounds as she worked herself toward orgasm. Some of the women stayed to watch her cum; others wandered off to get into their uniforms. Minnie came and I filled her with semen. Afterward we sat together, me catching my breath, and she wiping the cum off her pussy and thighs.

"That was perfect," she told me.

"Wonderful," I said, "Now go out there and write tickets." She hit the streets and that very day she broke a department record.

The next girl to approach me was Meagan Tytebred. Meagan was a cute athletic woman of about twenty-five. "I'm going to be straight with you, James," she said. "I see what you been giving to Helga and Minnie and I want in on it." I told her that as a fellow officer she could count on me.

"What exactly do you want?" I asked.

"I want cock. Pick your hole. But there is more. I have this leather collar and a leash. Would it be possible for me to get naked except for the collar and a set of knee pads? Then I could get on my hands and knees and you could lead me around the locker room by the leash in front of the other women. My tits would hang down, everybody could see my anus, and you could order me to do things."

"Like what?" I asked.

"Like to suck your dick, or lick your butt hole, or kiss one of the other girls' pussies. You could have one of the girls spank my ass while I suck you or lick your balls. Or you could have me fondle your balls while your fuck Helga or you could order me to eat Minnie's pussy while you fuck me up the ass. Things like that."

"If that is what you want?"

"That's exactly what I want," she said.

After that came Janice, then Adrian, then Juanita. One by one, each of them came to me with ideas about how I could make them better law officers. Mornings and evenings became filled with team building and morale building activities. As a result, productivity jumped. We put illegal parkers on the run. Parking ticket income to the city rose and then fell as people adapted to the new enforcement regime. The citizenry began taking their new respect for parking into other areas of their lives. Litter disappeared from the streets. Vandalism ended. Muggings were rare and serious crime began to decline. People were polite to each other. The women in blue had changed the city, but change is not always welcome to those who make their living off of chaos.

One Monday I was called in to the office of Captain Dorothy Natron. Dorothy was the highest ranking officer in the parking division. She was a heavy set woman with large breasts and large thighs. She still wore the old style uniform with jacket and skirt. In the division, her word was law. She told me that she had two important matters to discuss with me. The first concerned things that were happening in the Department.

We had been part of an important new project to replace all the parking meter poles with new breakaway poles that would give way when hit by a person or a car. Statisticians said that the new poles would reduce the alarmingly high parking meter death rate by half. The project was being pushed by the Department and Commissioner Filopad. Dorothy had been committed to the change ever since I joined the force.

"We have trouble," Dorothy said to me. "You know, William, that the regular cops have been using our girls for a little pussy when the wife wasn't giving any. Nobody minded all that much. The girls here can write tickets all day, suck a cop dick on the lunch hour, do the shopping after work, cook for the kids, and do the old man in the sack at night. All in a days work. And now with you here, they are even better than before. The problem is that the girls have been harassing the cops. Do you know Officer Narihuts? He was a regular at the meter maid pussy store. Well the girls have taken to calling him Officer Tiny-Dick. They do it to his face. There are others. I've heard of Frank LittleCock, Adam No-Dick, Officer Fred BB-Balls and a bunch of other names. They have a particularly nasty one for this beat cop named Bruno. Helga carries a picture of your cock in her wallet. She has been showing it around in the force telling the men that unless they are swinging wood like yours there is no reason for them to be coming around. Cops are insecure, immature, and sensitive men. They hold a grudge. I am afraid that they will try to get even by sabotaging the meter pole project."

"What can I do?" I asked.

"Talk to the girls. Remind them that all the men and women in blue have to work together. It won't hurt the girls to fuck a cop with low self esteem, and it could mean the difference between getting the break-a-way meter poles or not."

"I will talk to them, and I am sure they will cooperate," I said.

"Thank you William," she said. "I am counting on you."

"Captain, you said there were two things you wanted to talk to me about."

"Yes," she said. "It happens that I have a really hairy cunt. I'm talking a fur cave down there, and I am not wearing panties under my under my skirt today—just a garter belt and stockings. I know you do tension relief exercises with the most of the girls. I have been very tense myself lately and thought you might allow me to sit on your face."

"It would be my pleasure, Captain." I lay on my

back across the big desk in the Captain's office. She climbed up, straddled me so I was looking up her dress into the blackness of her hairy snatch. She slowly squatted, placing the dark lips of her cunt on my mouth.

"Find my clit and suck it," she said. I felt like I had been hit in the face by a hot barber towel. The engorged clitoris was easy to find. I took it into my mouth, sucked it, then ran my tongue across the tip. She began to undulate, moving her sopping wet genitalia up and down my face. The juices ran down my cheeks and chin as she let loose with a slow singsong moan. I thrust my tongue out when I could find her hole, but she didn't need my help. "Stick a finger in my ass," she ordered.

I gurgled an answer into her snatch. Her ass was a cop ass. It grabbed my finger like a pair of handcuffs and held tight. It was not an easy orgasm for her. She worked my face up and down, back and forth and then, using her hips, simply pounded my face with her cunt. She came in a torrent of moaning obscenities. When she was done she climbed down from the desk, straightened her skirt, and sat back down in her chair. I had the Captain's vaginal fluids dripping off my face onto my uniform.

"I made quite a mess of you," she observed. "I owe you for that. If you want to cum in my mouth some time, just ask. Otherwise, you are dismissed."

I went into the locker room still dripping with the captain's cunt juice, much to the delight of my sisters in blue. When the jokes at my expense were over they dried me off and cleaned me up. That night in the locker room I called a meeting after showers. The naked women gathered around me and I explained to them what the Captain had said and how everything we had worked for was at stake.

"No matter how small and pink their dicks," I explained, "you women have to remember that they are your brothers in blue. How would one of you feel if I refused to fuck you because your tits were too small or your pussy too loose? We are in this together. Let that beat cop know you care and that you respect both what he does and what he carries between his legs." Many of the girls, knowing they had been guilty, hung their heads in shame. "So what are you going to do tomorrow?" I yelled.

"Hand jobs," yelled one.

"Blow jobs," yelled another.

"Rusty trombones," Minnie said. The girls fell silent.

"Rusty trombones?" Helga said. "What is that?"

Minnie explained, "Where you get on your knees and tongue the guy's ass while reaching between his legs and jerking him off."

"And rusty trombones," they yelled in unison. I put up my hand to quiet them.

"Mostly girls, just fuck them," I said. "So what are you gonna do?"

"Fuck cops," they yelled back.

"I can't hear you."

"Fuck cops," they chanted. With asses bobbing and tits bouncing they yelled, "Fuck cops, fuck cops, fuck cops," until they were sweaty, exhausted, and could yell no more. The sight of all that tit, ass, and pussy moving in sweaty unison for the good of the Department made my dick hard as a rock. One by one each of the girls came up, put a hand on my erection, and renewed her vow to law enforcement.

Over the next three days my girls fucked and sucked like only meter maids can. They fucked the beat cops behind the donut shops. They sucked off the detectives and took it up the ass from the undercover guys. They did the swat team in a massive group fuck and suck that was so athletic it sent two of the boys to the hospital. Helga and the Captain double teamed the Chief of Police right in his office. But the hero was little Minnie Crolesmack. Over the three day period that followed my little talk she fucked fourteen cops, gave eleven blow jobs, took it in the ass six times, and ate seven pussies down at the central precinct secretarial pool. For her valiant effort, Captain Dorothy gave her the Parking Division medal of honor for having let more officers on her in a three day period than any meter maid ever.

The effort was not in vain. Self esteem in the police department shot up and crime took a holiday. Better yet, two weeks later we heard that the break-away meter poles were going into production. The holiday season was upon us, and to celebrate the great year, we planned a party.

The Friday of the party we pushed the lockers and benches out of the way to make room for the festivities. The girls made a gourmet Christmas dinner and arranged it on a big table we borrowed from central precinct. They made a butterball turkey, sweet potatoes with little marshmallows, green bean casserole with crunchy onions on the top, cranberry sauce in the shape of the inside of a can, and a bowl full of McDonald's apple pies for dessert. I had never seen such food. Captain Natron came as Santa, a role that fit her due to her large belly. Lacking a Santa suit the girls had stripped her naked and painted her red. She came in with big red tits hanging down on her big red belly and wearing black boots she had borrowed from the fire department. She had Christmas tree ornaments hanging from her nipples and had decorated her ample pubic hair with tinsel. Her big tits and belly jiggled like a bowl full of jelly as she pointed at Helga booming, "HO, HO, HO." Meagan Tytebred had traded in her leather dog collar for a small horse harness and, naked except for the harness, knee pads, and a Rudolph nose, led our painted Captain into the party. Swedish Helga wore nothing but her Viking hat and nipple ornaments, claiming that it was a Norse tradition, but most of the girls figured it was just an excuse for proving once again that she had bigger tits that anybody except the Captain.

We ate and drank until we could eat no more. Then we had the department talent show. A couple of the girls had written a song about "the littlest penis" that brought tears to my eyes. A young Asian woman who was new and had come to the corps after retiring from gymnastics showed how she could lick her own pussy. Juanita did the old pick-up-a-beer-bottle-with-your-cunt trick, as if anyone thought she couldn't. But it was the Captain who topped everybody when, after a fair amount to drink and a lot of encouragement, she put a grapefruit up her vagina and squeezed until the juice flowed. Meagan caught the juice in a tumbler and drank it. As the last drop of grapefruit juice disappeared down Meagan's throat the crowd went wild. All the Captain had to say about it was that at least the Women's Army Corp had taught her something.

That Christmas we thought that the parking division had nowhere to go but up. We had made peace with the regular cops. A memo came around saying the new parking meter poles were being manufactured in a factory in Romania and morale among the officers had never been higher. Unfortunately, our hopes for the future were soon to be dashed.

"Hamster-dick," I said out loud. I had suddenly remembered what they used to call Bruno. He jerked his head around from the front of the police car to stare at me.

"What did you say?" Bruno demanded.

"Ah . . . I said yams sure make me sick."

"You said 'hamster-dick,'"

"No," I protested, "I didn't say hamster-dick, because why would I care if a guy has a little wrinkly pink dick like a hamster. It wouldn't even matter to me because I don't even think about things like that."

"You are a dead man, James," he told me.

When the got to the station house Bruno dragged me out of the car and into the booking area, giving me hard punches to the soft parts of my body the whole way. They took my wallet, my belt, my shoe laces, and my keys. I was fingerprinted and photographed. After the mug shot I demanded my phone call. "I want to call a lawyer," I told the officer in charge of my paperwork.

"What lawyer would take a goat-fucker as a client?"

"I didn't fuck a goat," I protested. "There aren't any goats in this city."

"Mrs. Mohammad says you fucked a goat in front of her. Are you saying she is a liar?"

"Yes," I said. "She is a liar if she says there was a goat. I was just eating breakfast."

"What about this?" he said handing me the picture of Candace Pantz.

"That is a young woman I am trying to find. I am a

private detective."

"I thought you were a meter maid," he said.

"That was a long time ago. Now I am private detective trying to find Candace Pantz."

"So why did you show this picture to Mrs. Mohammad?"

"Just in case she had seen Candace."

"If Mrs. Mohammed wanted to see Candace Pantz she would just go down to Totally Naked Women Here like anybody else. She wouldn't have to get a picture of Candy's cunt from you."

"That's the point," I told him. "Candace isn't at the club any more. She disappeared."

"And fucking a goat is going to help find her?"

"There is no goat in this case."

"Tell it to the judge," he said and pushed the phone to me. I dialed my office and got the answering machine. I left a message for Teena and tried another number. The officer stopped me. "Just one phone call," he said.

"All I got was an answering machine," I protested.

"Tough luck." The officer dragged me to a holding cell at the far end of the building and threw me to the floor inside. My face was throbbing from my collision with the street outside Mohammad's Pig and Pancake and my internal organs were screaming from the beating I had taken from Bruno on the way into the station house. I lay curled on the floor waiting for the pain to subside. The cool cement of the cell felt good on my face, so I stayed on the floor of the cell until the pain became tolerable. When I opened my eyes to evaluate my circumstances I realized that I was not alone. On the bottom bed of the bunk beds sat a plain looking woman with her legs curled underneath her.

"Mr. James," the woman said, "are you awake?"

"How long have I been out," I asked, trying to focus my eyes on my cell mate.

"About half an hour," she said. "Remember me?"

I did. "Brett," I said. "From Otto's." She uncurled her legs and sat on the edge of the bed. She was wearing a modest white blouse and a navy blue knee length skirt.

"That's right," she said. "What are you in for?"

"Public sex with a goat," I said.

"Ewe?" she asked.

"Yeah me. Can you believe that?"

"No," she said, "Not you. Ewe. Were you fucking a ewe or a ram?"

"I wasn't fucking a goat at all. Bruno Hamster-dick and this woman in a burka trumped up the charge as some kind of joke."

"What were you really doing?"

"I was eating breakfast at the Pig and Pancake and looking for Candace Pantz."

"Candy Pantz works at Totally Naked Women Here. Why were you looking for her at Mohammad's Pig and Pancake."

"I thought Mrs. Mohammad might have seen her."

"When Mrs. Mohammed wants to see Candy Pantz she goes to Totally Naked Women Here like everybody else."

"But Candy Pantz is no longer there. She is missing and I have been trying to find her."

"So you fucked Mrs. Mohammed's goat?"

"I didn't fuck any goat. I told you it is all trumped up."

"It's easy for men to fuck a goat. You can just grab a ewe, hold her still, and stick your dick in. For a woman it's not so easy. A goat doesn't get an erection just because you show him your ass, you know. You have to get him hard with your hand first and hope he stays that way."

"You tried to fuck a goat?" I asked.

"Just once. Mrs. Mohammad and I were drunk and she dared me to do it. She tried to get me to suck it's dick I told her that it was her goat and if she wanted its dick sucked she should suck it herself."

"Mrs. Mohammad drinks alcohol and sucks goat dick?"

"Only on special occasions. She is from Alabama. I don't think she ever got used to city life. But why are you in here?"

"I told you, Brett. For sex with a goat, but I didn't do it."

"I mean why are you in my cell. You are a man, I am a woman and there are no guards around. You are probably going to brutally rape me any moment now."

"I am not going to rape you," I told her.

"That's exactly what men say just before they tear off your clothes, spread your legs so that they can leer at your helpless quivering pussy, and then ram their huge throbbing cocks inside you, and—."

"I am not going to do that," I interrupted.

"And then force you to suck their reeking dicks while humming the Star Spangled Banner and—."

"Stop," I yelled. "Brett. I am not going to rape you."

"I've been brutally raped before," she said.

"I'm sorry, Brett." I struggled from the floor. The pain in my face and body returned. I sat beside her on the bed and put my arm over her shoulder.

"It was awful," she said. "Two huge men. Weight lifters. They took turns raping me over and over. They made me do horrible and disgusting things to them. I can tell you what they made me do."

"No, Brett," I said, putting my hand over her

mouth to stop her. "You don't have to talk about it. Did you go to the police?"

"I did," she told me. "I went to them and told them everything those men did to me. It took hours just to describe it. Then I told the rape counselor, and then my therapist, and then the people at the coffee shop where I go, and then the people at Otto's, and each time I told it I had to relive the horror. And after all that the police wouldn't prosecute the bastards."

"Why not?" I asked.

"The prosecutor said I was asking for it."

"That is horrible," I exclaimed, "What did they say: that you were dressing provocatively, or that you let the guys buy you a drink? That is crap. No woman asks to be raped and the full force of the law should have fallen upon them."

"I know you are right William. But the prosecutor said that when the woman asks for it by putting the request in writing, it makes the prosecution very difficult. I shouldn't have written that letter, and had it notarized, and sent the men money afterward. I know better now."

"You are a strong woman, Brett," I said.

"I would feel better if you would put your hand on my pussy."

"Well . . . " I said, "just for a minute." She took my hand in hers, pulled the crotch of her white panties aside and placed my hand on her labia. It was clean shaven and I could feel genital jewelry. She held my hand tightly in place and looked into my eyes.

"Does holding me like this disgust you?" she asked.

"No. Of course not," I told her. "You feel very nice.

"If I disgust you and you wanted to punish me, I would understand."

"I don't want to punish you," I said.

"You could punish me because my tits are too small or because I let Mrs. Mohammad seduce me."

"Mrs. Mohammad?"

"She is very hairy down below. Afterward I was pulling black hair out of my teeth for a week."

"Brett," I said, hoping to change the subject, "why are you in here? What did you do?"

"Oh, I didn't do anything. I volunteer here whenever the police need to train new officers on the proper technique for body cavity searches. It is my way supporting the force."

"No, Brett," I mean why are you in the men's wing of the jail.

"William," she said still holding my hand tightly against her cunt, "this is the women's wing."

"God damn it," I swore. "Bruno put me in the women's wing. It is another of his jokes designed to humiliate me."

"Could I touch your penis?" Brett asked.

"Not now, Brett," I said. "I have to get out of here." She clamped her thighs on my hand.

"Is it because I don't have any tits?"

"I don't care about your tits, Brett. If it bothers you so much why don't you go to a plastic surgeon and buy some."

"I can't," she said, lifting her blouse to look at one of her nipples. "It is against my faith."

"What does that mean?"

"The book of Lascivious," she said. "Reverend Sister Babylon read to us from the Book of Lascivious. Sybil was wandering the dessert in search of the City of Bone and the Lord spoke to her, 'Sybil honey,' he said, "Do not puteth the sheep's wool in your tunic to make your titties what they be notteth, for your body is my temple, and each woman shall shake only what I have given to her, as she enters the City of Bone.' So Sybil took the fleece from her tunic and went into the City of Bone and was met by many Boners who praised her and heaped many precious pearls upon her face."

"What kind of church do you go to?" I asked.

"I follow Reverend Diana Babylon at the Holy Dereamer Pentecostal Gnostic Church of the Tribulation. You could come to services with me some time." She reached down and squeezed my hand hard against her vagina.

A voice boomed through the bars, "Mr. William James, take your hand off that woman." A large black woman in a guard's uniform was standing outside the cell door. Her blue uniform hugged her muscular frame so tightly that you could see her bra and panty lines in relief. She opened the door with one of the keys on her ring, grabbed me by the collar, and threw me against the bars on the far wall. My face smacked hard against the iron and pain reverberated up and down my spine.

Brett curled back on the bunk against the cell wall and said to the guard, "He said if I didn't let him touch me, he would rape me?"

"That's not true—"

"Shut up, James," the guard said. She sat on the edge of the bed where Brett had her knees wrapped in her arms. "Did he hurt you?"

"It sort of hurts down there?" she whimpered as she directed the black guard's hand toward her crotch. "You should make him go away and then come back and kiss it better." The black woman got off the bed and walked to where I had slumped on the floor.

"You come with me," she said, pulling me to my feet by the shirt. She marched me down the hall toward central booking, slammed me into a chair, and handcuffed me to the chair legs. From my position I could see the counter. Teena and Mrs. Milpy were talking to the duty officer. The black guard approached and the four of them held an extensive conversation which I could not hear. Mrs. Milpy was wearing a red skirt, spiked heels, and a blouse that showed off her cleavage. She motioned the female guard away from Teena and the duty officer. Mrs. Milpy whispered earnestly to the guard, pointing to me as she talked. The guard smiled and nodded at what Mrs. Milpy told her. The two of them returned to the desk while Teena signed papers. Coming over to where I sat the guard said, "I am so sorry about the way I acted back there, Mr. James." She unlocked the handcuffs. "My name is Deshawnawanda Jones. I could find a way to make it up to you if you wanted to meet me sometime. Maybe after I get off my shift. But for now, you are free to go." I rubbed my wrists. "And you can count on me to let Officer Hamster-dick know that he was out of line in putting you in that cell."

"I just want to go," I said.

"Deshawnawanda Jones," she said, "You won't forget, will you."

"I won't forget, Officer Jones," I told her.

I was still hurting. Mrs. Milpy and Teena helped me out of the building and into Mr. Milpy's BMW. Mrs. Milpy drove while Teena massaged my shoulders from the back seat. At the office they escorted me through Otto's and up to the office where the two of them tended to my cuts and bruises. Mrs. Milpy ordered up coffee and scones from the little bakery down the street.

When I was feeling better the ladies explained that Mrs. Milpy had called the office looking for me just after Teena had gotten the phone message. Mrs.

Milpy had a vehicle and bail money, so she picked up Teena and they came to the station together to get me. Mrs. Milpy posted bail but the jailers couldn't find me due to Bruno having put me in the women's wing. Officer Jones finally found me and brought me out.

"I put in a good word with my sister," Mrs. Milpy said, "the kind of word that means you won't have any more trouble from her."

"Thank you Mrs. Milpy," I said. When the food arrived they spread it out my desk. I took my chair and the two women sat in the client chairs.

"So what happened to you in the big house?" Teena asked. Both women leaned forward to hear the story allowing me to look down both blouses at the two sets of tits beneath: Teena's firm white ones and Mrs. Milpy's ponderous black ones. "Did you get raped?" Teena asked. Both women shivered at the thought, sending all four breasts in motion. I explained to them that it would take more that a couple crooked cops and a few ex-cons to hold me down and stick dicks in my ass. Out of concern for Brett's reputation, I kept quiet about her and the fact that I had been in the woman's wing. When she finished eating Mrs. Milpy left the office for home giving me the thumb and little finger 'call me' sign and then the finger in and out of the mouth 'blow job' sign, both behind Teena's back.

"She is so nice," Teena said after Mrs. Milpy left.

"What did she tell you?"

"She told me how much she admires you. She said that Mr. Milpy has hired several different detectives to take pictures of her having sex with men and you have been the kindest and most supportive of them all. She told me what a gentleman you always are and how, when she has the blues, you tell her she is beautiful and make her feel better. It made me very proud to work for you."

"I am pleased to hear that, Teena," I said.

"Mr. James," she continued, "I need some advice from you about this thing with Otto."

"What is it?"

"You know that Otto would like me to be part of the fund raiser Friday night at the bar where I would get on the pool table and jiggle my breasts in front of people to help raise money. Well he and I went into the back room to talk about it. He had me take off my blouse and jump up and down because he wanted to make sure that they were really as big and jiggly as they looked when I had clothes on. Then he squeezed them for a long time to make sure that they were real. After that we had the idea that we could raise more money if at the end of the show I pulled down my pants and showed everybody my buttocks and my vagina. So I pulled down my pants in front of Otto and wiggled my butt in several different ways trying to figure out which would be the most entertaining. At one point I was naked, legs spread and bent over holding my ankles. He came up behind me saying he was going to check me for shaving stubble, but instead he put his penis inside me. It was totally unexpected so I was off my guard. Before I knew it he was holding me by the hips and having sex with me. I tried to stop it but he has a very persuasive penis and I quickly went from 'Otto, please stop,' to 'Harder, Otto, harder.' We went at it for a while with me bent over. Then he picked me up and put me on my back on a table they use for cooking. It was awfully hot in there. My titties were bouncing, I was sweating, and Otto was pounding me with his cock. In the midst of it all I made a mistake. You have to understand that sometimes in a situation like that a woman can get excited and yell something like, 'Oh, Mr. James, fuck my hot cunt,' but she wouldn't mean William James, the man she works for. She would mean some theoretical William James who is kind, and caring and sexually attractive, but not her boss. Well that happened to me, and Otto heard it and made some comments about it, and I wanted you to hear it from me before you heard it from him because when we were talking afterward and having a cigarette he may have gotten the totally wrong idea that I had fantasies about him and you doing me at the same time, one of you doing me doggie style while I sucked the other one's cock. And the truth is, I have never had those kinds of thoughts and all I want is to be a good detective's assistant."

"I know that you do, Teena," I told her. "Anybody can have a slip of the tongue. If Otto brings it up, I will tell him that between us it is all business."

"Oh, thank you Mr. James. I won't mention it again, and I will tell that nasty Otto that he shouldn't be drawing conclusions from the things I say and putting his cock in me when I don't expect it."

"You do that," I told her. "But I need to go see Patty Pantz. Find me the address of that place where she works."

"Are you going to a library?" Teena's eyes widened.

"Yes, Teena. I'm going to a library."

"Well, you be careful. Maybe you should take your gun."

"I will be careful, Teena. Get me the address."

I got the directions to the Mulberry Street Library and headed to my car. At Otto's, the afternoon crowd was drinking and swapping lies about their bikes. Otto tried to get my attention as I went through the bar, but I waived him off mouthing to him that I had no time. The Gremlin and I hit the road. I found a parking spot a block of so from the library and put a quarter in the meter. It was an older meter, but it had the gold tint of one of the new breakaway poles. The question was would it really break away or was it death trap waiting to spring. I shook the pole and thought of people like Teena who were putting their bare asses on pool tables to stop needless parking meter deaths while crooked politicians slept like babies in their adjustable Posturepedic beds. There were still scores to settle around that, but this wasn't the time.

The building looked innocent—a simple stone building with the words 'Mulberry Street Public Library' over the ornate wooden double doors. Someone driving by, if they noticed the building at all, might have thought it was a bar, or a strip joint, or a pig and pancake place. But if you looked closely you saw the local drug dealers and hookers crossing the street to avoid walking in front of it. I checked out the neighborhood and when the street seemed empty I ascended the granite steps to the front door and walked in. It was a library, alright: books everywhere. There wasn't a soul in sight. I crossed the foyer and slipped into an aisle marked 'Philosophy and Religion.' My eyes fell on a book written by a guy with the same name as mine. I thought it might be a detective novel but it was something to do with religion. I heard footsteps and pretended to be reading the book. As I turned the page I came upon a piece of notebook paper that had been hidden inside. I pulled out the sheet. In a green magic marker someone had written, "Drop the Pantz case. Or Else." I knew right then that I there was more to this than just a missing dancer. I put the book back on the shelf, keeping the note for further study.

I worked my way to the back of the building and there she was. Patty Pantz was sitting behind the reference desk in matching navy blue skirt and jacket. She had the white blouse and rimless glasses that screamed 'librarian.' Behind her an older woman wearing sweater and full flowered skirt was making copies. Peggy saw me and waved. I slid along a wall toward her and was almost to her desk when I heard a deep male voice.

"Hey pal, let me see your card."

"I turned and found myself facing a muscular blond man in a blue blazer. He wore a name tag that read, "Ebenezer Jones, Library Security."

"What card is that?" I asked.

"Don't get smart with me pal," he said. "Library card. You think you can just walk into a library like you own it. Let's see the card."

"Listen Jones," I said. "You got me. I don't have a card. My name is William James. I'm a private eye on a case and I'm working for that librarian over there."

"Miss Pantz?"

"Yeah, Patty Pantz, and I have to talk to her about the case."

"She's a reference librarian. Are you sure you aren't some pervert trying to get a look at her." While we spoke Patty came out from around her desk and approached us.

"Mr. Jones," she said to the guard, "this man works for me."

"He can't stay here without a card, Ms. Pantz. I have a job to do here." She looked at me.

"Meet me at the coffee shop down the street," she said, "in ten minutes."

"Move it, James," the guard said, pushing me across the library and out the door.

I decided to use one of my psychological detective tricks on him. "Jones," I said. "That's an unusual name. You wouldn't be related to a police officer named Deshawnawanda Jones, would you?"

"Deshawnawanda is my sister," he said. I stared at his white skin. He got my meaning and said, "I was adopted. How do you know Deshawnawanda?"

I gave him my card. "You talk to her," I said. "She will vouch for me. I just met her this morning at police headquarters, and I want you to know—man to man—that I did not fuck her."

"Really," he said.

"Honest to God."

"Dude, that was really white of you. I can't tell you how many sleazeballs I have thrown out of here for trying to get a look at the librarians without a library card and when I tell them to get out and stay out, they come back with something like 'That's what I said to your sister last night after I fucked her.' That hurts my feelings. It seems to me that Deshawnawanda has not had good luck with men and it's good to hear there is a man out there who has not fucked her. If you ever want to apply for a library card, I could put in a good word for you with the people upstairs."

"I may take you up on that, Ebenezer."

"Call me Eb," he said. "Could I ask you a question before you go?"

"What is it, Eb?"

"How do you get into the private detective business? I thought that if I ever give up this library security gig, I might try my hand at the PI thing."

"Call me any time," I said, pointing to the business card in his hand. "I'd be glad to give you some pointers."

I ordered two cups at a coffee place called "Black and Strong." Patty arrived before the coffee. Heads turned as she walked to my booth. For many of the ghetto folks in the coffee shop it was first reference librarian they had ever seen. She slid her worsted wool librarian bottom across the seat of the booth and stared at me through rimless glasses with those big blue librarian eyes. "Are you ready for me to pay my bill?" she said in a low sultry voice. I felt her shoeless foot running up and down my calf.

"I came to tell you about my trip to Totally Naked Women Here," I said. While she played footsie under the table I told her about the Chesty Tits-a-lot, Ivanna Blackcock, Finger Mi, and of course Vagina Smooth. I explained that like most strippers each of them had a heart of gold and was using the dancing job to work herself through school so she could be of service to mankind in some completely selfless way. I told her about Bjorn Frow and his wanting to become a private detective. And, I told her about the card with the name of Reverend Dianna Babylon of the Holy Dereamer Pentecostal Gnostic Church of the Tribulation.

"But what does it all mean?" Patty asked.

"I don't know yet," I admitted. "I need to know more about Candace. Tell me what she was like as a child. What was it like growing up as her sister?"

"It is not easy to tell, but I suppose you must know it all," Patty began. "Candace and I came from an average household in the suburbs of a city not much different than this one. The Pantz family was just one of a thousand average families out there trying to make a go of it. There was Candace and my brothers, Marty and Yancy, and me. My mother was a stripper, like her mother before her. My father was a door-to-door flashlight repairman. My parents brought in enough money to put food on the table and pay the mortgage on a three bedroom ranch style home that looked exactly like all the others in the neighborhood. We were a traditional family. We expected that the girls would become strippers and the boys would become door to door flashlight repairmen. All of the kids did right by them except me.

"Mother worked at a family oriented strip club called Tits and Taffy where they had thirty-two different flavors of salt water taffy. As little girls we would go down and watch her work. She was so beautiful and everyone expected Candace and me to follow in her footsteps. My sister Candace took naturally to the profession. As a little girl she would try and shake her tits before she even had any. She would pull down her panties and wiggle her little pink butt at any uncle who would take the time to watch. When we were teens, mother would send us girls to stripper camp every summer. Candace would be so excited about the new crop of pasties and thongs. It was as if she had been born with a brass pole between her legs. And at camp it didn't matter what we did: flashing the boys' side of the lake from the canoes, making the tassels spin in opposite directions, or working the pole at the nightly stage shows, Candace was always the best.

"Just as Candace took after mother, the boys took after father. It seemed like they had flashlights in their DNA and there wasn't a portable illumination tool they couldn't fix. In addition, both of them had the personalities like father, temperaments that endeared them to the bored housewives they met while working door to door on hot afternoons. We got many a letter from women suggesting that my brothers could do things with a long black flashlight that changed those women's lives forever. Lots of the women customers signed up for a regular flashlight service plan and the boys thrived.

"I was the problem child. I was clumsy and couldn't dance like my sister. I hated going to stripper camp every summer and making a fool of myself. I loved my mother. I tried to want to strip, but I just couldn't. Feeling inferior to my siblings and a disappointment to my parents I started falling into bad ways. It started harmlessly enough with books. In the beginning it was the *Cat in the Hat* and *Green Eggs and Ham*. As I got older it was *Little Women* and *Little Men, The Scarlet Letter, Madame Bovary*, and *A Photo History of Gigantism in Male Genitalia*. My parents were concerned but hesitant to step in. They knew that many young people go through a reading stage and mine was simply more prolonged than others. In addition, it was an era when parents were encouraged to allow their children to explore alternate life styles and get it out of their systems. But for me it wasn't just reading. I built makeshift shelves in my bedroom and cataloged my collection of children's books according the Dewey Decimal system. It was not simply reading that attracted me, it was libraries.

"As I advanced in school I began skipping class so that I could hide among the books at the school library and watch the librarians go about their business. My grades suffered. I started hanging around with the other library-heads. Then one day the assistant principle caught me masturbating in the aisle as I watched Mrs. Slumcut check in books. I was suspended from school and when they let me return I was banned from the school library. I started skipping school altogether and spending my days in local public libraries. I was caught doing the same thing as before while looking at the women who worked behind the reference desk. They reported me to my parents and my library card was permanently revoked. My parents sent me to treatment, a twelve-step program for library heads, but I just went through the motions. When I got out of treatment, I ran away to the city where I lived on the streets. I made counterfeit library cards, and I sneaked into libraries. But with my picture on the banned list, I didn't get in often. I hung around outside the libraries staring at the buildings I was not allowed to enter. Sometimes I would go through the library dumpster at night looking for worn out books or discarded late notices. That's what I was doing the night I first saw Rita Hardswallow.

"It was about eleven at night and I was smoking out behind the Elm Street Library. The library had been closed since eight o'clock but there was still a light on inside. The shades on one of the windows had been left just open enough to let me look inside. I could see the librarian. She was wearing a mid-calf plaid flannel skirt and a plain white blouse. Her hair was in a tight bun, and she wore those tight fitting rimless glasses that leave nothing to the imagination. She was looking into the face of a large man in a janitor's uniform. They did not speak. She unbuttoned her blouse and by undoing the clasp on the front of her bra, exposed her firm white breasts to him. He reached out and touched them. Then he signaled for her to turn around. She did as he directed and leaned over the reference desk. With one hand he lifted the plaid skirt to reveal dark stockings, a black garter belt, and her alabaster nakedness beneath. In the light of a single lamp, her buttocks shown like a harvest moon. I was mesmerized and started to masturbate in the cold night air. The man ran a finger along the inside of her thigh. As he did it she spread her legs. He put his hand between the white thighs and cupped her labia in his hand. He unbuttoned his pants and took out his cock. It was long and beautiful. She had a hand between her legs and was fondling her clitoris in preparation. He moved close and inserted himself inside her. As he did, she arched her back to meet him. He held her by the hips and in increasingly deep thrusts proceeded to fuck her from behind. I worked my pussy with my hand as he worked hers with his cock. I had cum twice on my hand when he put her on her back on the desk, and holding her ankles in his hands, drove his cock into her pussy from the front. I had a clear view of her wet cunt as it accepted every thrust of his organ. I could tell from the spasms in her hips when she orgasmed. She came two or three times and then lay there motionless on the table. When she moved no more he pulled out.

"The librarian slid to the floor so she was on her knees in front of him. He put the cock in her mouth and she sucked until he ejaculated, filling her mouth with cum. She swallowed what she could and the excess ran down her chin onto her heaving bosom. I came again in my hand. It was the most satisfying orgasm I had ever experienced. She sucked the last few drops of semen from his dick, at which point he pulled away, put his cock back in his pants, and disappeared. She took a small towel from the desk and wiped her face and her crotch. She pulled down the dress and put her breasts back into the bra. Then, with a librarian's efficiency she locked the desk drawers, turned out the lamp, and went out into the night.

"I knew that night that I was hopeless. I wanted to be a librarian and I didn't care what the world thought about it. I didn't care that it would bring shame upon my family or that I would never be welcome in respectable society. But, how could it ever happen. I didn't have a library card. I had been banned from the public library for life. I lay there against the library dumpster crying and wondering if it wouldn't be better for me and my family if I just ended it all. And then I heard a voice.

"'What's the matter, girl,' the voice said. I looked up. It was the librarian—the very same one who had been up on the desk just an hour earlier. She was still wearing the plaid dress and the rimless glasses. To me, she was the most beautiful woman in the world.

"'Nothing,' I said.

"'Then why are you crying?' she asked, as she sat down beside me against the dumpster. 'I've seen you out here before. What do you do out here?'

"'I can't tell you,' I sobbed."

"She put her arm around me and took a handkerchief from her skirt pocket to dry my tears. 'My name is Rita,' she said, 'Rita Hardswallow, you can tell me.'

"I told her everything: how I had been banned from libraries, how the only thing I wanted was to be a librarian, how I had watched her earlier and masturbated, and how she was the most beautiful woman I had ever seen. My story burst forth in a torrent. When I was done she leaned against the dumpster and lit a cigarette.

"'The life of a librarian isn't easy,' she said. 'You become one of society's outcasts. You will see things that most people cannot even imagine. You will do things that would make a maggot vomit. People will come to you day in and day out, year after year, demanding you to respond to their most intimate and private requests. You cannot choose to be a librarian, you are called to it and if the call comes, it cannot be resisted. And when you answer the call, you turn your back on all that you have known and all that you have accepted as good and true, for then you are no longer of the day-to-day world. You are *librarian*.'

"'I am called,' I cried. 'The call has been with me as long as I can remember. I want to answer it. Rita, I need to answer it. Can you help me?'

"And thus began my apprenticeship into the hushed world of librarianship. She sneaked me in the back door each morning where I began in the stacks, that area of the library where the public never goes. I met other librarians. They clothed me in librarian clothes and put me to work in the back doing the most menial tasks. I cleaned the floors, emptied the garbage, and performed cunnilingus on other librarians. There was a training area in the very rear of the stacks where they would strap me to a table, run their hands over my naked body, and let Jerome the janitor have violent sex with me while they watched. I was never allowed to speak or make any sound. We live and work in a silent world. Despite the physical strain and the long hours I never complained for no matter what I suffered in the library, I never wanted to be on the outside again. Eventually they fabricated fake ID and a fake high school diploma for me so that I could enter formal librarianship training. I finished the five year course in three years due largely to applying my new skills to the cocks of my college professors.

"My family turned me out, so Rita set me up in an

apartment with another librarian. We were completely isolated from society, going to the library early every morning and returning late at night too exhausted to do anything but fall asleep. Slowly I developed the skills of a librarian. My Kegel muscles became stronger and stronger, my throat relaxed during insertion, my anus graciously accepted whatever sought entrance. After four years they took me to the library administration building for testing. There I demonstrated my skills to the library administrators. One of the tests involved my being tied naked to a hook in the ceiling and being spanked and then fucked by men in masks. It took me three trips to administration building before I could complete that portion of the training in complete silence. Once I had been fully tested by library administration I was sent to see Commissioner Filopad for final approval. He is a small but impressive man. I found him to be very strict. He spent several hours with me and I was quite sore afterward. But when I left I was a city librarian.

"The next morning when I arrived at the library the other librarians stood in line to hug and congratulate me. That morning, in my tweed skirt, clunky shoes, and rimless glasses I walked out of the stacks and quietly took a seat behind the small desk by the front door. At long last I was *librarian*.

Like all rookies, I started out in circulation, but I had talent and advanced quickly. I made reference desk in just over three years, making me the youngest librarian in the city to hold such a prestigious position. Everything I had dreamed of that night by the dumpster had come true.

"I settled into the quiet and predictable routine of the reference librarian. Each library card has a special symbol on the back indicating what level of service the patron is entitled to receive. All requests are made in an elaborate code. For instance, if a customer asks to find out the population of Somalia, it means that he wants to fuck me between the tits. If he wants to know the boiling point of Freon, that means that he wants he wants anal intercourse. If a woman comes and asks for the number of crewmen on the first voyage of Columbus it means that I should suck her nipples while fingering her down below. It a man, a woman, and a German shepherd come in and ask how many bricks there are in the great wall of China it means . . . well, you get the drift. There are over ten thousand requests, and the librarian must know the meaning of each and be able to respond. Mistakes are severely punished. We have a regular by the name of Mr. Milpy who comes in once a week and asks for the height of the largest Egyptian pyramid. That means I should lean back in my wheeled chair, spread my legs, and put a stapler in my cunt."

"Mr. Gerald Milpy?" I asked.

"Yes, do you know him?"

"I do," I said. "What kind of people come to libraries?"

"All sorts of people. A lot of government officials come to the library. Prominent businessmen. The decision about who gets a library card is made down town at library administration. The process is very secret. We take applications and send them down there, but we never know who will be approved and who will not. All I know is that the richer and more powerful you are the more likely it is that you are carrying a library card somewhere in your wallet."

"Do the police have cards?" I asked.

"No," she said. "Police don't use libraries. Because of a long standing agreement, police take their business to parking enforcement. We librarians look down on the meter maids as untrained, undisciplined, and noisy, but the police like their trailer-trash enthusiasm. They say there's a certain captain at parking enforcement who can juice a grapefruit with her cunt."

I pushed for a change of subject. "How did you end up living with your sister?'

"I had been working at the reference desk for about a year. My family hadn't spoken to me since they learned that I was librarying for a living. For a while that was okay because I made the other librarians my family. But I missed my real family and thought about them often when alone in my bed at night. One evening I was driving around the city thinking of mother and I saw Totally Naked Women Here. I thought of mother and Candace and pulled into the parking lot. It was my way of remembering a normal family life like I had before the library. I took a seat away from the stage and ordered a club soda. When I looked up the stripper was facing away from me bent over with her legs spread. I thought to myself *I know that butt*. It was larger and mature, but that was the same little butt I used to see every Christmas when little Candace would be pulling down her new Christmas thong to wiggle her ass for our Uncle Mort. When she turned and faced the audience I saw that I was right. The butt was attached to Candace.

"She finished her show and came to my table carrying her thong in her hand. She was still as beautiful as ever. The reunion was awkward. She had moved to the city and become a respected exotic dancer. I had become a librarian. But blood is thicker than those social distinctions. She didn't want to be seen at her work talking to a librarian so we went to a nearby bookstore to talk. We talked and talked, me with my plaid flannel skirt and my hair in a bun, her in her miniskirt and spiked heels. Like a good girl she had dropped out of high school to work with mother at Tits and Taffy. However, when the taffy market crashed the place closed. Mother, who had been working her way through engineering school for twenty-five years, gave up the stripping altogether and became a nuclear power plant designer. Candace felt hemmed in by stripping for the same audience every night in the same little suburban tittie clubs. One day she got on a bus and came to the city to make her fortune. Mort, our uncle, knew her talent and immediately put her to work.

"Because both of us had no time for anything but our careers, we were both living alone. We decided we would get an apartment together. She tried to keep secret from her co-workers the fact that she was rooming with a practicing librarian, but the word got out. Fortunately, the other strippers had hearts of gold and accepted me as if I were a normal person."

Patty and I had both finished our coffees. Patty's eyes shined in the white florescent light of the the coffee shop. There was a teardrop in the corner of her eye as she thought of her sister. I took out the piece of notebook paper that I had found in the book at the library and handed it to her. She read it and said, "Drop the Pantz case, or else? Or else what? William? Who wrote this?"

"I thought you might be able to tell me," I said. "I found the note in a library book by a guy with the same name as mine."

"William James?"

"Yeah, but I didn't write it?"

"*The Varieties of Religious Experience*," she said. "What about them?"

"Was that the name of the book?"

"I think it was," I said. "Is that a clue?"

"Maybe," she said. "What do you think?"

"I think I want to search your sister's room at your apartment. We may find something there."

"Okay, we can do that now." I left the coffee shop with Patty and walked openly down the street with her to the Gremlin. People could think what they wanted. Maybe she was a librarian, but she was a person first. When we got to the Gremlin the meter had expired and there was a parking ticket under the windshield wiper. I pulled it out and looked at it. Someone has scrawled in green magic marker across the ticket the words, "Drop the Pantz case, or else." I folded the ticket and put it in my pocket. We got into the car and she gave me directions to her apartment. We had driven a few blocks when she said, "William, if you asked me how old Attilla the Hun was when he died, I could blow you while you drive."

"That is very unsafe," I said, remembering my years with the force. "Many a driver has swerved off the road and been killed by hitting a parking meter that would not break away because of getting sucked off while driving." Patty pouted and said she was sorry we brought it up.

Patty and Candace shared a small two bedroom apartment above a flashlight repair shop. She took me up and made coffee while I looked around the apartment. "Our bedrooms are in the back," she told me. I opened the first of the doors. "That one is mine," she said. I was looking at a small bedroom with nothing in it but a plain bed. No dresser, no night stand. Patty appeared behind me with the cups of coffee. "I live a simple life," she said. "I plan to put some straps on the four corners of the bed in case I have guests some day, but I haven't gotten around to it."

"No books?" I asked.

"No," she said. "No books. When we moved in, Candy demanded certain rules. One of them was no books in the apartment. She accepted the fact that I was a librarian, but she would not tolerate my bringing it into our home."

I went to the next room and opened the door, "This is where Candace sleeps," Patty said. The room was the opposite Patty's. The large bed was covered with pillows and stuffed animals. There was a dresser and night stand piled with colored bras and thongs. She had plastered the walls with strip club promotional posters. Most of them featured a woman called Seamy Frigg. Patty pointed to one of them, "That is our beloved mother," she said. "Frigg was her stage name."

I pushed the stuffed animals and old thongs aside looking for a clue. Nothing seemed out of order until I reached between the mattress and box springs and felt something hard. I pulled out a book. Holding it up to Patty, I said, "What is this?" Patty was shocked.

"I didn't put it there. I have been true to my word. No books in our home."

"If you didn't put it there, Candy must have," I said. Patty put her hand on my penis and looked into my eyes.

"You really are a detective, aren't you?" The book was a black leather bound volume with the words "Holy Bibble, James King Edition" printed in gold on the front.

I handed the book to Patty, "You are the librarian. Tell me what this is?" She opened the book and examined the first few pages.

"The library has lots of Bibles, of course, but I have

never seen a Holy Bibble. I says it is the word of God translated from the ineffable by James King. All rights reserved and copyright 1978. It was privately printed. Let me read a bit of it." She climbed onto Candy's cluttered bed and opened the book. "You can sit down there," she said pointing to the end of the bed. "Feel free to look up my skirt while you wait." She lifted her knees and spread her legs as she read. She was wearing the same black stockings and garter belt I had seen in my office when we met. Once again she had no panties. I looked up her dress and had the feeling that I had seen that pussy somewhere before. I let the thought pass and waited for her to finish reading.

"Well?" I finally said, "What is it?"

"William," she answered, "Are you familiar with the regular Bible?"

"Of course I am familiar with the Bible," I told her, "What do you think I am—some kind of guy who never finished high school and was driven out of his home town by the Women's Philosophy Club and caused his football team to lose the state championship and doesn't even know what's in the Bible?"

"Of course I don't think that, William," she said. "This book is like the Bible, but different. Do you remember Adam and Eve in the Book of Genesis?"

"Of course I do?" I said.

"Well listen to this. I will start right after woman is created from Adam's rib. She started to read.

"And the man and his wife were naked, and were not ashamed in their nakedness. The woman who was called Eve had big firm titties and soft hair between her legs. And the man, who was called Adam, had a big cock that was never soft or limp. Yet Adam did not put his cock inside Eve's pussy, and Eve did not sucketh upon Adam's cock. And Adam did not put his mouth upon the woman's crack. Now the serpent was the subtlest of the creatures made by God and the serpent came to Adam and said to him, 'Why do you not fucketh that hot babe with the bit tits?' and Adam did not answer because he knew not of what the serpent spoke and wanted to be left alone to rub his penis with his hand. For God had forbidden the man to eat from the tree of knowledge and thus he was stupid. The serpent went to the woman and said, 'Why do you not compel Adam to puteth his cock inside you?" And she did not answer because she did not know of what the serpent spoke and wanted to be left alone to rub between her legs with her finger. For God had forbidden the woman from eating from the Tree of Knowledge and thus she was also stupid. And then the serpent offered to the woman fruit of the tree of knowledge saying that if she ate she would know what to do with the member that sticketh out from Adam's groin and she ate the fruit. Then Eve took the fruit to Adam and he ate and their eyes were opened and they knew they were naked. Then Adam saw that he should put his cock inside of Eve and she did lie upon the ground and he did fucketh her so that they did not have to rub themselves. And when they were done she tooketh his cock in her mouth and sucketh it and it was good for both of them. And after they had eaten the fruit of the Tree of Knowledge the man and the woman fucketh and sucketh in the Garden of Eden from morning to night like the bunnies in the field. And God saw what they were doing and said to them, 'You have eaten of the Tree of Knowledge and now you have fucketh and sucketh all throughout my Garden and frightened the animals with your moans and groans and made a big mess.' And God expelled them from the Garden and told them to go do their fucking and sucking somewhere else and they were cast out. And after Adam and Eve had been sent away, God looked upon the Garden of Eden and saw that it was untended, and that it was unwatered and that it was overgrown. And to return the Garden to the way that it had been formed by his perfect hand, God created gay men."

She stopped reading. The story of Adam and Eve didn't seem like the one I remembered, but I waited for her to comment.

"It is some alternate version of the King James Bible," she said, "possibly a modern gnostic offshoot."

"Gnostic?" I asked.

"A word from the Greek meaning 'knowledge.' It implies secret knowledge. Gnostics attach themselves to mainstream theology asserting secret doctrines and gospels unknown by the greater body of the church membership. In early Christianity there were many gnostic sects. On of the groups treated semen as holy."

"Was Candace a gnostic?"

"She did have a phase in which she thought she wanted to become a nun. She bought a habit, a rosary, and a cross. But after the restraining order, I thought she had given it up."

"Vagina Smooth mentioned a restraining order," I said.

"Yes," Patty said, "I was here when it was served. The Catholic Church was not pleased."

"So what kind of church uses a Bibble?"

"There is a name and address stamped inside the front cover. It says, 'Reverend Sister Diana Babylon, Holy Dereamer Pentacostal Gnostic Church of the Tribulation, 1700 Pine Street.'"

"Did Candace go there?"

"Not that I know of," she said.

"It looks to me like I will have to talk to Reverend Babylon."

"Do you think she knows where to find Candace?"

"It could be," I said.

Patty reached between her legs and fondled herself. "When you are looking for a missing person do you ever fuck the missing person's sister on the missing person's bed?"

"Sometimes I do," I said, "but in this case I think that going to this church would be more useful,"

I left Patty on the bed playing with herself. Outside the rain was falling hard on the city, driving the hookers and drug dealers inside. The mean streets were wet, empty, and gray. I sloshed my way to the Gremlin. There was a sheet of paper stuffed in the passenger door handle. I pulled it out and climbed into the car. I opened the soggy sheet of paper. It was lined notebook paper with the words, "Drop the Pantz case, or else," written in green magic marker. As I was reading the note the passenger window exploded inward sending broken glass across my lap and onto the front seat. I looked over and saw a bullet hole on the inside of the passenger door. I cranked the engine of the Gremlin and got the hell out of there.

When I was out of the neighborhood I called the office. Teena answered. She sounded like she had a mouth full of marbles. "It's William," I said. "What's wrong with you?"

Her voice came back to normal, "Oh nothing," she said, "I was eating a muffin. It was a muffin."

"Okay," I said, "have there been any calls?"

"Mr. Milpy called. He wants a report and more pictures. Mrs. Milpy called and wants to know when you are resuming her surveillance."

"Anything else?"

"There was this other call. A young woman imitating a man with a deep voice said, 'Drop the Pantz case, or else,' and then hung up. Do you know what that is about?"

"Not really," I told her, "but I think that person just tried to kill me."

"Oh William," she cried, "are you in danger?"

"I think so," I told her. "I am going to Totally Naked Women Here, and then to church."

"To church?" she said.

"To church. I will see you at the office tomorrow?"

"So you won't be back into the office today?"

"No."

"I will stay here working. I will get to that filing as soon as I finish this muffin. You can count on that."

The rain was coming down hard, soaking me through the broken window of the Gremlin. I drove to the industrial district and into the parking lot of Totally Naked Women Here. The parking lot was empty. I pulled my hat over my eyes and ran for the door.

The club was warm inside. The soft neon on the wall and the floodlights around the stripper pole was a welcome respite from the gloom of the library. I took off my overcoat and shook off the rain. Bjorn Frow came up to greet me wearing the too-small tuxedo: the uniform of his profession. "Good evening, Mr. James," he said. "Wet night out there."

"Yes it is Bjorn," I said, laying my coat over a chair.

"You seem to be wet only on your left side," he observed.

"Good observation," I said. "You will need to catch those kinds of details if you want to be a PI. Someone shot out my car window trying to get me off the Pantz case. It comes with the job." I looked around. A couple of guys sat at the bar drinking. Two men sat at tables near the stage waiting for the next stripper. "Is Vagina Smooth here?" I asked Bjorn.

"Jane Madison," he said.

"What?"

"You don't use her real name out here in public."

"Okay, is Jane Madison here?" He nodded over his shoulder. Vagina was walking onto the stage wearing only a red throng. I left my coat and took a seat at the edge of the stage. Vagina saw me and smiled. She approached me and leaned over so her bare titties dangled in front of me. She squeezed her nipples. "Hello William, it is so good to see you," she said. "Have you found Candy?"

"Not yet," I said, "but I spent the afternoon with her sister."

"The librarian?" She bounced her breasts in her hands.

"Yeah," I said, "the librarian."

"What did you think about her?" She turned around and bent over to I had a view of the red thong running up the crack of her ass. She looked am me through her spread legs with her hair hanging on the stage.

"She wants to find her sister?" I said.

"What I mean is did she offer to perform unspeakable sexual acts on you?" Vagina pulled the crotch of her thong to the side allowing me to see her labia.

"Well," I said, "she *is* a librarian after all. I just keep my mind on my job." Vagina spread the lips of her pussy with her fingers so I could see the pink inside. "I need to know, Vagina, did you ever see Candace reading a book called the Holy Bibble?"

"Do you mean the Bible?" she asked as she pulled down her thong and wiggled her ass.

"No, the Bibble, rhymes with 'nibble,' written by James King." She pulled her buttocks apart to expose her pink anus.

"I don't remember her reading at all. Maybe she read the Bibble?" She turned around and leaned over so her tits hung in my face.

"I think this church with its Holy Bibble has something to do with her disappearance."

"What are you going to do?" She licked her nipples as we spoke.

"I am going to church." I put a folded dollar on the stage.

She picked it up with her buttocks, and looking over her shoulder said, "You be careful, William. Take Bjorn with you. He can keep you safe."

I left the stage to find Bjorn while Vagina finished her dance. I explained to him what I had learned from the examination of Patty and Candy's apartment. He agreed to go with me if I would give him some detective work to do in return.

I had time to kill so I had the kitchen fix me a burger. When Vagina was done with her dance she put on her robe and joined me at the table. We ate and talked while Chesty Tits-a-Lot and Finger Mi went through their routines. When I was finished eating and the girls were done stripping, the four of us went back in the girls dressing room and played Scrabble until it was time for me to go.

Outside in the parking lot the rain continued. The upholstery in the Gremlin was soaked, and while I had been inside someone had stolen my hub caps. We decided to take Bjorn's truck. Bjorn drove a huge four-wheel drive pickup with monster truck tires. I climbed the chrome ladder into the passenger seat and Bjorn brought the behemoth to life. We plowed through the rain to the edge of the industrial district where rundown motels with free porn hide the U-pull it junkyards out behind. The building at 1700 Pine Street was a windowless gray concrete structure sandwiched between a Romanian sausage factory and a tampon manufacturing plant. There was nothing to identify it as a house of the Lord except for a small neon cross above the green metal door. Bjorn parked on the street fifty yards past the building and I climbed down from the truck.

The interior of the church held a stage and about a hundred folding chairs. Twenty or so of the chairs were occupied when we got there. The stage had a wooden speaker's podium with a neon cross on the front identical to the one above the door. A silent man in a suit handed us a program. Bjorn and I took seats in the next to last row and sat quietly waiting for service to start. The room began to fill. A well dressed African American couple took the two seats between me and the middle aisle. The man wore a gray striped suit and red tie. The woman was packed in a white blouse and dark wool skirt. Both of them wore strong cologne. Two small Asian women who appeared to be mother and daughter took the seats on the other side of Bjorn.

At nine o'clock the lights dimmed and generic religious music emanated from a boom box behind the podium. The crowd stood. A spotlight came on and the Reverend Diana Babylon walked on to the stage. She was a small blond woman wearing sheer white robes that did not conceal the firm round breasts beneath. She carried book I recognized as James King's Bibble.

She stood behind the podium and spoke into the microphone. "Our scripture lesson this evening is from the Book of Jonah," she said. And she began to read, "The Lord came to Jonah and said to him that he should go to the City of Belli for there were many whores there and that Jonah should fuck them in the name of the Lord so that they should know the only true God. But Jonah knew that the whores of Belli were all fat and he did not want to fuck them because his heart was hardened against fat whores and his cock was not hardened so he ran from the Lord and took a boat to the city of Pussi. The Lord sent a great storm upon the sea but Jonah had gone below deck and was asleep. The captain of the ship came to him and asked him what the hell was going on and whether Jonah's God had sent the storm. And Jonah said that the storm was probably sent by his God to punish him for going to Pussi, so the sailors took Jonah and tossed him overboard into the water in order that the seas would calm. And then the Lord sent Jonah a great white whale who took Jonah inside of her many times and the whale had huge tits for Jonah to put his cock between and a giant pussy that did cleave to Jonah and the great whale did swallow Jonah many times and made him cummeth in her ass. And for three days Jonah did spend his seed in the great white whale and then she did let him go. And thereafter Jonah understood his duty to the Lord and he did go to Belli and did fuck the fat whores so that the whores of Belli thereafter knew the power of the Lord."

"Praise be the Lord," yelled the woman next to me.

After the scripture lesson, we sang hymns. Then we were directed to greet our brethren in the congregation. The black woman next to me turned and said, "May the Lord be with you." I reached out my hand to shake hers. She reached out her hand, but instead of shaking mine grabbed me by the crotch. "The man next to me is not my husband," she said. "He's my brother. Not my brother like in a black man, but my brother like we both came from the same mother. He has been fucking me in the ass all week. It is disgusting. Do you like my tits?"

"Very nice," I said.

"I suck my brother's cock," she said. "He says it's not incest as long as he doesn't do my pussy." I looked past her to her brother. He seemed to have his hand up the dress of one of the female ushers. "My name is Flaba Brown," she said. I heard a commotion behind me and turned to look. The two Asian women next to Bjorn had gotten his fly open and were hopping up and down in excitement.

"Little black dick," the mother was repeating as she pushed her daughter's head toward Bjorn's crotch. "You suckee little dick."

"What did you do?" I demand of Bjorn.

"Nothing," he said. "They pulled my pants open." The younger of the two small women had clamped her mouth on Bjorn and was not going to let go.

The mother was repeating, "Miji suckee suckee."

The lights came down and the music began again. Reverend Babylon took the stage and Flaba Brown took her seat next to me. Bjorn sat with the young Asian still clamped to his cock.

"Sinners," Reverend Babylon yelled into the microphone. "You know who you are. The reamers and the reamed. You men have put your cocks inside the holes of many women and you are not satisfied. You put your seed into the mouth of your woman, and into her pussy, and into her anus, but you are not satisfied for you are not pure. So you look upon your neighbor's wife, and your wife's sister, and the waitress down at the coffee shop so that you can put your cock in their holes hoping that you shall be satisfied. And you put on your good suit and your new shoes but what you really seek is pussy that will satisfy you. You are lost, for you can never capture the satisfaction that lies in Lordly copulation until you have been cleansed of all your unclean fucking—until you have been dereamed.

"And you ladies. You get up and paint your eyes so that they will attract a man and you color you lips red so that it will look like a cunt. And you put on your pushup bra so your bothers can see you tits. And you wrap yourself tight in your new clothes so that your husband will want to put his big cock inside you. And you fuck your husband but then you look to your husband's friends, and the mailman, and the Mexican who does your gardening and you go and suck them so that they cum in your mouth and you whisper to your boss at work that you like it up the ass. But you can not find the satisfaction that comes from copulation in the Lord until you are cleansed—until you are dereamed by the Pentacostal power of Gnostic Tribulation."

Reverend Babylon went on in the same vein for about half and hour, walking up and down the stage, her breasts bobbing beneath the sheer white gown. The energy in the crowd came to a fever pitch and the worshipers rose to their feet shouting and waving their arms. Flaba Brown, next to me was chanting and swaying to the rhythm of Diana Babylon's hypnotic sermon. Suddenly Flaba pulled open her blouse, unleashed her giant black breasts from her bra, and thrust them toward me as I sat there in the chair.

"Praise the Lord and grab the titties," she yelled at me as her undulating melons hit me in the face and knocked me over backward onto the floor. I felt a hand slide down my pants and grab my cock. The Flaba fell upon me. I grabbed Flaba's breasts and pushed them.

I could see Bjorn. He still had the young Asian woman clamped to his cock with the mother screaming, "Suckee, suckee, you little bitch." I turned back to my own attacker. The big black woman had her dress up, and her naked black ass was descending on my face. A moment later I was buried in pussy and asshole. She was too strong and heavy for me to push her away. I felt my way around her butt and thighs looking for a handhold beneath her dress while she slathered my face with vaginal fluid. Somebody was jerking my cock, but blinded by the Flaba's crotch and skirt, it could have been anybody. I put a finger in her anus hoping it would force her off me but it just encouraged her. There was nothing to do but get a breath when I could and wait. Soon the preaching calmed and a glimmer of light appeared. Flaba rose to her feet and I sat up. We returned to our chairs. I wiped my face on my sleeve while Flaba buttoned her blouse over her still quivering tits. Bjorn was pulling his pants up and the Asian mother was wiping semen off her daughters face. Little Miji's mother bowed thanks to Bjorn over and over.

Reverend Babylon then invited the members of the congregation to be blessed and dereamed. Flaba whispered to me, "It makes you a virgin again, so that next time is like the first time." Anyone who wished could approach the stage and receive a dispensation from the Reverend that would absolve them from all unlordly copulation. Flaba and her brother joined the line to receive the blessing. Little Miji and her mother joined. At the stage Reverend Diana put her hand on the heads of each person who kneeled before her and removed the stain of copulation. Bjorn and I stayed in our seats.

After the dereaming the plate was passed and money flowed. Bjorn and I rolled out eyes at each other as we saw the stacks of twenties accumulating in the collection plate. Despite the bad address and the plain cinder block church, the Reverend was not doing too badly. At the end, the music played softly as the congregation chatted and filed out of the building. Bjorn and I waited for the crowd to clear and went up to the door from which Reverend Babylon had appeared. A large man in a black robe guarded the door.

"We'd like to talk to the Reverend," I said. He opened the door without comment and allowed the two of us inside. Reverend Diana Babylon was lounging stark naked in the kind of over-sized leather recliner you might buy for your grandfather at Sears. She was smoking a Marlboro and fiddling with the remote to her television. Bjorn and I stood just inside the door until she picked a channel showing a basketball game.

"Approach," she said. Bjorn and I stepped forward.

"I am William James," I said. "I'm a private detective—."

"I know who you are," she interrupted.

"You do?"

"I know everything. I saw you in the back with Flaba Brown and her brother. What a whore she is. Her brother is even worse. The two of them live together. He fucks Flaba in the ass and claims it's not incest. I can't even believe it. Do you think I'm cute?"

"You are very attractive," I said.

"I could afford a boob job," she said. "I think my tits are too small."

"Your breasts are just fine," I told her, "I came here to ask you about—."

"I know that," she interrupted again. "You are looking for Candy Pantz."

"That is correct," I said. "How did you know?"

"I told you, I know everything. But I don't know where Candy went so I guess I don't know everything, but I know everything except that."

"Did she attend church here?"

"Candace was studying to be a sister." She tapped the ash from her cigarette and glanced up at the basketball game on the television. "We were studying the parable of the man from the mountains and the Lord spoke to her and called her to become a Bride of Chris."

"Of Christ?" I asked.

"No. A bride of Chris. Our savior. The parable inspired her to make Chris her personal savior."

"I don't know that parable," I said.

Reverend Babylon puffed on her smoke then reached down and scratched her crotch. "Your friend is staring at my pussy," she said. I looked at Bjorn.

"Stop staring at the Reverend's pussy," I told him.

"I wasn't," he said. "She's naked. I was just looking at her."

"I'm right here," she said to Bjorn. "You don't have to talk about me in the third person. And you were looking at my crotch. Did you think you were going to get to stick that black dick of yours in me?"

"I wasn't thinking anything?" Bjorn protested.

"Bjorn," I said, "Go out and guard the truck."

"Gladly," he said. He turned and left the room,

"He wanted to fuck me," she said when he was

gone.

"Tell me the parable of the man from the mountains," I said.

"The parable is from the Holy Bibble. A woodsman, his wife, Edna, and his two helpers came down from the mountains and they met Chris on the road. And the woodsman said to Chris that his hands were cold from work in the mountains and that that hands of his workers were cold but they had no flint or matches or butane lighters with which to make a fire to warm themselves. They had heard of the Holy Chris performing great miracles so they asked him to make a fire so that they could warm their hands. Then Chris looked to him and asked why do you ask me for fire to warm your hands and the hands of your helpers when you have with you your wife, Edna, and you could warm your hands upon her pussy and your helpers could warm their hands upon her titties. But the woodsman objected and said to the Holy Chris that if he were to warm his hands upon the pussy of Edna she would be made cold and would shiver and when it came time to fuck, her pussy would be cold. And he said if I allow my workers to warm their hands upon her titties she will become cold and will shiver and rubbing her titties will make the workers want to fuck her and then I will have to watch them every minute so that they don't go off in the bushes with her and fuck. Then Chris said to the woodsman that he must look to the blessings given him before he asked God for another and the woodsman asked of what blessings did the Holy Chris speak. And Chris said his wife, Edna, had a pussy that was always warm no matter how many cold hands were put upon it and that her titties were always warm and that no matter how many men put hands upon her titties she would not fuck any man but her husband although she might give a blow job now and then. And the woodsman turned to his wife and asked if what the Holy Chris said was true and Edna said that it was true and that before she was married many men had warmed their hands upon her pussy and she did never shiver, or push them away, and never did her pussy become cold. And she said that many men had warmed their hands upon her titties but never had her titties become cold and that she had never fucked a man who warmed his hands upon her titties but had given a blow job now and then. And the woodsman asked of his wife why she had not told him this and she said he ought to have known without her having to ask. So the woodsman warmed his hands upon the pussy of Edna and the helpers warmed their hands upon her titties and her pussy stayed warm and her titties stayed warm. And the woodsman realized that he was blessed. And Edna was much pleased that she could be a blessing to husband and was thankful to the Holy Chris for opening the eyes of her husband to the blessings he had, and she got on her knees before the Holy Chris and gave him a blow job, and when she was done the Holy Chris baptized her face in the spirit of the Lord."

I pondered the parable unsure what it all meant. The Reverend snuffed out her cigarette. "So that story made Candace want to become a nun?" I asked.

"A sister. A bride of Chris. But not a nun. I have signed a legal consent order agreeing not to use the word 'nun.' Catholics can be very litigious. But our sisters get to wear cool black outfits just like real nuns. And trust me, the underwear is a whole lot better here."

"How's that?"

"Hose, garter belts, crotchless everything, nipple rings, piercings, vaginal jewelry. Anything that will enhance a woman's sellibacy."

"Celibacy. You mean no sex?" I asked.

"Sellibacy with an 's'–the capacity for being sold. Candace was to learn to sell it for the greater glory of Chris the Lord."

"The 'it' being . . . ?"

"Pussy, ass, blow jobs, butt fucks. Things that men want from women and that women want to give to men."

"It sounds like prostitution to me?" I said.

"It looks like that from the outside. However, a prostitute is interested in getting money. Our sisters seek solace in sellibacy because they cannot find sexual satisfaction unless the man is paying for it. Candace had boyfriends. She could love them and satisfy them in the bedroom and get pleasure from doing so. But her ultimate desire was to sell her poon for money. She could do it for love, but she could not get that long hard orgasm she so desired. What made her hot, was to know that she was trading pussy for cash, that her crotch was a commodity, and her titties for sale. With money on the bedstand or the dashboard of the car she would orgasm hard and long. But selling it is a dangerous and degrading business, particularly if you don't need the money. So she came to us and we provided a spiritual answer."

"How so?"

"I don't really understand Candy's problem. You touch my clit with a man's dick, or a tongue, or a finger, or an unbalanced washing machine on the spin cycle . . . or a dildo, or a hamster or a peanut butter sandwich and I cum like a research libraryian at a statistician's convention. No problem. But that wasn't the way it was for Candace. She needed more than just a weekly dereaming to clean away her sins and reset her orgasmic mechanism. She needed the deeper kind of spiritual approaches we can only provide through meditation, study and the sisterhood."

"How does that work?'

"She had studied the Bibble and taken the classes. We planned last Sunday to send her out of town to the convent where she could learn the art of sellibacy. But she never showed up."

"Where is this convent?" I asked.

"Just outside the city in a small town called Fumbuck. She would have spent six months there doing spiritual training, but she disappeared after her shift at Totally Naked Women Here, and hasn't been seen since"

"What do you think happened?'

The reverend rolled sideways on the recliner and lifted her leg. She had a neatly trimmed clamshell of a cunt. "Probably kidnapped," she said. "Maybe she is being held hostage by four of five bald, middle aged men with big fat stomachs and being forced to suck their dicks while they rest their big beer bellies on her sweet little head. And while she tries to breathe and chokes on the dicks, the others take turns fucking her from behind or giving her tongue in her asshole. And after she has sucked and fucked them all she has to go into the kitchen naked, with cum running from her cunt, and cook them all macaroni and cheese."

"Why do you think that would happen?" I asked,

"No reason," she said. "It just seems to happen to a lot of women, so I thought it might be happening to her."

I gave the reverend my card. "If you hear from Candace, you will give me a call, won't you?"

"I sure will," she said. "She is one of my flock. I want to see her safe . . . . So did you want me to fuck me while you are here?"

"Could I take a rain check?" I said. "I really need to go."

"Sure," she said, "I will make a note of it. One dip in my pussy for Detective Williams James."

I left the Reverend's office through the only door and found myself in the main church area. The lights were low and everyone was gone. I walked down the center aisle toward the exit when I heard the words, "That's him." It was Flaba Brown and her brother. "He pulled down my under things and put his mouth on my love spot." The black man stepped forward to face me.

"Did you molest my sister?" he demanded.

"I didn't do anything," I protested. "She knocked me down and sat on my face. I was lucky not to be suffocated."

"Are you trying to say that my sister is a fat nigger slut who sat on your face and takes it up the ass from her own brother . . . and I don't mean brother like in another black person, but her biological brother."

"I am not trying to say anything," I said.

"Well, you apologize," he demanded.

"Let's make him come home with us," Flaba said "and make him apologize there." I decided that a trip home with Flaba and her brother was not going to be productive, so I made a run for it. Neither of them were fast. I arrived down the street at Bjorn's truck with the two of them panting far behind me.

"Let's go," I said to Bjorn. He turned the key and the truck roared to life. We left my two pursuers shaking their fists at me from the sidewalk.

"Did you learn anything?" Bjorn asked.

"A lot." I proceeded to tell him about Candy's intention of becoming a bride of Chris.

"But does that bring us any closer to finding her," Bjorn said.

I had to admit that it didn't. I comforted myself with the fact that I had only been on the case for two days. Considering that the day had begun with me being beat up by Mrs. Mohammad and being sent to jail, I felt okay about my progress. I told Bjorn that in the morning I wanted him to contact Ebenezer Jones and go with Jones to see Mrs. Milpy. I explained that Ebenezer worked in library security, a job not unlike strip club security, and that they shared and interest in becoming private detectives. Mrs. Milpy, I explained, would show them what to do.

As we drove home through the dark streets of the city, I heard a sound in the truck that seemed out of place. It was a wet sound, not the sound of a motor or tires on streets. Bjorn pulled the truck up in front of my apartment and rather than jumping out I turned on the dome light in the cab. There between Bjorn's legs was little Miji, dick in mouth, smiling up at me with her round Asian face. She spit out the cock, smiled at me and said, "Miji suck little black dick."

"Bjorn," I said, "what's with that?"

"William," he answered, "I think I'm in love."

Chapter 3

When I woke up on Wednesday morning my body was still throbbing from the beating I had taken at the hands of Mrs. Mohammad and Bruno. I could taste Flaba Brown's hairy black vagina. I made some instant coffee on the hotplate in my room and headed for the office. The streets were foggy. I slipped through Otto's unnoticed and limped up the stairs to my office. Teena was in the office putting papers into the bottom drawer of her file cabinet. She was bent over so that her ample butt hung out below the hem of her miniskirt. Her thick shaved pussy lips peaked out from between her legs.

"Teena," I said, "wear some underwear for Christ's sake." She jerked to attention and pulled down her skirt.

"Did you see my vagina just now?"

"How could I help it," I said. "You had it hanging out there like a flag on the Fourth of July."

"I did not, and I didn't know your were coming in. You should have knocked."

"Teena," I said, "this is my office. I don't have to knock. And it is a place of business. Any member of the public can walk in here without knocking, and when they do the first thing they see is not supposed to be your naked ass."

"You are right of course, Mr. James," she said. "I am so sorry." She pulled down on her short skirt which barley covered her pussy when she was standing upright. "You could spank me," she said. "That might help. I respond well to spanking. I could lean over your desk and you could—."

"That's enough, Teena," I said. "I do not want to

spank you. Just wear some panties when you come to work."

"Will you come to Otto's on Friday and look at my breasts and my vagina when I dance for the fund raiser?"

"I will be your biggest fan," I told her.

"When I dance at the fund raiser, do you think the men in the audience will get boners?"

"I am sure they will, Teena," I said. "Today, however, we have a detective agency to run." I told her about the meeting with Patty Pantz, finding the Holy Bibble in Candy's room, and the trip to the Holy Dereamer Pentecostal Gnostic Church of the Tribulation. I told her about the gunshot to the window of the Gremlin and the notes in green marker trying to warn me off the Pantz case.

"It sounds very complicated," she said, "and dangerous."

"It is, Teena," I said. "Candy worked her Saturday shift at Totally Naked Women Here and never made it home to the apartment she shared with her sister Patty, the librarian. She was supposed to report the next day to the convent in little town of Fumbuck to become a Bride of Chris. She never showed up. Her co-workers were all strippers working their way through school and everyone of them has a heart of gold. She herself was on a spiritual journey and kept the Holy Bibble as the only book in her bedroom. No one has demanded a ransom."

"How did she leave?" Teena asked.

"What do you mean?" I asked.

"When she left on Saturday night. Did she drive a car, take a cab, ride the bus?"

"Mmmmm," I said. "Good point. Maybe it is time to talk to my buddies on the force?"

I left the office and headed to my real office: the city streets. Otto's was empty except for Bret sitting at the bar. She motioned me over.

"Where you going, William?" she asked.

"I'm taking the bus over to Totally Naked Women Here to pick up the Gremlin. I had to leave it there last night."

"Can I come along," she asked. She was back in the skin tight riding clothes that showed off her athletic physique and her lack of tits. Seeing me eye the outline of her nipples she rubbed one of the bumps and batted her eyelashes at me.

"I don't think so," I said. "I can't work with dames following me around."

"Come on, William," she begged, "Twenty four hours ago we were cellmates and your hand was up my skirt clamped on my privates. Now you can't even ride the bus with me?"

"Oh, all right," I told her. She hopped off the seat and put her arm in mine. The city was shrouded in fog. We walked down the street outside Otto's and waited at the corner for the number sixteen bus.

"That secretary of yours," Brett said, "is she gonna show her shit at the fund raiser this Friday?"

"Teena is looking forward to dancing," I said.

"Otto is fucking her, you know."

"I am aware of that."

"He says she could suck a golf ball through a garden hose."

"I wouldn't know," I said.

"I figured you were fucking her too. She is hot. I love those big tits of hers. If I was a man, I'd fuck her. In fact, I'd fuck her woman to woman if she was so inclined, or she could fuck me with a strap-on."

"You will have to talk to her about that."

"If I was you, I'd give her the business doggie style. But you do what you want. When the bus comes, how about you and I sit in the back and I will jerk you off."

"Brett, it is eight o'clock in the morning. We will be on a city bus."

"I can suck you. I suck a great dick. Lots of slobber and snot."

The graffiti-covered city bus arrived and I followed Brett inside. The seats were empty, but the center aisle was packed with standing Catholic school girls in white blouses and plaid skirts. They hung from the overhead rails, blocking but refusing to take any of the empty seats. As we paid our fare the girls turned their heads to face us. Each pony-tailed head sported an angry stare.

We had to push through the schoolgirls to get to the unblocked seats at the rear door. The closest girl made a growling noise under her breath and glared at me. Brett, undeterred, pushed and elbowed a path through the plaid skirts telling one of the larger girls to "move her fat ass or go home limping." The girls made way for Brett, the way a crowd makes way for a crazy person, but then closed back in to block my way. As I pushed through, they stuck out their butts and elbows to hinder my passage. Hands grabbed my ass and my crotch. The large one who had drawn Brett's ire grabbed me by the ears and pulled my face between her breasts. With my head wedged between her young tits, I heard a voice whisper, "Drop the Pantz case, faggot." I reached out for any hand-hold and felt, in the sea of adolescent flesh, the hard barrel of a snub-nosed pistol. I yanked my head out of the big one's knockers, and looked down into the highly shined patent leather shoes they all wore. In the reflection off the shoes I could see that under the plaid skirts they wore identical thong underwear. I felt a hand on my cock outside my pants. I threw myself forward, knocking two of the girls into bus seats and emerged into open air at the back of the bus. I took a seat next to Brett on the back seat. The girls stared at us with cold Catholic school girl eyes. A little blond closest to us grabbed her crotch with her hand, thrust her hips in our direction, and stuck out her tongue.

"Come here you little cunt," Brett said in a stage whisper. "I'll give you something to hold that is a lot better than that stinky little snatch of yours." The girl gave us the finger and turned away. A grumble went through the group. "Catholic gang bitches," Brett said to me. "Can't ride a goddamn bus in the city any more without having some Catholic girl gang trying to stick something up your ass. Did I ever tell you about the time a dozen of them cornered me at the public playground over on Beech Street."

"No, Brett," I said.

"I won't go into it now. The memories are too painful, but I don't mind saying that I had to eat a lot of girl-gang pussy that night in order to get out of there alive. They say that girls the worst, and having been gang-raped by both, I can say that they aren't all that wrong."

The bus lurched to a stop. The doors opened and the schoolgirls left through the back door. Outside, nuns with nightsticks hurried them into Saint Darlene's School for Girls, an old brick schoolhouse with bars on the windows. Just before entering the school the little blond turned and flipped us off one last time. Seeing the finger in the air one of the nuns cracked her hard across the shins with a nightstick. The girl winced and disappeared limping through the door.

After the exodus of Catholic school girls, the bus was empty. Brett said, "No one would notice if I was to honk on you meat for a little. I told you, I can suck a cock like nobody's business."

"Not now, Brett," I said. "I'm working."

"Well if you change your mind just grab me by the ears and push my head into your crotch. It will be a secret signal between the two of us that you want me to blow you."

"I'll keep that in mind," I said.

The creaking bus bumped and bounced its way to the warehouse district and the parking lot of Totally Naked Women Here. Bret and I got off and walked across the lot to the Gremlin. Both the drivers side and passenger windows were now gone. While Brett watched, I got in. The seat was soaking wet. I put in the key and the car roared to life.

Brett was standing outside the passenger side window. "I'm going inside for some biscuits and gravy," she said.

"Totally Naked Women Here serves breakfast?" I said.

"Not as good as Mohammad's Pig and Pancake, but not bad, and you get to look at pussy while you eat."

"They have strippers during breakfast?"

"Sure," she said, "not the good heart-of-gold kind of stripper who dances for the night crowd, but something breathing with tits."

I turned off the motor and followed Brett into the club. The lights were turned up to bright. Several of the tables were occupied by men eating bacon and eggs. Up on the stage a heavy set middle aged Hispanic woman was leaning naked against the stripper pole chatting with the diners and smoking a cigarette. There was no music. Brett led me to a chair at the stage.

"*Hola* Brett," the naked Hispanic woman said

"*Hola* to you, Esmeralda," Brett answered.

"Who's your friend?"

"William," she said, "William James. He is the detective trying to find Candy Pantz."

"Pleased to meet you," she said. She leaned over and cradled her large brown breasts in her hands. "Like Mexican tits?"

"I do," I said, "and yours are quite attractive."

A voice came from behind us asking us if we wanted to order. Brett and I ordered the biscuits, gravy, and coffee. The waitress disappeared. Esmeralda stood back up and held her left breast in her hand. "No they are not. I'm too old for this stuff, really. I can't even dance anymore. At night I work as the cook, but it makes me feel good to get naked up on a stage now and then."

"You still look great," Brett said.

Our breakfast arrived. The waitress put the food on the edge of the stage. Brett and I pulled up our chairs to eat. Esmeralda came near us and squatted flat footed in front of our plates. She had thick black hair on her cunt. "We make the best plate of biscuits in the city," she told me and she was right. Both the biscuits and the gravy were delicious. I devoured the food with Esmeralda's hairy brown snatch looming in front of me.

"Esmeralda," I said with a mouth still half full of biscuits, "when the girls leave here at night, how do they get to their homes?"

"By cab," she said.

"Always," I asked.

"It is part of their pay. It is too dangerous to walk

or leave their cars in the lot. They always get a cab."

"Then Candy Pantz left here by taxi on Saturday night?"

"I don't know for sure, but that is what usually happens. They are not allowed to get rides from customers." She was holding her breasts in her hands staring at her nipples.

"What cab company do you use?"

"Yellowchecker."

"Yellowchecker Taxi Company?"

"Yeah," she said.

I left Brett at Totally Naked Women Here chatting with Esmeralda and started up the Gremlin. I thought about the Yellowchecker taxi company as I headed toward the avenues to check in on Bjorn, Ebenezer, and Mrs. Milpy.

The cold morning air whipped through the broken windows of the Gremlin and the wet seat soaked my pants. I drove out of the industrial district and into the opulent residential neighborhood where the Milpy's lived. When I arrived at the house, Bjorn's huge pick-up truck was parked in front. I parked the Gremlin behind his truck and went to the front door of the house. The door was unlocked.

I heard noise coming from the kitchen. I walked through the large living room toward the sound. In the kitchen, Mrs. Milpy had set up a tripod and video camera in one corner. Mrs. Milpy was laying on her back on the kitchen table with a long patterned dress pulled up to her belly button. Ebenezer Jones, the guard from the Mullberry Street library, was holding her black ankles in the air and was rhythmically fucking her on the table. The top part of the dress had been pulled down to expose her breasts and they were moving like tiny twin waterbeds. Mrs. Milpy wore a

brightly patterned wrap over her hair giving her a
Mrs. Butterworth look. Her head was tilted off the far
edge of the table and Bjorn had is cock in her mouth.
Little Miji was standing on a small stool running the
camera. Miji was wearing a tight red sleeveless blouse
but nothing below the waist. Bjorn was the first to see
me.

"William," Bjorn said, "come on in." Ebenezer
turned to look without taking his cock out of Mrs.
Milpy. Miji waved energetically from behind the
camera.

"Hello, Bjorn," I said. "It looks like you and Eb
figured out what to do."

Mrs. Milpy spit out Bjorn's cock and raised her
head. His cock wasn't as small as everyone made it
out to be. "Hello William," she said. "Come to check
up on your boys?"

I walked over to the table. "I wanted to make sure
they were providing the services you paid for, Mrs.
Milpy. They are both new to the business." Eb
continued to fuck her gently as I talked.

"What they lack in experience," she said, "they
make up for in creativity."

"And you are getting good pictures?"

"Very good pictures," little Miji yelled from behind
the camera. "Much fucking and sucking. Very good."

"How is the search for Candy going?" Mrs Milpy
asked. As she spoke Bjorn absentmindedly slapped
his dick against her cheek.

"I am on the case today," I told her. She turned her
head and licked Bjorn's balls for a moment. "And I
have a new lead."

"Good deal," she said. "Do you like my Aunt
Jemima look today?"

"Very nice," I said.

"We are going to do country school teacher and the cowboys later."

"I'm sorry I can't stay for that," I said.

"Me too. You would make a wonderful cowboy. But at least stick a dick in Aunt Jemima's mouth before you go." Bjorn stepped away. I pulled out my cock and put it in her mouth. She made a suction with her cheeks and pulled it in. I let her suck on the tip for a minute or so, then tipped her head back and pushed it down her throat. She gave me that wide eyed look of surprise that only black people can do well. I hadn't fucked anybody for a while and had a lot of semen waiting to get out. I let go early and shot it on to her face.

"Good picture," Miji exclaimed. "Much semen."

"You are still the best," Mrs. Milpy said wiping some of the cum off her face with the hem of her dress. "Now Bjorn, get that little black thing of yours over here." He stepped up and returned his cock to her mouth. Mrs. Milpy started sucking and gave me a thumbs up.

I looked to Ebenezer. "And Eb, I still haven't fucked your sister."

"Thanks man," he said, "and thanks for letting me go out on this job for you."

"You treat Mrs. Milpy right," I ordered, "Her husband is one of my most loyal customers."

I wiped off my cock at the kitchen sink with a tea towel while my two assistants and their new camera person continued to make porn for Mrs. Milpy to show her husband. As I left I could hear her yelling about white men fucking her nigger cunt. It meant she was about to orgasm. I jumped in the Gremlin and drove the streets thinking about the Pantz case.

Without a destination something in my unconscious mind took over and I found myself in front of the city parking division. Some of the girls were coming back to the station for lunch. Once you have worn the badge, the love of blue never goes away. Seeing the girls in their parking enforcement uniforms I pulled over to the curb, leaned over the steering wheel, and sobbed.

I remembered the days after that Christmas party where Captain Natron had juiced a grapefruit with her vagina. Everything was good. The parking girls were servicing the cops and I was servicing the girls. The workmen were installing the new breakaway parking meters and the city was calm. Then one day Captain Natron called me into her office. I thought she just wanted to sit on my face, something she had taken to doing fairly often, but when I arrived in the office there was a young woman seated in front of the captain's desk.

"William," the captain said, "this is Wilsha Dewet. She was a secretary over in city procurement. I would like you to hear what she has to say." I sat in the chair next to her. "Wilsha," the Captain said, "Tell Mr. James what you told me."

"Everything?" Wilsha asked, staring at the captain.

"Everything," the Captain said. The young woman was blond, about medium height, wearing a knee length blue dress. She held a small leather briefcase in her lap. I guessed her to be about twenty-two years old. She turned to me to speak.

"Well, Mr. James," she said, "about a year ago I graduated from community college and started looking for a real job. I had good grades and good secretarial skills. My sister worked for the city and liked it. The pay wasn't great, but the work was steady and she got good benefits. So I watched the papers and when an opening came up I applied. The opening was for an administrative assistant—that's what they call a secretary these days—in the procurement department. I took the civil service test for the position and did well enough to get called for an interview.

"It was my first interview for a real job. I'd worked in fast food during school and cleaned houses while going to college, but I was ready for a career. I was very nervous before the interview and called my sister many times for advice on how to handle it. I bought a new business skirt and jacket. The morning before the interview I bathed, I put on my best perfume, I shaved my legs and armpits, and I shaved my pussy twice, just in case I missed a hair the first time. Then I put on my silk garter, my best lace stockings, and my new suit.

"I got there early. The interview was to be with Harold Litclicker, the assistant director of city procurement services. I was terribly anxious. I was afraid my typing wouldn't be good enough or my tits wouldn't be big enough or I didn't have enough experience. After about an hour of waiting and sweating it out, Mr. Litclicker invited me into his office. He was an older man with white hair. Just his look put me at ease. He asked about my education, my prior work history, and how many boys I had fucked while going to college. They were the questions my sister had prepared me for. After the first few questions, I pulled my skirt up a little and spread my legs so that he could see my well-shaved snatch. When he asked me where I wanted to be in five years, I told him that I wanted to working for a kindly older man who would mentor me and let me suck his cock.

I then showed him how I was able to put both of my ankles behind my head. That got him out from behind the desk. He dropped to his knees in front of me, licked my hole for about twenty minutes, and offered me the job.

"I started the next day in the secretarial pool in procurement. The department was headed by Commissioner Filopad. The commissioner asked me into his office one day to blow him, but for the most part I stayed at my desk and did my job. My job was to handle the purchasing for the parking meter replacement project. When the bills came in, I reviewed them and, if they were in order recommended them for payment. Our two biggest vendors were the company that provided the new meter poles and the company that disposed of the old ones. The provider was a company called ACME Meter Poles, Inc., and disposal was done by Acme Pole Disposal, LLC. As the months went by I handled hundreds of these invoices and I notice that both sets have the same printing error when printing a dollar sign. It becomes clear to me that the invoices for the two companies are being printed on the same printer. I start paying attention to these invoices, and I notice that certain numbers seem to match. Right after ACME Disposal charges the city for destroying five hundred old poles, ACME Meter Poles charges us for five hundred new ones. I look up the two companies at the state corporation division and both of them are owned by another company named Hydamuny Inc. I start thinking that something funny is going on

"Now, ever since I started working there I stop in now and then to see Mr. Litclicker and let him run his tongue up and down my crack. The next time I go see him I am up on his desk with my legs spread. He has his face in my snatch and I decide to tell him about what I found out. The moment I mention Hydamuny Inc. he pulls his face out of my crotch and won't have a thing to do with me. He tells me that he will look into it and I should forget it. I can hardly get my dress down before he rushes me out of the office. The very next day I get transferred to the secretarial pool at the sanitation department. I go to see Mr. Litclicker about my transfer, thinking I may have done something wrong and to tell him that he is welcome lick my asshole too if he wants, but he won't even see me. Now I have been around and I know the kind of men who like to lick young pussy, and this man is one of them. If he is turning down pussy like mine, he is scared of something."

Willa turned to me, hiked up her skirt and spread her legs. She was right. A clit licker like Litclicker would never turn down pussy as young and smooth as Wilsha Dewet's unless he was scared of something.

Wilsha continued, "I did my best over in sanitation. They put me in charge of the lunch and break room. A week later I was fired. They said I failed to keep the napkins sanitary, but I swear that those were the most sanitary napkins in the whole city. It was a setup."

Captain Natron looked at me. I could tell she thought the young woman was telling the truth.

"All I ever wanted," Wilsha said, "was to find some nice quiet bureaucracy where I could start at the bottom and fuck my way to a nice salary and six weeks of vacation a year. Is that to much to ask in America?"

"You did nothing wrong," Captain Natron said, "and that is not too much to ask. The day a young girl in this country can't try to advance herself with hard work, good looks, and pussy is the day I move to

Romania."

"Thank, you," she said, "I just don't know what to
do. I have no job. I have no future. And it is all
because I tried to do the right thing. I haven't slept for
days from the worrying."

"First things first," Captain Natron said. "I am
going to ask William to take you back in the meter
maid locker room and fuck you stupid. You let him
bone you until you are cross-eyed and can't walk
straight. He has the dick to do it, and it will take your
mind off all this. While you are doing that, I'm going
to look into what you have said. And if there is a job in
this city that you can do, I'm going to make sure that
you get it."

I escorted Wilsha to the parking division locker
room. Helga and Minnie Crolesmack were undressing
for their evening showers. I whispered to them a short
version of what had happened to Wilsha and what the
captain had ordered. The two naked meter maids
introduced themselves to Wisha and invited her to
shower with them before she got boned. Wilsha
agreed and I got to watch as they helped the young
woman undress. They dropped her skirt and
stockings. She had upturned breasts with the kind of
nipples that never went completely soft. Her pussy
was a perfect smooth clam shell and her butt as round
as a basketball. I am not really the most enthusiastic
of cunt lappers, but one look at Wisha and I wanted
nothing more to bury my face in her crotch. Old
Litclicker had not let her go without a good reason.

In the showers the girls took turns lathering each
other, an exercise that had far more to do with arousal
than to cleanliness. Wilsha bounced Helga's big
Swedish boobs in her soapy hands while tiny-titted
Millie fondled Wilsha's young titties. I soaped up their

pussies, and each of them took a turn at lathering up my cock and balls. After drying each other off, I laid Wilsha on the designated fucking table at the end of the locker room. Helga and Minnie held her hands as I spread her legs and put my hard cock at the entrance to her cunt.

"Don't worry, sweetheart," Helga said, still naked from the shower, "William is the best."

I pushed my cock inside her and she gasped. Her cunt clamped on me like a velvet vice grip.

"It's too big," Wisha cried.

"You will be fine," Minnie said. "I have a little tiny cunt like yours. Just relax and let him work." Wilsha closed her eyes and I pushed until my balls snuggled up against her ass. I started with a slow rhythmic motion designed to loosen her up and bring her slowly to the place where I could give her the kind of pounding that the Captain had ordered.

"That a girl," Helga said, rubbing her Swedish finger across Wilsha's nipples. The young woman's pussy unclamped. I picked up the pace, slapping my hips against the soft inside of her thighs. I took hold of her ankles to give myself a straight shot at the pink hole between her legs. Wilsha started panting and moaning underneath her breath. In a couple of minutes I was slamming my cock into her with all the power my hips could generate. The slapping sound echoed down the locker room, and she avalanched into orgasm. As she came, I rammed my cock deep inside and held it there. She cried out and squeezed the hands of Minnie and Helga. At each orgasmic aftershock her cunt grabbed my dick. I waited until all the cunt squeezes had subsided and then started all over again.

I fucked Wilsha for nearly forty-five minutes before

finally delivering a thick load of semen into her cunt. When I finally pulled out she lay on the table motionless. As I wiped myself off, a couple of the girls helped Wilsha, who was now cross-eyed and jelly-kneed, to a lounge chair against the wall. They covered her with a blanket and she fell into a long deep sleep. The Captain was right. For a few hours she wouldn't be worrying about her troubles.

The Captain was gone by the time Wilsha and I finished so I went on about my job and didn't think about it too much. Two days later I was doing my rounds on parking patrol when I heard a loud crash a couple of streets over. I jumped into my three wheel meter cart and drove toward the sound. I arrived at the accident about the same time as the ambulance. There I saw a woman lying on her back on the sidewalk bleeding. A solid metal parking meter pole extended from her crotch like a big metal dick. She was dead. The paramedics pulled her off the pole and gave her CPR, all to no avail. I saw a young dope dealer who worked that corner and pulled him aside.

"What happened?" I asked.

"Dude, it was horrible," he told me. "I was standing there waiting to sell some grass and I hear this crash. That lady had been riding one of those little scooters when this black car hit her. The scooter swerved, hit a pot hole in the street, and threw her in the air. The wind caught her dress and for a moment all I could see was this hairy pussy flying toward me. I thought it was my damn lucky day, a big ole pussy coming right at me, so I put up my hands to catch it thinking to myself that it is like a baseball game and if I catch the pussy I will get to take it home and fuck it. Well, there I am with my arms out to catch it, but between me and the pussy is this parking meter. Instead of falling into my arms, the pussy slams into the meter pole. The woman slides down to the sidewalk, and I see that that she is pretty much dead."

"The meter pole didn't break away on impact?" I demanded.

"No way, man," he said. "It held solid as a rock."

I was devastated. Everything that Wilsha Dewet said came back to me. I went home. The papers the next day were filled with the story. The dead woman's name was Dorothy Ledspregs. She was a middle-aged woman with a checkered past who had turned her life around and dedicated herself to bringing young men to Chris. She had an apartment across the street from the athletic center for City High School. After practice each day she would invite young men to her apartment to talk to them about purity and committing their lives to the church.

"Yeah, she was great," one of the boys interviewed for the story said. "She had pictures of her younger years when she smoked and drank liquor and had unprotected sex with black men. She would warn us about the dangers of drugs and loose women. Sometimes she would show these old films of herself doing bad things. She was really cool." The newspaper article went on to say that she had continued to have minor struggles in her life, struggles that resulted in some families obtaining court orders to keep her away from their young sons, but for the most part she was a valuable asset to the community struck down in her prime by a reckless driver and a parking meter pole that would not yield to her oncoming body.

I wasn't able to see Captain Natron for a couple of days. When we finally met she closed the door behind me as I came in. I thought she closed the door because she wanted me to go down on her, but once again I was wrong. "This is big," the Captain said, "and the whole city is locked down. Anybody who talks is gone. The word is out on Wilsha Dewet. She's fucked, and I don't mean by you on a table in the locker room. She will never work for government in this city or any other city. Forget her. We have to look out for ourselves."

"What are they going to do?"

"There will be a blue ribbon investigation, and they will find that the meter pole was an isolated failure."

"The police are going along with this?"

"They are. I am, and so are you. Don't be a Pollyanna, William. It is time to watch out for yourself. Forget Wilsha, forget Mrs. Ledspregs. Protect yourself."

I went home to my apartment, heated up some canned chili, and tried to forget about the whole thing. I came to the city to work, not to be a hero. The next day I put on my uniform, put on a stiff upper lip, and went to work as usual. A pall had fallen over the locker room. We were like zombies. Nobody was fucking. Nobody was talking.

Once in my cart I threw the ticket book on the floor. I wasn't going to write any more tickets until I knew for sure what was going on with the parking meter poles. I went to a place in the city where all the poles were old—not yet replaced. They were simple hollow steel poles—thick, durable, and unbreakable, with old fashioned look like a galvanized pail. Then I went to a part of the city where the new ones had been installed. These were also solid in appearance but had a newer shinier look with a very slight gold tint.

I bought a pipe cutter from a woman named Bill at Bill Dykes Hardware. It was hard for me to do intentional damage to a parking meter, but desperate to know what was happening, I cut two poles for study. One was an old pole. The other was one of the break-away poles. Back in my apartment I went over each with a magnifying glass. The old poles had a tiny mark stamped at the bottom. The stamp said, "Acme Steel." The new poles were better looking than the old, but the new finish with the gold tint came off easily with some fine sand paper. When the finish was removed from the bottom, I found the same stamp at the bottom. The stamps on the older poles had been worn down by weather and use. The stamps on the newer ones had too. The new break-away meter poles were the old meter poles with a new finish.

Wilsha Dewet had been right. The old poles were being taken down, refinished, and reinstalled with the city being charged for every step in the process. I loaded up the two meter poles and took them down to the police department. No one would look at the poles or listen to my story. I took them to the district attorney. I couldn't get past the receptionist. I had to take the law into my own hands.

Commissioner Filopad had scheduled a press conference to address the unfortunate death of Mrs. Ledspregs. He was going to appear with the young men who she had helped to the ways of righteousness. I took off early on the Friday of the press conference, went home and pushed one of the new meter poles down my pant leg. My plan was to sneak it into the press conference and force Filopad to face the evidence.

It is not easy to walk while trying to hide a parking meter pole in your pants. I took the bus down to city hall where the press conference was being held. I limped off the bus in front of city hall and headed up the stairs to the front door. A hooker being let out of jail walked up to me and snickered, "Hey, pal, is that a parking meter pole in your pants or are you just happy to see me."

"I'm happy to see you," I said, not wanting to let on about the meter pole.

"Dumbass," she said.

I limped into the conference and, unable to sit, stood against the back wall. One of the young men described in the newspaper was telling the press corps how Mrs. Ledspregs had led him back to his church. Half way through his speech his mother dragged him off the stage muttering about a "fucking whore." When the young man was gone Commissioner Filopad took the stage. Filopad was a round man about five and a half feet tall. He was bald, heavy and well dressed. An officer in blue standing on the stage lowered the microphone for him. He proceeded to say that the blue ribbon committee had investigated the meter pole death of Mrs. Ledspregs. The death of Mrs. Ledspregs was a tragedy for her family, none of whom could be here today, and for the community as well. However, in no way was the death a reflection on the breakaway meter pole project. The failure of the pole that killed Mrs. Ledspregs was an isolated failure unlikely to ever reoccur. He said that all poles had been inspected and parking meter deaths were a thing of the past. Everything Filopad said was a lie.

I reached in my pants for the parking meter pole. I got a grip on it and pulled, but it wouldn't come out. During the bus trip and the walk into the building the pole had become entangled with my clothes and wouldn't budge. Filopad finished the presentation and the reporters were throwing him softball questions. I pulled frantically at the pole with no result except to draw the attention of those around me. Seeing no other way to complete my plan, I dropped my pants, regretting that I had not worn underwear. With my slacks on the floor I pulled the pole free. Naked from the waist down I rushed the stage holding the pole aloft and yelling, "Hey Filopad, look at this."

No one, however, was looking at the meter pole. A woman screamed. Another yelled, "It's the biggest thing I've ever seen on a white man." Two policemen took Commissioner Filopad to the ground to protect him. "It's huge," someone yelled. "It can't be real, can it?" "It's an implant."

And then I was buried in policemen.

The headline in the paper the next morning was, "Crazed Male Meter Maid Attacks Commissioner Filopad." The story that followed was no more accurate than the headline.

The police took me to the edge of town, beat the hell out of me, and threw me down the pit of a farmer's outhouse. I spent most of the night trying to climb out and the next two days walking back to the city. When I got to my apartment there was a package waiting for me outside the door. It held the contents of my locker down at parking enforcement. The girls had all signed a get well card and Captain Natron sent a letter explaining that if I ever came close the parking enforcement building again I would be arrested. She wrote that it might be better if I moved to Romania.

I put down the letter and got in the shower. While washing the shit out of my hair I reviewed what had happened. Right there I made a vow to myself that I would dedicate the rest of my working life to fighting corruption. The next day I returned to city hall and applied for my private investigators license.

I raised my tear-stained face from the steering wheel. Someone was knocking on the window. It was Captain Natron and Helga. I rolled down the window.

"Is that you, William?"

"It's me," I said. The Captain went around the car and slid into the passenger seat. Helga got in the back seat.

"You can't be here," the captain said. "You will be arrested."

"Something brought me here," I said. "I need your help." I told them about the Pantz case. "You in parking enforcement are everywhere. You see things. You hear things. You smell things. You feel things when they get shoved up your vaginas. I need your eyes, your ears, your noses and your vaginas."

"You can count on my vagina," Helga contributed from the back seat.

"Shut up, Helga," the captain said. The captain turned to me. "She misses you a lot."

"I miss you a lot too," I said to Helga.

"All the girls miss you," she said from the back seat.

"We will do whatever we can," the Captain continued. "I will put the word out to the girls. If there is any information out there about Candy Pantz, we will find it. But you have to stay away from here. I could be fired for even talking to you. If we learn something we will get the information to your office."

"Thanks," I said, "Now, get out of here. The last thing I want is for any of you to suffer on account of me." In a moment, the two of them were gone. I drove slowly back to my office. Private investigation had my heart, but parking enforcement would always have my soul.

I drove back to the office and wound my way through the ten-speeds outside of Otto's. Inside the bar the noon-time drinkers were swilling vodka smoothies. Up in my office, Teena was at her desk reading *Striptease for Dummies*. There was a wet spot and a pair of men's jockey shorts on the carpet next to her desk.

"What's that?" I asked, pointing to the white shorts.

"Oh that," she said, "Uh, that is . . . that is the underpants you told me I had to wear. Yeah, I went and got some underpants." She got up from her chair, bent over and stepped into the leg holes of the jockeys.

"Those are men's jockey shorts," I pointed out.

"Sure they are," she said. "It's all the fashion these days. You know how hot a girl can look in a man's dress shirt or a man's t-shirt. These days the hot thing is girls wearing men's jockey shorts." She pulled up the underwear and lifted her skirt. "See," she said, "and I can use the fly to scratch myself if I have an itch."

"They are too small and they look used," I said.

"I couldn't afford a new pair," she pouted, "and this was the only size they had at the consignment shop."

"How about the wet spot on the carpet."

"I spilled my coffee," she said.

"All right," I said, "come in the office." I told her about the morning at Totally Naked Women Here and the Yellowcheckered cab company. I told her about how Bjorn and Eb had taken over the Milpy case so I could concentrate on the missing Pantz.

"Do you plan to leave Ed and Bjorn in charge of Milpy?" she asked.

"I think so," I opined. "They seem to be doing a good job."

"I don't think Mr. Milpy will like that."

"Why not?" I asked.

"He only trusts you, and he is very particular. Very demanding and stern."

"Mr. Milpy?"

"Oh, yes. He could be very upset if he finds you are having your assistants handle his case."

"Well, we will see," I told her. "Today I want to concentrate on the Pantz case."

"I have been thinking about that," Teena said. "What if some of the people you have been talking to have been lying to you."

"What do you mean?"

"I mean not telling the truth. It happens."

"But most of the witnesses are strippers with hearts of gold. They wouldn't lie."

"What about Reverend Babylon? She isn't a stripper. She said Candy never arrived at the convent. What if she did?"

"Reverend Babylon is a woman of the cloth," I said. "She would not bear false witness."

"She bares everything else," Teena said. "Why not a false witness?"

"You have a point."

I went to get the Gremlin. Brett was in Otto's drinking when I left. As I walked through the bar she grabbed her ears and made an "O" with her mouth. I waived her off and hit the streets.

Twenty minutes later I was on the road to Fumbuck. The little town was about fifty miles outside the city, a two hour drive for the Gremlin. I turned the radio to right-wing talk and leaned back in the seat to enjoy the ride. I was in farm country with rolling hills and gentle streams. The sight of the fields, and farms and animals brought back the happiest days of my life.

After listening to the football game outside the window of the farmhouse and knowing that Cuckold Falls could have won that game if I had been there, I headed down the country roads to make my fortune. I found work on the farms and spent that winter sleeping in barns and storage sheds. They were cold nights, occasionally warmed by a lonely farmer's wife. Time passed, the snow eventually melted, and spring came.

One sunny morning I was walking along a country road when out of nowhere a tall blond boy about my age appeared beside me. He was a lanky kid wearing bib overalls and oversize farmer's boots.

"Where you goin'?" he asked. I had grown wary of strangers, but I was also lonely, and he was the first person my age I had seen in a long time.

"Down the road," I said, "wherever it takes me."

"Where you live?"

"Wherever I lay my head at night."

"You don't have no home?"

"Not that I can go back to," I said.

"My name is Frank," he said, "But everybody calls me Hayseed." He pointed to a red barn in the distance and said, "I live over at that place. You want to come for lunch."

Frank took me to his farm, and introduced me to his parents, Carl and Carla Fudrucker. The Fud-ruck-ers fed me, offered me a room in their big farmhouse, and invited me into their lives. Carl Fudrucker was a heavy set Santa Clause of a man who greeted every day in his farmer's life as a gift from God. And he had good reason. Mrs. Fudrucker was a big-bossomed, pink-cheeked farm wife, who cooked, cleaned, gardened, and brought happiness into the lives of everyone she met. The other resident was cousin Milli. Milli was a red-haired, freckled-faced girl of sixteen, born and bred for the farm life. After a few days together, Hayseed, Milli, and I became inseparable.

It was a good farm and a warm spring. There were animals to feed in the morning and crops to tend in the afternoon. Yet with all the work there was also time to lay in the pasture and watch the clouds go by. Hayseed, Milli, and I had finished our chores early one afternoon and gone out to the cow pasture by the creek to enjoy the sun. We all wore blue denim overalls. Hayseed and I, because of the warm spring, were naked beneath. Milli wore a t-shirt beneath hers to cover her breasts.

"Milli," Hayseed said as we lay in the grass together, "have you shown William your titties yet?"

"No," Milli said blushing, "he ain't even asked to see 'em."

"Well, show 'em," Hayseed said. "Milli has been growin' her titties for about a year now and they is coming in real good." Milli unhooked the straps of her overalls and pulled her t-shirt over her head. Her young titties were firm, round, and just as covered in red freckles as her face.

"Do you like them, William?" she asked, averting her eyes from mine.

"They are beautiful," I said.

Hayseed turned to me. "Let's fuck her."

"Oh, no you don't," Milli responded, leaping to her feet. "You can't fuck what you can't catch." Holding her overalls up with one hand she took off running across the pasture with her freckled breasts bouncing in the spring sunshine. Hayseed and I jumped to our feet and took off after. She was fast. We pursued down the creek, across the pasture, and into the orchard. When she got too far ahead she would stop and taunt us by bouncing her young boobies at us with her hands. We might never have caught her if she hadn't tripped over a branch in a clearing in the apple trees. As she tried to get up and run again, Hayseed made a flying tackle at her ankles. He held her face down on the grass after the catch and sat on her while we all caught our breath.

When we are all breathing normally again, Hayseed rolled her over and, sitting on her hips, held her wrists against the warm grass. Looking into her face he said, "Nice tittles, freckleface. How come those nipples are all hard?"

"Not because of you, fart breath," she said.

Hayseed slid off her and worked around so that he was kneeling above her head all the time holding her wrists to the ground. When in position he said, "William, pull off her overalls?" She kicked at me ineffectively as I approached. The loose overalls slid off easily leaving her in nothing but white cotton panties and farm boots. "Get the panties," Hayseed said.

"You bastards," Milli exclaimed, "you leave my panties alone."

"Milli," Hayseed said, "we can't fuck you with your panties on."

"Well, go behind the barn and beat off then," she protested. I grabbed her cotton underwear at both hips and pulled it off. She clamped her legs together. "William," she said, "I thought you were a nice boy. Not a fuckboy like Hayseed."

"Don't listen to her," Hayseed said, still holding her down by the wrists. "Spread her legs." I grabbed her ankles, then spread and lifted her legs. She had a smooth young pussy dusted with red hair and covered, like the rest of her, with freckles. "See, she's a frecklepussy," Hayseed said.

"You are both boogerheads," she responded.

"Go ahead, William," he said, "fuck her." I let go of Milli's ankles and pulled off my overalls. She clamped her legs back together.

At the sight of my erect penis, Hayseed said to her, "Well, look at that, Frecklepussy. William has a big ole dick."

"I'm glad somebody around here does," she said.

"You spread your legs now like a good girl," he ordered.

She opened her thighs a few inches and batted her eyelashes as me. "You want to put that big nasty thing inside of little ole me?"

"I do," I said, "if you don't mind."

"Maybe if you tell me I have pretty titties," she said.

"Just fuck her," Hayseed said reaching down to grab her by a nipple.

I gently opened her legs and kneeled between them. I took my cock and placed it at the entrance to here cunt. She was very wet, and as I eased my dick inside her I said, "You have beautiful titties." I then lowered myself pushing my cock all the way inside her. She wrapped her arms around my neck, pulling me against her, and moaned. She had a tight wet pussy that had a mind of its own. It grabbed my cock and held it tight. I started doing her in slow motion, gradually increasing my speed. At times I would stop with my cock all the way inside, with my balls pushed against her pink ass, and let her squeeze me with her pussy muscles. I picked up the speed and force and gave that sweet freckled pussy a good farmer pounding. She lifted her legs, grabbed her ankles, and took it like only a farm girl can. She moaned, she panted, she cried out, and she screamed. I came hard and long inside her. Afterward I lay on top of her letting my orgasmic aftershocks pump that last few squirts deep inside.

When completely soft I rolled off onto the warm meadow. She lay there in the grass catching her breath, her hips still making spasmic thrusts at a cock that was no longer there. When her breathing slowed and her hips stopped moving she looked at Hayseed. "What's wrong with you, cousin? Don't tell me you gone fag on me." He slid out of his overalls. His cock was rock hard and almost as big as mine.

"If you're ready for the real thing, Frecklepussy, I am ready for sloppy seconds."

"Then why don't you just shut up and fuck, fart breath." she said. He climbed on top of her, and she lifted her hips to take his cock. He fucked her hard and fast from the opening thrust. The sound of their hips crashing together echoed through the trees. She panted and yelled, "Give me that cock, you fucking bastard, son of bitch, cunt licking, sister sucking fuck." They pounded and writhed against each other in the afternoon sun, sweating, grunting and moaning until Milli came again, yelling obscenities to the spring sky.

"I'm going to cum," Hayseed panted.

"Not in my cunt, you bastard," she growled. "Do it in my face."

"Are you ready?" he asked.

"Fuck yes, I'm ready," she said. He pulled his cock out of her freckled hole and rose on his knees. She sat up and grabbed his dick with her hand and pumped it hard. The semen shot out in a solid stream across her freckled face and the thick white ooze dripped down her cheeks and chin. When most of it had found her face, she put her lips to the tip of his dick and sucked until Hayseed's penis started soften. When fully drained he fell backward into the grass. Milli scraped the semen off her face with her fingers and rubbed the sticky liquid on her tits.

We sat in that meadow for the rest of the afternoon. Milli fondled our testicles and we talked about life, love, and what we wanted to be when we grew up. That night the Fudruckers fed us meat loaf and mashed potatoes. We watched television sitting on the floor together while Mr. Fudrucker read the paper and Mrs. Fudrucker knitted. I had worked hard that day, fucked hard, eaten well, and gone to sleep in a warm bed. Life was good.

Farm life went on. Calves and piglets were born; the crops were planted. Hayseed and I helped Mr. Fudrucker in the fields while Milli helped Mrs. Fudrucker with the cooking and cleaning. In the late afternoon, when Hayseed and I were finished with our chores Milli would come down to the barn to see us. We would talk about our days, relax, and share of cold RC. More often than not Hayseed would say to me, "Let's fuck Frecklebutt."

"You guys stay away from me," she would say and sprint up the stairs into the hay loft. We would follow her up, chase her over the hay bales avoiding the handfuls of hay she would fling at us until one of us caught an arm or an ankle. We would strip off her clothes and have our way with her. More often than not, once we got her naked we would bend her over a blanket-covered bale of hay we had arranged for just such a purpose. I would fuck her from behind while she sucked Hayseed's dick. We would each cum, me in her pussy, Hayseed in her mouth. Then we would take a rest and do her again with the positions reversed.

Milli was a truly remarkable girl. Her throat opened to for cock as if her mouth had no other purpose than to please a man. If you were still, she would suck you harder than the milking machine. When she was on her hands and knees or laid across the hay bale, she would lift her chin, straighten her neck, and give you a direct shot at her throat. I could push my cock deep into mouth and hold it there while she forced herself to swallow. The effect was to undulate the full length of her tongue up and down the bottom of my cock. She liked it when I held her head like a basketball and directed the sucking. Sometimes she swallowed. Sometimes she would pull back, demanding that we spray our cum on her face and tits.

What was most amazing about little Frecklebutt was her astounding pussy. Hayseed and I fucked her twice most every afternoon. If we finished work early and were feeling creative, we might do it four or five times. There were days we rode her so hard that she would waddle back to the farm house for dinner bow legged and sore. On warm nights we took her back to the hay loft for another round before bed. Milli orgasmed hard and often. She never turned down cock, and never quit until both of ours were drained dry. And in the house at night she would sneak out of her bed in the predawn morning to come to my room and ride my morning boner until the sun rose. But no matter how many times we fucked, her pussy was always as tight and warm as that first afternoon in the orchard. The Lord had blessed that tight freckled pussy of hers. Hayseed and I were the beneficiaries of that blessing.

Those were beautiful days of youth, fresh air, good

food, and wonderful fucking. Hayseed, Milli and I grew strong and healthy. The only fly in the ointment was a girl named Muffy Holcorn who lived on the farm down the road. Muffy was an attractive thickset girl a year older than Milli. She had brown hair, large breasts for her age, and the kind of round butt that said she would someday be fat. Muffy had a cousin in the city, and went to visit for a month or two every summer. While in the city she had picked up a disdain for the farm life and lorded it over the other farm girls. She took particular pleasure in tormenting Milli.

"Come here you little freckled cow," Muffy said to Milli one day when they saw each other at the soda fountain in the little village close to the Fudrucker farm. Milli reluctantly took a seat at the fountain next to Muffy. "What you wearing them bib overalls for? Did you think this was a barn you were supposed to clean out?"

"No," Milli said, "I just wanted a root beer float, and I like my overalls."

"Well, you sure better stay on the farm, because if you were in the city no man would even look at you like that. In the city you can't just go up in the hay loft and pull down your pants. You have to get seduced."

"How do you do that?" Milli asked.

"The man asks you out on a date to a movie and a restaurant. Then you shave your legs and your arm pits and your pussy and you put on your Sunday dress with frilly underwear and pantyhose. Then you spray yourself with perfume so you don't stink and when the man comes he has a suit and a tie and he is wearing cologne that smells like fruit. Then you go to a movie and he puts his arm around you and feels your tits in the movie and if you want to you can feel his dick, but if you want to play hard to get you don't do that. Then you go to a restaurant with men waiters and a special dish that is not on even on the menu and you eat dinner. And after you eat he pays for the dinner and then takes you to a real motel where they have this thing where you put a quarter in the slot and it makes the bed vibrate. And then when you fuck him you have been seduced."

"I don't have any pantyhose," Milli said.

Muffy was a constant headache to Milli, wearing fancy clothes that she got in the city, and always demeaning Milli for her lack of sophistication. One time when her cousin, Darlene, came to visit the two cousins caught Milli in town, dragged her behind the drug store and pulled down her pants. They spread her legs, ridiculed her freckled pussy, then bent her over a pickle barrel and put a corn cop in her anus. They said it was her country dildo and she better get used to it because it was the only cock a freckled country cow was ever gonna get. Milli escaped their grasp holding her overalls in her hands and ran away with the orange corn cob still poking out her freckled ass. During the getaway she ran by the old men who sat on rockers in front of the general store, and they all agreed that there hadn't been a naked woman running down the street of the village with a corn cob up her ass since that awful spring of sixty-three.

Back at the farm, Milli told us the story through her tears. She was humiliated and ashamed. For weeks we planned revenge. We had an elaborate plan to kidnap Muffy when one Saturday she just dropped in our lap. Hayseed and I were up the hay loft screwing Milli when we heard a car in the barn yard. We took our dicks out of Milli and went to the window to see who it was. There was Muffy Holcorn knocking on the door of the farmhouse. As it turned out both

Mr. and Mrs. Fudrucker had gone to town. I quickly pulled on my overalls and headed out of the barn.

"Hello, Miss Holcorn," I said to her. "Can I help you?" Muffy was wearing a pink sweater, flared skirt, panty hose, and red patent leather shoes.

"You must be, William," she said, "the new boy that the Fudruckers took in. Is Mrs. Fudrucker here? My ma sent me over to borrow some canning jars."

"She's up in the hay loft," I said. "You best come up there and ask her about them jars. I'll show you the way." I motioned her toward the barn and she walked beside me.

"My cousin, Darlene, lives in the city," she told me as we walked. "That's where I bought this dress and these shoes."

"They are nice," I said.

"In a year or so I'm going to move to the city and wear clothes like this every day." I didn't respond. "I bet you'd like it a lot to have a pretty girl like me on the farm, you having nobody but Hayseed and that little freckled girl, Milli, to look at." She danced away from me and twirled to make her skirt flare outward. We got to the barn and I pointed her to the stairs that led to the loft. She took a step. "You can walk behind me up these stairs, but you don't be tryin' to look up my dress now," she said.

"I won't," I promised.

She pushed open the trap door to the loft and stepped up. Hayseed jumped her from behind a stack of bales and grabbed her by the arms. Milli was sitting half way up a staircase of hay bales stacked against one wall. She had put her overalls back on but wasn't wearing a shirt. We could see her red nipples on either side of the denim bib. Muffy spotted Milli and the two women glared at each other. Hayseed held

Muffy tight.

"Last time I seen them freckled titties that girl was buck naked with a corn cob up her ass," Muffy sputtered. "Ain't that right, Milli?"

"Hayseed," Milli said, "hang her from the rafters." I tossed a rope over one of the rafters of the barn. Hayseed managed to get one end around Muffy's wrists while I pulled back on the other end so that Muffy's arms lifted above her head.

"Hayseed," Muffy said, "you don't pay no attention to that little frecklebutt girl. She don't know nothing but farm ways. You know you always liked me, Hayseed. Why you go listening to her?" He said nothing. When she was suspended on her tip toes I tied the other end of the rope to one of the wall beams.

"Lift her skirt," Milli ordered. Hayseed was behind her and I was beside her. I reached for the front hem of the flowered skirt.

"Oh no you don't, William," she said. "You leave my clothes alone. I won't have no boys lifting up my skirt." I raised the hem of the skirt to her chest so her undies were visible from the belly button down. She was wearing sheer panty hose with red bikini panties.

"William," Milli said, "you keep holding the skirt up. Hayseed, pull down those panties." From behind, Hayseed took the panty hose by the waist band and pulled the hose and panties down just far enough to expose Muffys ass and vagina. The underwear and hose stretched taught against the outside of her thighs just below her crotch.

"Hayseed," Muffy protested, "you stop that. I am going to tell Mr. and Mrs. Fudrucker."

"William," Milli said, "tell me if she really shaved all the hair off her pussy."

"Don't you dare," Muffy yelled at me. "Don't touch my pussy or anything else." I cupped her labia in my hand and squeezed.

"Don't feel any hair at all," I told Milli. "I think she really did shave it all off."

"So what if I did?" Muffy protested. "That's what all the city girls do."

"Okay William," Milli said, "let loose of the skirt." I complied and let the hem drop so that she was covered.

"That's more like it," she said to Milli. "Now tell Hayseed to pull up my panties and maybe I won't tell on you guys."

"Hayseed," Milli said, "I want to see Muffy's tits."

"No," Muffy yellled.

Hayseed reached around from behind and lifted the sweater to expose her white bra. He then undid the clasp at the back and her tits fell out of the bra into view. She had heavy breasts that even at her young age had begun to sag. They jiggled as she struggled.

"Muffy," Milli said, "you got a pair of big ole knockers there, don't you?"

"Please, tell them to cover me," she begged.

"Hayseed," Milli said, "I bet you'd like to paw them tits some, wouldn't you?"

"I wouldn't mind that none, Milli," he answered.

"Stay away from me," Muffy cried. Hayseed reached around her from behind and balanced Muffy's hooters in the palms of his hands.

"They are awful big and soft," Hayseed said.

"Well you squeeze 'em good," Milli ordered.

"Oh Hayseed, stop this," Muffy pleaded. "If you stop now, I promise I won't tell."

"William," Milli said, "you can feel her titties too."

Hayseed let one drop and I took it in both my hands. It was smooth and warm. Her brown nipples were erect. We bounced, stroked, and jiggled her big tits as Muffy moaned in protest.

"It sure is nice," Milli said to Muffy, "watching them boys play with your titties. Makes me want to touch myself." Milli put her hand beneath her coverall bib and squeezed her left nipple. Then she said to us boys, "Strip her."

"Oh please don't tell them to do that," Muffy pleaded. She realized that pleading to Hayseed and me was not going to work. The key to her prison was in Milli's hands. Hayseed pulled her skirt to her ankles and lifted her feet out of it. "I don't mind if you touch my titties," she pleaded, "but please don't touch me down below."

"Strip her naked," Milli said.

"Oh, oh, oh, no." Muffy cried. "Please Milli. I'm sorry about the things I said, and about the corn cob. I really am sorry." We untied her hands just long enough to get her out of the bra and sweater, then returned her wrists to the rope. Hayseed pulled off the pantyhose and red panties. When we were finished her naked breasts stood white and bare in the dusty afternoon sunlight.

"You being a city girl," Milli started, "maybe you think that a girl should have a corn cob up her butt. But here on the farm we have different ideas about what goes up a pretty girls asshole. William, show her." I unsnapped my overalls and let them drop to the floor. My cock was at attention.

"Oh, my god," Muffy cried, "it's huge. Please Milli. Not that. I will do whatever you want."

"Grease her up," Milli said. Hayseed took two fingers of the lubricant we used for milking the cows and slathered it up the crack of Muffy's ass.

Feeling the lubricant being pushed into her hole, she begged of Milli, "Anything Milli. I promise. I will do anything you want and I won't tell anybody."

"You would suck these boys cocks?"

"Yes," she said meekly, "if that is what you want."

"You would get down on your knees and lick my freckled pussy."

"Yes," she said.

"Yes, what?"

"Yes, I will get down and lick your pussy."

"My freckled pussy."

"I will get down and lick your freckled pussy."

"Well, in that case—"

"Oh, thank you, Milli," she said.

"In that case, William, fuck her in the ass."

"No." she protested, "Please Milli."

I moved behind her and spread her ass cheeks. She had a good full butt. The crack and hole oozed lubricant. "No, please no," she cried as I put my cock against her anus. It tightened.

"Just relax," I whispered in her ear. I reached around and cupped her pussy in my left hand for leverage, then I slowly forced my cock into her asshole. Her anus tightened on the head of my dick. I remained still with my cock stuck about an inch in. When her butt muscle relaxed again I pulled her ass all the way onto my erection. She let out a deep hopeless sigh that told me she had given up the fight.

"At least," Milli said, "you ain't running down a public street with a nasty old corn cob sticking out your butt and giving the old men at the general store something to talk about."

"I am so sorry I did that, Milli," she panted. Her asshole stayed loose and I started moving my cock in and out. Unwillingly she began to respond.

"Okay, Hayseed," Milli said. "You fuck her front side." Milli said nothing. Hayseed dropped his overalls and approached her from the front.

"Please, Hayseed," she said, "be gentle."

He put a hand on her breast and looked deep into her eyes. "You know I will," he said. He bent his knees to get low enough to get his cock into her cunt and pushed inside her. I felt his cock next to mine through the thin flesh wall that separated her cunt from her ass. As he pushed in, I pulled out and as he pulled out I pushed in.

"They are too big," she moaned.

Hayseed put his mouth to her ear. "They are just right. You have a big ass and greedy cunt. Just relax and feel the rhythm."

"Okay, Hayseed," she whispered. "I trust you."

As we continued to fuck, she produced a rhythmic moan that was first unintelligible but then morphed into the words "Oh Hayseed, oh Hayseed . . . Fuck me Hayseed, fuck me." I finished first, shooting a stream of semen up her ass. I pulled out and walked up the bales to sit by Millie. As Hayseed finished he put his mouth to her ear.

"I love you," he whispered. "I have loved you since we were little."

"Oh Hayseed," Muffy said, "I love you too." As she said it, he came, filling her shaved cunt with his stuff. Hayseed pulled his cock out of Muffy and untied her wrists. Semen was dripping from her both her holes as she fell to the hay loft floor panting. Hayseed kneeled beside her and comforted her until she caught her breath. He then took a handkerchief from his pocket and wiped the white ooze from her cunt and her asshole.

"Are you all right," he asked.

"I think so," she said, feeling her pussy and her butt. "William was very gentle, and you, Hayseed, you were fabulous. I think I orgasmed about ten times."

"Your pussy is the best," he said. She put her hands around him and pulled him close.

"Thank you for saying that, Hayseed. It's exactly what I needed to hear." She lay next to him in his arms with her legs spread to let her crotch dry. I got some RC cola, passed the bottles around, and returned to my seat on the hay bale next to Milli. "I want to tell you, Milli," Muffy said, "that I am really sorry for what Darlene and I did to you and all the things I've said. The fact is that I was just jealous of you being over here every day spending time with Hayseed. I have had this huge crush on him since I was a little girl and we used to play doctor behind the church after services."

"You remember that too," Hayseed said.

"Like yesterday," she told him. "So Milli, if you still want me to kiss your pussy to make up for what I did, I will be glad to do it. But I have to say that I never put my mouth on another girl's pussy before, so I don't know if I would be any good."

"Muffy," Milli said, "you don't have to lick my pussy. I just said that to humiliate you and get even for what you done with the corn cob. Now that I heard why you did it, it don't seem to matter. And I never had a girl's mouth on my pussy either. I just said that cause I heard it once and thought it would make me sound sophisticated."

"I wouldn't mind, really," Muffy continued, "I seen your pussy when we was doing you with that corncob behind the store and it was awful pretty. That made me even more jealous."

"It ain't pretty," Milli protested. "It's just a freckled farm pussy. Good for fucking, but not for dressing up pretty like yours."

"Do you really think mine is pretty?" Muffy said, putting her fingers between her legs and spreading her labia with her fingers. "I think it's getting fat on the outside."

"And your titties are beautiful too," Milli said. The freckled girl stood and stepped down the bales to the loft floor. Muff stood to meet her.

"You can touch them," Muffy said to the other woman. Milli unhooked her overalls, let them drop to her ankles, and stepped out. The two women embraced. Milli took Muffy's large breasts in her hands and held them like melons.

"That feels wonderful," Muffy said. The two young farm girls kissed long and hard. Muffy then playfully pushed Milli back down on a hay bale, dropped to her knees, and lifted Milli's legs to fully expose her freckled cunt. I put my arm around Milli and fondled her breasts while Muffy applied her mouth to Milli's crack. Milli purred and squeezed my hand as the other woman's tongue found her clit.

Milli looked into my eyes and said, "You like to watch this, don't you?"

"Yes," I said.

"I want you to watch," she responded. She lifted her hips and pushed her cunt onto her new friend's face. Muffy licked, kissed, tongued, bit, and fingered Milli's hole until Milli cried out in pleasure. After Milli's first orgasm, Hayseed would not be kept apart from his new love. Muffy was on her hands and knees eating pussy, her pendulous tits swaying beneath her, when Hayseed approached and took her doggie style from the rear. Muffy arched her back to make her pussy available, and Hayseed plowed her thick farm cunt with his cock. With each thrust he drove Muffy's face hard into Milli's freckled hole. Muffy cried out. Milli cried out, and the three of them came together in a writhing mass of naked farmer flesh.

In the days that followed Muffy came over every afternoon. She threw away her fancy city clothes, bought herself bib overalls, and let soft brown hair grow back on her pussy. Most days we spent in the hay loft, but when the sun was high we often ran through the fields just enjoying life. We all went naked beneath our overalls. The boys cocks swung free in the loose fitting farmer clothes, while the girls' tits bounced beneath the scant cover of the bib overalls. The days grew longer and after a good dinner we would all four walk up the hill in the pasture. There the girls would go to their knees and suck our dicks as we watched the sun go down over the ripening corn.

The month after Muffy joined us, was one of the best times of my life. Hayseed and Muffy were in love, but no one was jealous. I fucked Muffy as often as I wanted and Hayseed still fucked Milli at least once a day. The girls sucked each other's tits and licked each other's pussies, both for their own pleasure and the boy's entertainment.

And then it all came to an end. One day the police came during dinner time and broke into Mr. and Mrs. Fudrucker's bedroom. The room held a wall full of video equipment. It turned out that the hay loft was filled with hidden cameras. Everything we had done was on tape. Mr. and Mrs. Fudrucker had been filming it all and showing it as porn every Friday night in the basement of Fraternal Odor of Possum Meeting Hall in town. One day Muffy's father got drunk and wandered down there only to see his daughter up one the screen taking it up the ass while eating pussy.

Mr. and Mrs. Fudrucker went to jail. Muffy was locked in her bedroom and told she couldn't come out until she was thirty. Milli went to a foster home. Hayseed and I went our separate ways. He went south never to be seen again. I went north to join the service.

I downshifted the Gremlin as I passed the sign announcing that I was entering the village of Fumbuck. Fumbuck was one of the thousands of one street towns that dot the farmlands west of the city. It was not much different than the place near the Fudrucker farm where Milli went for a root beer float and ended up with a corncob up her ass. But it wasn't the same town and that was a long time ago. I was a boy then. When I entered Fumbuck I was a man with a case to solve. I pulled into the parking lot of the Fat Sow Tavern, a country watering hole sandwiched between the feed store and the tractor dealer. As I came through the door conversation stopped and all heads turned. Twenty sets of female eyes followed me from the door to the bar stool.

The tavern was filled with women. Most of them wore variations of plaid shirts and blue jeans. A few wore the gingham dresses common among farm women. A huge female bartender who was six feet tall if she was an inch waddled down the bar to take my order. Her heavy breasts wobbled under her Fat Sow t-shirt.

"What'll it be?" she asked without making eye contact.

"RC cola," I said, "neat." She went to the glass case

behind the bar and got a bottle of RC. She opened the soda and poured it in a glass in front of me.

"We don't get much call for RC. You must not be from around here."

I threw back half the glass of cola. "I'm from the city," I said, "I'm looking for the convent of the Holy Dereamer Pentacostal Gnostic Church of the Tribulation."

"You mean that whorehouse out behind the hardware store?" she asked. No one in the place had said a word since I entered, but every ear was tilted toward our conversation.

"I believe the building houses women who have chosen to live their lives as the brides of Chris," I said.

"I call 'em whores," she said, "Disease-ridden whores. You got a problem with that city boy?" An ugly but muscular woman in bib overalls two stools down stood and faced me.

"Sow," she said to the bartender, "you want me to throw this asshole out of here?"

"Sit tight there, Denise," the bartender said. "If the man wants to drink an RC, he can drink an RC." I gave the woman down the bar my power stare. She flipped me off and sat back down on her stool. Her girlfriend beside her in a blue gingham dress hung on her shoulder and whispered something in the ugly woman's ear that made them both chuckle.

"I'm a detective," I said. "I'm looking for this woman." I took the picture of Candy Pantz from my coat and put it on the bar.

"Some lost whore, I suppose," the barkeep said without looking at the picture.

"She was an exotic dancer," I said. "She finished her shift one Saturday night and never arrived home."

The barkeep said, "Probably kidnapped by a dyke

motorcycle gang and made a sex slave. While we sit here and sip our drinks, she is tied down in some cycle repair shop with a gang of hairy lesbians each taking a turn at rubbing their fat cunts against her pretty little face."

"Why do you say that?" I asked.

"Just seems to happen a lot," she said. "I'm surprised it never happened to me the way things are theses days."

"Please," I said, "look at the picture." I pushed it across the bar toward her. She looked and then pulled away in shock.

"What's the matter, Sow?" asked the woman down the bar from me.

Sow looked at her friend. "It's the pussy. It looks just like Poopsie." The woman with the gingham-clad girlfriend moved down the bar and looked at the picture.

"Is that Poopsie?"

"Who is Poopsie," I asked.

Sow came back to the picture and put her hands on the bar. "Poopsie," she said, "was my only true love. You might figure that I've had my face in a lot of pussy in my life, detective, and you are right. I've had my tongue in every snatch in this room—more than once. But all that licking is just a vain attempt to recapture what I had with Poopsie."

The patrons of the bar got up quietly and gathered around as Sow continued. "I was living in the city. I had just gotten a job as a welder down at the docks. The money was good but I was lonely."

"How lonely were you?" the ugly woman said, her girlfriend still draped on her arm.

"I was so lonely that one more than one occasion I let a man between my legs just to feel the warmth of another person." The gathering crowd at the bar made vomiting noises to show their disgust. "Then one day I had to stop in at the human relations department to take care of some insurance matters and there sat Poopsie. She was the sweetest, sexiest lipstick lesbian I had ever seen. She had this little blue business skirt wrapped so tight across her sweet ass that when she turned her back to me to get a tax form, I almost came in my pants. She knew I was interested. She batted her eyelashes, wiggled he butt, and bounced her tits. We finished our business, I asked her out and the whirlwind began.

"We were fire and ice. She had the smoothest little clam-shell pussy, just a wisp of hair, and when she lifted her skirt to show it, all you could see was crack. I am the opposite. Mine is the grand canyon of cunt, the kind of dark hairy place an outlaw band could hide for years without being found. I got thick black pubic hair, and my inner labia hangs out like a theater curtain. I loved her sweet smooth crack as much as she loved my hairy one. I would suck her perky tits and she would lick these big danglers of mine. I would run my tongue across her clit until she came. She would put her whole hand inside me and fist me until I could barely walk. We got an apartment and settled in to make a licking and lapping life together.

"Then came a time when she had to work late a lot. One day she came home looking tired and I thought it would be a good idea to cheer her up. I lifted her up on the kitchen table, raised her skirt, and went down on her. When I got into her little crack something was different. There was a musky, salty taste that I hadn't encountered before. I didn't think too much about it figuring it was just the taste of the long hours she had been working.

"A few days later she had to go to an evening business meeting. I was horny that night. When she came in I was waiting for her naked. I grabbed her, gave her a deep kiss, and pushed her down on the coffee table in the living room. I lifted her skirt and pulled down her panties. When I pulled her legs apart to get a look at that sweet tight cunt of hers I saw, to my horror, white semen oozing from her crack.

"We fought and we cried. She said it was a moment of weakness with one of the men she worked with. She just wanted to be reminded again why she was a lesbian so she went to his apartment and did him. She told me it was horrible, that his balls were hairy and his cock was disgusting. She said she never wanted to have anything like that in her vagina or in her mouth again. She begged me to forgive her and kiss it all better. I reluctantly agreed. I went down and used my tongue to clean the cum out of her cunt. I did it for love.

"I thought that was the end of it, but it was only the beginning. A few days later I was at my lunch hour out in the ship yard. She came to me with tears in her eyes. She begged me to kiss her and as I did I tasted that taste again. She said that she had slipped again and that I had to kiss away the pain. We went into the women's bathroom and I went to my knees in front of her. She lifted her dress. Her snatch and thighs were covered in semen. I was disgusted, but she begged me to lick it all off and do her clit until she came. I did as I was asked.

"That night I demanded to know what had happened and she told me she had once again 'slipped' and given in to the dark side of herself that was driving her toward dick. 'But how did you get so much on you?' I demanded. 'In your pussy, in your mouth, all over your thighs.' Then she admitted that there had been three men. She had offered up pussy and blow jobs to the accounting department, doing it on the work table in the copy room. She apologized profusely and we cried again. I forgave her and we swore we would start over with a clean slate.

"Less than a week later she came home from work with the downcast eyes and look of remorse that said it had happened again. She told me that this time it had been the men in the sales department, four of them, one after another. And this time there was another hole I would have to clean up. That night I sucked semen out of her asshole and swallowed it. I had reached a new low. After that we didn't even bother pretending it wouldn't happen again.

"Pretty soon she was bringing the men back to the apartment. One day she arrived with a couple of the welders I worked with. She had promised that if they came over they could watch while I ate her out. I should have left the moment she came up with the idea, but I loved her too much. I let them strip me and let the men touch me. The pulled down their pants and showed me their disgusting meat sticks. I was repelled, but I didn't stop. Poopsie and I did sixty-nine on the living room floor while they sat in the recliners drinking beer and stroking their balls. They fucked Poopsie switching off between her pussy and her mouth. Between the two of them they managed to cover my darling in Teamster semen: her face, her tits, and her crack. When they were done, I got on my hands and knees over her and licked it up. While I was bent over cleaning up the cum with my tongue, one of them got on his knees behind me, pushed me down onto Poopsie, and rammed his cock, still wet from Poopsie, in my ass. I just lay there on top of

Poopsie while he fucked me in the butt. I could have stopped him easily, but I didn't have the will to do it.

"The next morning Poopsie left for work early. I called in sick. I was nauseated from eating cum and my asshole hurt so much I could hardly walk. I packed my bags, jumped in my pick-up and said goodbye to the city forever. Driving aimlessly I happened upon a tavern for sale. I pulled over and used my life savings to buy this. And that is the story of Poopsie and the Fat Sow tavern. "

Sow ended her sad story and the audience applauded. They had heard it many times before.

"So is this Poopsie?" I said, pointing to the picture of Candy.

"Naw," she said, "it is close, but it's not her. I just love telling that story."

"And we love hearing it, Sow," said the woman in the gingham dress.

"And you never heard from Poopsie again," I asked.

"Never did," she told me. "I opened this lez bar. The farm women welcomed me with open arms and open legs. This is my life now."

"No more cock's up the ass then."

"Nope," she said, "well, maybe a couple of times after hard drinking with old man Thomas down at the hardware store. But what a woman does drinkin' don't really count. I will admit, though, that on some winter nights when the wind is howling I have dreams of that big welder's meat in my ass and little Poopsie giggling in evil pleasure underneath me. But other than Mr. Thomas and a few dreams it's been nothing but clean pure country pussy for the Sow."

"You will keep an eye out for Candy Pantz, won't you?" I asked. "If you see her just contact the folks over at the convent."

"You mean the whores?"

"Brides of Chris," I said.

"Whores."

"Okay, whores then." I gave up. "If you see Candy Pantz, tell the whores."

"I will do that," Sow said. "And drop in again when you have the time. There are a couple of girls around here who go both ways. A good word from me and you are pretty much guaranteed to get lucky."

"I will do that," I said.

I left the tavern and crossed the street to the hardware store. The place was empty except or an wiry tanned old man reading a tittie magazine behind the counter.

"Can I help you?" the man asked.

"Are you Mr. Thomas?'

"John Thomas," the man said.

"My name is William James," I said. "I'm a detective. I'm looking for this woman." I put the picture of Candy on the counter. He looked it over. "I was over at the Fat Sow. The barkeep over there mentioned you as someone who might have seen her."

"You talked to Sow?" he asked, still examining the picture.

"I did," I told him.

"Did she tell you I fucked her in the ass?"

"She mentioned that," I said.

"Loose mouthed bitch," I said. "She tells everyone she sees. Now I can't get a regular woman to take a second look at me. Trust me son, your reputation is all you have. I spent twenty years working this store being a credit to the community, good church goer, and getting it fairly regular from the local farm women. One stupid drunken night I decide to fuck the

Sow in the ass and all that is down the drain. Next thing I know there's an article in the weekly newspaper right under the stock report with the headline, "Hardware Store Owner Cornholes Fat Sow in the Plumbing Aisle.' Now the farm wives just laugh at me and make pig noises."

"How about the picture?" I said.

"There weren't any pictures, thank God."

"I mean the picture in your hand, the picture of Candy Pantz."

"I think she has been in here before," he said, "but then she was wearing clothes. Hard to tell if the woman with clothes was the same one as here with her legs spread."

"When was this?"

"If it was the same woman, it would have been just a few days ago in the morning. Came in here and bought some batteries. Then I think she headed back toward the convent."

"The convent of the Holy Dereamer Pentacostal Gnostic Church of the Tribulation?"

"Whatever they call it," he said, "I'm a Methodist myself."

"Where is the convent?"

"Just go around back of the store and follow the path." I headed toward the door. "And if you see Sow, tell her to go fuck herself."

I left John Thomas Hardware and followed a small walkway around the building. Near the back door of the store a small path let toward the farmland that surrounded the village. I followed and was reminded again of the wonderful days I'd spent on the Fudrucker farm with Milli, Muffy, and Hayseed. The path led to a grove of trees. Hidden among the trees was a large white farm house with a porch that wrapped around three sides. A porch swing creaked in the gentle breeze. Behind and to the left of the farm house stood a red barn with a round silo attached and a rooster-shaped weather vane on the top.

I stood on the porch and looked around. There were no signs or insignia to indicate that this was the convent except for a copy of the Holy Bibble sitting on the porch swing. I knocked on the door and waited.

A small black woman in her mid thirties answered the door. She was wearing a clean white blouse and a dark skirt. She wore eyeglasses and had her hair pulled back tight against her head.

"May I help you sir," she said.

"My name is William James," I responded. "I am a detective and I am looking for a missing woman."

"Oh," she said, "you are the Mr. James that Reverend Babylon prophesied would come here. Please come in."

My host escorted me to a well furnished living room at the front of the house. A big window looked out on to the path I had just walked. I took a seat on the couch and the woman took a seat in an upholstered chair across from me. A low coffee table lay between us.

"My name is Verjen," she said, "Verjen Merry." She handed me her card. It said she was Sister Verjen Merry, Mother Superior of the Convent of the Holy Dereamer Pentacostal Gnostic Church of the Tribulation. I tucked the card away in my pocket. A woman came in dressed in a nuns habit: black dress, white hood, and clunky shoes. She silently deposited a tray of tea and cookies on the table in front of us and disappeared. As the nun padded away the mother superior said, "Thank you, sister."

"I am looking for this woman," I said, handing her

the picture of Candy Pantz. "I think she was intending to come here." Sister Vergen Merry looked at the picture.

"Reverend Babylon made arrangements for this woman to come here last Sunday. She was to join the sisterhood and study with us. But she never arrived. I expected her, but this picture is the first I have seen of her. Reverend Babylon told us that we should cooperate with you in every way."

"Mr. Thomas at the hardware store said she might have been in his store a few days ago buying batteries."

"That is very interesting," Verjin said. "It suggests that she made it all the way out here to Fumbuck but never made it the last few hundred yards to the convent."

"How do you sisters get along with the residents of Fumbuck?"

"We keep to ourselves," she said. "We do have to shop in the village. We get groceries at the country store and batteries from Mr. Thomas."

"The owner of the local tavern thinks you are all whores," I said.

"Ms. Sow is very opinionated and seldom keeps her opinions to herself. She claims to be a lesbian, but the local paper reports that she has had repeated instances of sodomic intercourse with Mr. Thomas in the plumbing aisle. I don't think she understands the sisterhood or what we do here."

"What do you do here?"

"We are brides of Chris. We meditate, we masturbate, and we study the Holy Bibble."

"The Reverend Babylon said that Candy was coming here to learn sellibacy."

"Women become brides of Chris for a variety of

reasons. Some come to learn the spiritual technique of sellibacy. In fact, that is why I came here. Ms. Pantz, had she arrived, would have studied under me."

"Tell me about sellibacy," I said. She leaned back in her chair.

"It is probably easiest if I just tell you my story." She closed her eyes and began to speak.

In the old days my name was Betsy Smith. I was the assistant to a stock broker in the city. It was a good job and the business did well. Then the market collapsed and I learned that my boss had engaged in a lot of illegal transactions. The office was closed and everyone who worked there got sued by the investors who had lost money. I needed a good lawyer, a specialist. My story begins in the office of Mr. Jason Fredrick, a lawyer who specialized in stock-fraud litigation.

I had dressed carefully for the meeting with Mr. Fredrick. I was wearing my best blue skirt with matching jacket. I had been to the hairdresser the day before and had spent an hour that morning putting on my makeup. As we talked about my situation I realized that he was the lawyer I needed, but when he told me how much the legal fees would be for my case I was devastated. "There is no way in a thousand years that I can afford that," I said with tears in my eyes.

Mr. Fredrick was an average looking white man about fifty years old. He wore a dark suit and expensive silk tie. He was also the best lawyer in the city for my kind of case. After a pause that seemed like forever, he lifted his eyes from the paper in front of him and looked at me directly. "There may be a way," he said, "but it is highly unethical."

"What way?" I said.

"I might be willing to trade my services for yours," he said.

"What services could I possibly provide you?" I asked.

"You are a thirty year old African-American woman. You are somewhat overweight, but well dressed and well groomed. You have large breasts, thick thighs and a round rear end. These are female physical characteristics that I find attractive. Although not married now, I see from your record that you have been married once and had a child. Thus, you are familiar with sex but probably not cynical about it. If I were to have sex with you, I would not be destroying your innocence, nor would I would be patronizing a prostitute. That is what I want. If we could come to a firm agreement, I would be willing to trade legal services for sexual services."

He described me perfectly. I never sold my body because I never had to. I'd never given it a lot of thought, but the idea of selling sex didn't shock me. I'd used sex in relationships to get what I wanted from boyfriends and husbands. Sometimes what I wanted was love and attention. Other times it was a new dress or a new car. I didn't plan on walking away from Mr. Fredrick without hearing what he had in mind.

"What would I have to do?" I asked.

"I charge $250 per hour. Your case will cost many thousands of dollars in fees to resolve. In return, I ask that you come here for sex once a week for a year. It need not be as regular as that, but you must come fifty-two times. When you come here you will be ready, willing, and able to accept my penis in your vagina, your mouth, between your breasts, and in you anus."

I stopped him. "I don't do anal sex."

"Then we have no deal. But let me finish before you decide." I had lied to him. I'd taken it up the butt a few times. I didn't love it, but it didn't kill me either. "You will show up here ready to have sex involving any of those parts of your body. If you normally don't lubricate well you will apply KY jelly to you vagina before you arrive. You will always lubricate your anus. All your orifices should be ready for me when you arrive. You will participate in sex and remain until I let you go. Although I may engage in some light bondage, I will not do anything that is physically damaging or dangerous. You should plan to be here about an hour for each visit."

I squirmed in my chair. I knew I was going to take the deal. I liked the guy. I wasn't going to let keeping my legs together stand in the way of my case. On the other hand I didn't want him to think the decision was easy.

"And one other thing. You will have to earn your right to enter this agreement by performing oral sex on me today. After you do that, we will both have two days in which to repudiate the agreement. You will think about the deal and let me know if you want to proceed."

"And you will be able to withdraw as well?"

"I will," he said.

"Then I will have given you a blow job for nothing?"

"That's correct."

"So the blow job is a test to see if you like me?"

"You can walk away as easily as I can," he said. "You are tested no more than am I. You might find me repulsive. Your giving me a blow job will assure me that you know what you are getting into."

I pulled at the hem of my skirt and considered the offer. I had never given myself to a man for any other reason than love. A couple of those times, when I was younger, that love had been fueled by hormones and alcohol, but love nevertheless. I now had to decide whether I was going to do it for financial advantage alone. I thought that if I was ever faced with that question it would be a great struggle, but as I sat there in front of Jason Fredrick, the best stock fraud lawyer in town, the decision was so easy that it made me uncomfortable.

I looked at my hands in my lap. "I don't have a choice," I said. "I need you to take my case."

"Stand and come around the desk," he said. His voice was gentle and the eyes behind his wire rim glasses were kind. He looked to be in good shape for his age. I got up from the chair, walked around the desk, and stood before him. He looked me over from head to toe.

"What should I do?" I asked.

"Lift your skirt," he said. The blue wool skirt was tight enough that when I pulled it up, it clumped and stayed at my waist. Underneath I was wearing dark red underwear and pantyhose. They were underthings designed for business, not romance. He reached to me and ran his hands down the outside of my hips to my knees. He then brought his right hand to the inside of my thighs and moved it up slowly. I spread my legs enough to give him room and he cupped my vagina in his hand. He held me for a moment and then took his had away.

"Turn and lean over the desk," he said. He pushed his chair back to make room for me. With my skirt still around my waist I did as he ordered. I put my elbows on the top of the desk so that my rear faced him. My breasts hung down in my bra, and as I leaned over they rested on the top surface of the desk.

"Like this," I said.

"That is fine," he responded. I kept my legs slightly spread. I felt his hands run gently over my buttocks and along the inside of my thighs. Then he took hold of the elastic band at the top of my pantyhose with a hand on either side. He pulled down the pantyhose to just above my knees taking my panties with them. I kept my head down on the desk imagining him just staring at my bare ass. I knew that from his vantage he would be able to see the lips of my pussy peeking out from underneath the crack of my butt. A wave of sexual pleasure passed through my body. It was not attraction for this strange quiet man but for sexual contact itself. He put the palms of his hands on my buttocks and gently fondled them. Then taking a firmer grip he forced them apart giving him what I knew would be an unobstructed view of my anus. I felt as if I were a specimen being examined for structural integrity. Yet his touch was gentle, with no hint of hurry or roughness.

He took a hand off my butt and cupped my vagina, squeezing the lips gently together. The heel of his hand pressed against the entrance. An involuntary spasm shook my hips and he felt it. He took his palm off my pussy and parted my labia with two fingers. With my pussy lips open he would be able to see my pink insides. He let my lips fall closed and put a finger inside me. I was trying to remain non-responsive, but my vaginal muscles failed to cooperate and gripped his finger.

"You are exactly what I expected," he said. I swallowed hard. His finger was still inside me. I thought to myself, *That's not exactly the compliment*

*a girl wants to hear when she is bent bare assed over
a man's desk.*

"I feel very exposed," I said.

"That's because you are," he said. He pulled his
finger out of my vagina, and pulled my skirt down.
"Please stand up," he said. I followed the order. My
pantyhose and panties were still at my knees, but with
the skirt down I was modest again.

"Did you like what you saw?" I asked him, fishing
for compliments.

"I did," he answered. "Please take off your clothes."

"Right here," I asked.

He pointed to a small table set against the office
wall. "You can put your clothes over there." I walked
over to the table and started to undress. He leaned
back in his leather office chair, watching.

"I am not used to undressing in front of a man I
just met," I said to him as I took off my jacket and
began unbuttoning the blouse beneath.

"If you were used to it I wouldn't have offered you
this opportunity," he said. "I expect that you will be
shy and embarrassed, but neither ashamed of your
nakedness of humiliated by it." His statement made
me brave. I had a good body. My breasts had fallen
since my twenties, but he knew how old I was when
he offered me the deal. I was a bit overweight, but it
was flesh that gave a man something to hang on to. I
finished unbuttoning my blouse watching my hands
work on the buttons. I took it off and laid it on the
table with the jacket. Without looking at him, I
reached around with one hand and undid the clasp of
the bra. Leaning forward I let it fall down my arms
into my hands. Released, my breasts swung free and
visible in the law office. Keeping my eyes from his, I
laid the bra on the table. Naked from the waist up I

turned and looked at him.

He was looking directly at me. Our gaze met but he said nothing. I lifted the hem of my skirt far enough to get a hold on the elastic parts of my pantyhose and pushed the underclothes down to my ankles. Kicking off my black high heels, I pulled the pantyhose, one leg at a time, off of my bare feet so when I stood straight again I was wearing nothing but the blue wool skirt. I undid the clasp on the side and unzipped it. When it was loose, I looked at Mr. Fallon. His expression was unchanged. I let go of my hold on the loosened skirt and pushed it to my ankles. I stepped out of the circle of cloth at my feet and stood before him naked.

"I find you very attractive," he said. "Come to me." I approached him in the chair. As I got near he spread his legs. "Put your hands on my knees." I did as he ordered. Leaning forward made my breasts fall toward him. He reached forward and cupped them in the palms of his hands, judging their weight and firmness. He squeezed gently with his fingers. He then let them loose and said to me, "Get on you knees."

I went to my knees in front of him and rested my arms on his legs. I was facing the crotch of an expensive wool business suit. I looked up at him and our eyes met. He did not have to say a thing. I reached for his belt and unbuckled it. The suit was perfectly fitted and the button beneath the belt buckle slid open easily. I undid the zipper fly and pulled the two sides apart. Beneath he wore silk boxer shorts. I reached through the slit in the front of the silk shorts and found his cock. He had been slouched in the chair sufficiently to give me access to what I needed, but as I touched his penis he slid down even further, pushing his genitals in my direction. I pulled the cock out of his pants to where I could get at it with my mouth and put my fingers back in his pants to explore his testicles. He had large warm balls that felt good in my hand. I fondled them gently while pulling his pants as open as I could get them.

His cock was circumcised, about eight inches long, and erect. I took my hand off his scrotum and held the cock with both hands at the base. Then I looked up at him. Our eyes met and I smiled. I turned back to the cock in front of me and licked it gently by putting the tip of my tongue against the sensitive underside of the head. As my tongue touched his dick, it crossed my mind that this was my last chance to back out. He had been satisfied, if not overwhelmed, by my body. He was not going to use his two days to get out of the deal. If I sucked him off, neither was I. If I put that cock in my mouth it would mean fifty-two weeks of sex with this man. I looked at his cock one last time and then wrapped my lips around it.

The man had a decent tasting cock. I hadn't sucked a lot of dick, but enough to know that some taste better than others. I got my mouth around the head of his dick and made a suction while rubbing my tongue against its underside. I heard and felt a gentle gasp come from him. Still sucking gently just on the tip I lifted my face to look at him. I wanted him to see what I looked like with his cock in my mouth. Our eyes met and the tension drained from his face. He smiled with his lips and I smiled with my eyes. He reached out and ran his hand over my hair. As he caressed my head, I turned back to the job before me.

I pulled as much of the cock into my mouth as I could and held it there, forcing my tongue against the underside. For a moment I felt filled with his masculinity. It seemed to grow in my mouth as I held it, pushing back against my throat and tickling my gag reflex. I pulled away and then went back down on him. His dick responded and I could taste some pre-cum in my mouth. It was salty and satisfying. It made me feel nasty. I had been holding his cock at the base with fingers from both hands. I let go with one hand and put the free hand between my legs. While fondling my own pussy, I pumped up and down on him with my mouth.

There is a comfort that comes from sucking a man. His most precious possession is at your mercy. When I give a blow job, I am not worrying about whether I will get enough of what I want or anything like that. It is pure giving and the joy you bring is like no other. No man is happier than when he has just delivered a load in a good woman's mouth. The woman's reward is the look of happiness on face and satisfaction of a job well done.

I increased the speed of the in and out, pushing as deep as I could with every stroke. He started to breathe heavily and I felt the gentle touch of his hands on my ears. He started to direct my face, pulling me on to him and lifting me off according to what felt best to him. As in a dance where the man leads, I followed his direction.

He pushed hard into me one last time, almost causing me to gag, then pulled half way out and shot semen in my mouth. I took it in and swallowed. Then I wrapped my lips around just the head and sucked hard to get every last drop of cum. I kept sucking until his cock went flaccid and even then I held it in my mouth sucking gently on its softness. When I was sure there was no life left in his cock I leaned back on my heels and put my hand to my face. His semen was dripping from my chin onto my tits. I looked up at him.

"That was very good," he said. I leaned forward and took hold of his flaccid penis.

"Let me put this back where I found it," I said. I slid his cock into the boxer shorts and began buttoning his fly. He remained silent. I stood and walked to my clothes. I put on the bra first, then the blouse, leaving my pussy and butt uncovered as long as possible. He watched every move. I balled up the pantyhose and underwear and put them in my purse. Finally, I leaned over, stepped into the skirt, and pulled it up. Stepping into my shoes I was once again the shy black women dressed for a meeting with her lawyer.

When I looked over toward Mr. Fedrick he was reading one of the legal papers on his desk. I walked softly to the door and left without saying a word. His young blond secretary was at work at in the outer office.

"Goodby, Ms. Smith," she said.

"Goodby, Ellen," I said.

Walking out to my car in the office parking lot I felt something I had never felt before. My panties were in my purse and the fresh air swirled around my bare ass and cunt. I could still feel his finger inside me. The musky maleness of cock mixed with salty semen left a taste in my mouth that I never wanted to go away. I felt better about sex than I had in years. My ass was truly worth something. My cock sucking was no longer a hormone driven frantic act of desperation or the side dish for my infatuation with some man. I didn't love Mr. Fredrick. He as a good lawyer and a pleasant man, but I certainly didn't love him. This good, honest and intelligent man had traded his valuable services for the right to stick his cock in me. I felt talented, and powerful. If I was a whore then I was a good whore. I climbed into my car in the parking lot, hiked up my dress, and masturbated until I came. I had never cum so hard or so long in my life.

We went to trial in my case and Mr. Fredricks was brilliant. I sat at the table in the courtroom next to him for two days. He was fully worth every cent that he would have charged me. I didn't wear panties to court. Seeing him work and knowing that I was paying for his skills by giving him pussy kept me wet the whole time. After the trial I scheduled seeing him every Wednesday afternoon. As a merchant of sex I didn't have to worry about a relationship, about whether he was true to me, and whether I would get my nut or not. My product was my ass and as a merchant I only had to worry about giving my customer the service he deserved. I took the job seriously.

I have to say that at first I didn't know what I was doing. For the first Wednesday I bought myself a mini-skirt, fishnet stockings, and bright red patent leather shoes with heels so high that I could barely walk. Mr. Fredrick smiled when he saw me.

"If I wanted a streetwalker," he said, "I would have gone to the streets. One of the many things I find attractive about you is that your pussy is not available to anyone with a hundred bucks in his pocket. You should never dress to suggest that it is."

I was embarrassed and learned a valuable lesson. He didn't mind the hooker outfit so much that he wasn't willing to do me doggie style over the desk, however the next week I came in a simple dress and white cotton underwear. He was so pleased that he had me suck him off and then stay around long enough for him to recover and fuck me missionary style on the office carpet. It was a great session and the feel of him in my cunt and my mouth stayed with me for hours.

In the months that followed I learned my trade. He taught me the techniques for taking it in the ass and enjoying it. He taught me deep throat. Some Wednesdays his secretary joined us, and I learned to how to have sex with a woman in a way that is most pleasurable for a man to watch. It was the year that changed my life.

Before the year was over I began to expand my horizons. I paid my car insurance by blowing my agent. I got a twelve pound prime rib for a dinner party by letting the butcher lubricate me with bacon grease and fuck me between the tits. I paid for a year of gym dues by letting a guy do me doggie style while I licked his girlfriend's pussy.

At the time I thought I was born to be a whore. One weekend I put on a mini-skirt and a pair of ridiculously high-heel shoes and joined the hookers down on Seventh avenue in the city to see what it was like on the streets. There I realized that what I was doing was different. The hookers there were doing it for the money. They were driven by pimps, addiction, and poverty. They would have painted houses if it had paid more. I have always been able to make money, and I have never been in poverty. I was doing it for the sex and the sex was only good for me if I did it for money. I felt lost between the world of prostitution on one hand and plain-jane monogamy on the other. Downcast and depressed I turned to the church.

Reverend Babylon redirected my life. She led me to the Holy Bibble and showed me the way to Chris. She sent me here to study. I meditated and learned, leaning heavily on the story in the Bibble of the Semen on the Mount. And through my religious studies I found my way to sellibacy. I changed my name, took the vow, and have lived here ever since helping others use the Bibble to address their own needs. It is because of my story that Reverend Babylon sent Candy Pantz to me.

Sister Merry leaned back in her chair, signaling that her tale was done.

"That is an inspiring story," I told the Sister. "I am sorry that Candace never had the chance to hear it."

"She may yet," Sister Merry told me. "Sister Babylon has great faith—faith that you will find Sister Pantz and bring her to us unharmed." As she spoke the woman in the nun's habit who had earlier brought the tea and cookies came back into the room and whispered in Verjen Merry's ear. Sister Merry listened, then turned to me. "Sister Jizzebel has heard the prophecy that we here at the convent will be visited by a man with a very large penis. She wonders if you are that man."

"The size of my penis is my cross to bear," I said.

"The dude we expect has been blessed by God," Sister Merry said. Her colleague in the nun's habit blushed. "The prophecy says he once had a whole locker room full of meter maids begging for it."

"Those were my sisters in blue," I said.

"Well meter maids know a good cock if anybody does," she said. "They aren't reference librarians by any stretch of the imagination, but they still know a good piece of meat when they see one. If you are the man of the prophecy, we ask that we be allowed to look upon your blessings." Sister Jizzebel came to me and went to her knees beside my chair. She reached out and put her hand on my cock.

"Sister," I said to her, "your touch is very gentle." She was a young woman. Her body was concealed by the black nun's habit.

Sister Merry responded, "Sister Jizzebel does not speak to anyone but me, and then only in whispers. Her spiritual path is a vow of silence." Sister Jizzabel began undoing my belt and fly. "Sister," Merry said, "you should express thanks to Chris and the man of the prophecy by showing Mr. James your tits." Sister Jizzabel took her hand from my pants. She pulled on the sides of her habit, snaps came undone, and a flap in the front fell open exposing a firm set of pink breasts. She had large hard nipples surrounded by areola as big as the saucers beneath our tea cups.

"Your breasts are very beautiful," I said to the nun. She silently went back to the task of opening my pants without a word. When my fly was down she pulled out my cock and held it in her hand showing it to Verjen Merry.

"You are the man of the prophecy," Merry said. "Praise the Holy Chris." Merry took a small bell from the coffee table in front of her and shook it. A high pitched tinkle rang forth and I heard footsteps in the house. Three women came into the room and stood against the far wall with their heads bowed. One was a smallish Hispanic woman wearing a blue habit cut in the same style as the one Sister Jizaebel wore. One was a thin white woman in a kimono, and the last was a large breasted Asian woman in a nurse's uniform. None of the three said a word.

"The prophecy has come true," Vergen Merry said. "This is William James. You can see by the size of his member that he is the man we have been expecting to come here and bless our home." The three women raised their eyes enough to look at my cock, still in Sister Jizzabel's hand. Sister Merry looked at my dick. "We, the sisters of the Convent of the Holy Dereamer Pentacostal Gnostic Church of the Tribulation ask you, William James, the man whose visit has been foretold by the Holy Reverend Babylon, to honor us by putting your large penis in the vagina of Sister Jizzabel." Sister Jizzabel turned around, still on her knees, laid over the low coffee table so that her rear end faced me. She then raised the lower part of her habit to expose her anus and labia. She was wearing dark stockings with lace tops that held firm on her upper thighs without a garter belt. The effect of the stockings and the black habit was to frame her white ass in a very pleasing way. While I enjoyed the view she spread her legs to make the entrance of her vagina visible.

"You are very pretty, Sister Jizzabel," I said.

"Her fulfillment is in silent submission. You can speak to her but she will not answer," Merry said. "Each of the sisters has her own spiritual path. We can continue our conversation while you fuck her."

I have never been a religious man, but I never mocked those who chose the religious way of life. I certainly didn't come to the convent looking to fuck one of the nuns, but Vergen Merry's quiet confidence in her own spirituality took me by storm. I could not deny her request. I slid off the chair so that I was on my knees behind Sister Jizzabel. I took my cock in hand and ran the tip of it up and down the crack of her pussy. The three women against the wall raised their eyes enough to watch what I was doing. I took my cock and pushed it slowly inside the warm nun cunt in front of me. She arched her back as it went in but remained silent. He pussy gripped my cock like the hand of a vengeful God. I backed it out and pushed in again to begin a quiet respectful fuck that would honor the house of the Lord.

Sister Merry who was sitting on the other side of the low coffee table reached out and caressed Sister Jizzabel gently on the head. Merry then picked up her tea cup from the table and sipped its contents. Taking the cue I reached for one of the cookies and nibbled on it as I continued to bone Sister Jizzabel. The crumbs fell down my chest onto our now-wet genitals.

"Sister Jizzabel is here at the convent studying the parable of the ten virgins," Merry said. I told Merry that I was not familiar with the story

"The Holy Chris tells of ten virgins," she said. "These virgins went forth to meet the bridegroom. Five of the virgins were wise and five of them were foolish. The five that were wise shaved their pussies and took oil to lubricate between their tits and in their assholes so that when the bridegroom arrived they would be ready to fuck him and suck upon his cock. Five of the virgins were foolish and they did not shave their pussies or take oil to lubricate their between their tits and in their assholes. Instead the just sat around gossiping and touching their hairy pussies with their fingers and being really catty about other women.

"And at midnight there was a cry and behold the bridegroom cometh. And the foolish virgins said to the wise virgins, give us your razors so we may shave our pussies and let us borrow your oil so that we can lubricate between our tits and in our assholes. But the wise virgins answered saying there are not enough razors to shave your nasty cunts and there is not enough oil to lubricate your dried up assholes. The wise virgins told the others that they were dumb cunts and that they should go to Walmart to buy their own razors and get their own oil. And so the unwise virgins went to Walmart.

"And while the dumb cunts were down at Walmart the bridegroom arrived and the wise virgins went in the basement with him for his bachelor party. In the basement the wise virgins did dance naked on the table in front of him and his bowling buddies, and they did fucketh the bachelors and did sucketh upon their cocks and did take many penises in their assholes. After the bridegroom and all his friends had fallen asleep from having fucked the wise virgins so vigorously and in so many different positions, the unwise virgins came to the door of the basement and it was shut.

"The unwise virgins called out that they were ready and that they had shaved their pussies and oiled their assholes and they were ready to fucketh and that they were ready to sucketh on cocks so they would no longer have to touch their own pussies with their fingers. And the bridegroom raised his head from his drunken stupor and told them to get the hell away because there was no one awake to fucketh them and no longer did his buddies have erections upon which they could sucketh. And they did go away and some of them again touched their pussies with their fingers and some of them went lesbo and lay together one licking upon the crack of the other."

I listened to the parable, moving my cock in and out of Sister Jizzabel as Sister Merry told it. Jizzabel's silent submission made her pussy mysterious and enticing. Fucking her while listening to the parable of the ten virgins infused my dick with a spiritual warmth and fulfillment that was new to me. I felt as if

I could just stay there forever at the convent basking the light of the Lord and screwing the nuns.

"So what does the parable mean?" I asked Sister Merry.

"When sister Jizzabel's year of silence is over, she will explain it to us."

"Maybe it means you never really know when you will be asked to a bachelor party," I said. Sister Merry smiled an enigmatic smile like the Mona Lisa and changed the subject.

"Did you stop in town?" she asked.

"I did," I told her. "I stopped at the Fat Sow for a thirst quencher and information."

"Sow is quite the character," Sister Merry said. "She provides the wine for the convent. I pay for that by allowing her to call me Poopsie while she licks semen off my tits and thighs."

"She told me about Poopsie," I said.

"She tells everyone," the Sister responded. "She runs a lesbian bar but she is not as committed a lesbian as she makes out. If you go there again you should ask her to show you her vagina. It is one of the largest and hairiest vaginas I have ever seen. She won't mind—particularly if she has been drinking. She is quite proud of it. She would probably let you fuck it if you asked nice."

"The one I have my dick in right now is all I need," I said, still moving in and out of Sister Jizzabel.

"Did you hear that, Sister Jizzabel," Merry said. "Mr. James likes your cunt." Sister Jizzabel stayed silent but I could feel an increasing responsiveness to my thrusts. She was trying to stay still but found herself instinctively pushing her ass back to meet my cock on the in-stroke. Her hands which had earlier been palm down on the coffee table now had a white knuckle grip on the far edge. "Sister Jizzabel," Merry continued, "used to be a moaner. She moaned, and screamed and swore and grunted like a pig. All that noise, however, blunted her pleasure, so not only did she get evicted from a lot of apartments, she did not have satisfying climaxes. She is learning to hold the orgasm inside where it will explode silently and bring to her a kind of satisfaction, both physical and spiritual, that all the sweaty moaning and groaning never could."

As Sister Merry spoke, Jizzabel writhed on the coffee table. The muscles of her pussy gripped and released my cock in waves. Seeing what was happening, I took her by the hips and gave her eight or ten hard thrusts, enough to make me cum and fill her nun cunt with semen. She felt me orgasm inside her, finished off her own, and lay limp on the coffee table jerking from aftershocks that started in her crotch, moved up her body and out her arms, into her fingers. My dick didn't immediately go soft so I continued to gently fuck her limp body to prolong our pleasure and rid myself of the last tiny drops of cum. When flaccid I pulled my cock out and sat back up on the chair opposite Vergen Merry. Sister Jizzabel remained motionless in front of me, her vagina exposed to view with semen oozing from her hole.

The Asain woman in the nurse uniform left the room and returned with a bowl of soapy water and a sponge. She dropped to her knees beside me and silently washed my cock and balls.

"Who is this?" I asked Merry, indicating the nurse working on my dick.

"That is Sister Horenece. Horence Nitelytail. She will tend to your personal hygiene while you are here."

Eventually Sister Jizzabel revived. I stayed with the sisters for dinner and most of the evening. Except for Jizzabel who just sat there with a Cheshire Cat grin, we talked about the convent, the Holy Bibble and the little town of Fumbuck. They served a meal of fresh clams and bratwurst. We did a short Bibble study after dinner, the Sister in the Kimono gave me a blow job, and we played two games of Scrabble.

When I left the convent at about ten o'clock that evening, my Gremlin was still parked in front of the Fat Sow. I saw a light on in the tavern and walked inside. The place was empty except for Sow, who was doing paperwork on one of the tables. She looked up as I approached and said, "Well Detective, did you enjoy the whores?"

"My name is William James," I said. "You should call me William. They are not whores and you know it. They are Brides of Chris."

"Call 'em what you like," she said, looking back to her paperwork. "Would you like a nightcap?"

"I could do with an RC to help me sleep," I said. She got up and came back with a cold one.

"How come the place is so empty?" I asked.

"Farm women. A weeknight. The stupid bitches are all at home fucking their ugly husbands."

"I thought they were lesbians."

"Whores is what they are," she said. "This town don't have enough people to have lesbian bar with real honest to God full-time lesbians, so the farm women take up the slack in their spare time. It gives 'em a break from sweating and grunting underneath their hairy farmer husbands. They're all whores. That's what I say." Sow had been drinking.

"Sister Vergen Marry says you have a remarkable vagina."

"Well, loud-mouth whores like her are what's wrong with this town," Sow said. "Next thing you know they are going to put up a sign saying, 'Fumbuck: The Home of Sow's World Famous Giant Cunt.' They could advertise it like the Grand Canyon or the Great Wall of China as the only vagina visible from space. We could set up bleachers and folks could bring the kids."

"Now Sow," I said, "Sister Merry didn't mean it like that."

"I suppose not," Sow answered. "You want a look, right?"

"Yes, I do," I said. "if you don't mind."

Sow pushed the papers out of the way, lifted her big dress and climbed on the table. Laying on her back, she spread her legs. Her labia were like two rolled up beach towels lying next to each other. The huge lips were covered in wiry black pubic hair. Between the two rolled towels hung a pink avalanche of flowery flesh.

"Wow," I said.

"Speechless aren't you?" she said, "Most people are. A huge cunt is my cross to bear."

"I know that it isn't easy," I told her. I walked around the side of the table so she could turn her head and get a good look at me. I opened my pants, took out my cock, and held it for her to see.

"Jesus Chris," she said, "that's the biggest cock I've ever seen on a whi—"

"Stop," I interrupted. "Don't say anything. This, you see, is my cross to bear."

"I understand," she said, "I really do." For a moment we stared at each other, she spread-legged on the tavern table, me in the middle of the room with my cock in my hand. After a long but not totally uncomfortable silence she said, "I think it is destiny."

I took a position in front of her huge cunt. She reached between her legs, spread the lips and lifted the loose skin away from the hole. I laid my cock on her vagina, positioned it in front of the hole and pushed in.

"That is nice," she said. For me it was like throwing a penny in the ocean. Her cunt devoured my dick like it was nothing. She put her hand on her clit and fingered herself while I fucked her. We fucked for about twenty minutes. I brought her to orgasm and then came myself. My cum disappeared inside her never to be seen again as if she could swallow with her pussy. When we were done we took turns wiping each other off with a bar towel. I told her I had to leave. With a tear in her eye she asked me to come back some time and said we could do it again. As I walked out the door, there were tears in my eyes as well. Her invite to return was sincere, but we both felt in our crotches that we would never see each other again.

It was midnight before I was back on the road in the Gremlin. I pulled into the city about two in the morning, took a quick shower, and dropped to sleep. The morning comes early in the city, and the Pantz case awaited.

Chapter 4

I dragged myself out of bed the next morning famished. Nuns and lesbian farm women can really take it out of a man. No longer welcome at Mohammad's Pig and Pancake, I went looking for breakfast. The morning air felt good in my lungs so I walked the streets, eventually stopping at a hole-in-the-wall bagel and rib place I'd never seen before. The Mexican guy who ran it served up bad coffee and something close enough to food to get me going on the day. For an extra two bucks he said I could fuck his sister in the back room. His sister was better looking that his food, but I decided I should get back to work on the Pantz case instead.

On the walk back to the office I cut across Jimmy Hoffa City Park. The park was empty and fog still hung in the treetops. In the afternoon, the park would be filled with young mothers pushing their little bastards on swings. On this cold morning the place was deserted. I was passing the playground when I heard a familiar voice.

"Hey faggot," the voice said, "stop right there." Six Catholic school girls stepped out from behind the jungle gym. They were led by the little blond I had seen on the bus when riding with Brett. One of them was the large girl who had pulled my face into her tits. They wore the same plaid skirts, knee high socks, and patent leather shoes. The little blond leader twirled a rosary like a greaser swinging a bicycle chain. "Willam James," she said, "private dick."

"That's me," I said, "What's it to ya?"

"Private asshole, is what I say."

"Very private asshole to you," I retorted. *Ha,* I thought, *bet she didn't expect that.*

"You been told to drop the Pantz case. It seems you are not getting the message. There are people in this city who think you don't understand the seriousness of the situation." She walked toward me. I held my ground and thought about the best way to subdue her without causing her serious injury. I had decided to do the Siberian death chop when she caught me with a crushing right lead to the nose. I staggered back, felt a second blow to the temple, and was buried in plaid skirts, patent leather shoes, and soft Catholic schoolgirl flesh.

They held me down and blindfolded me. I was stunned by the shot to the nose and head, so they were able to lift and carry me from where I had fallen. When they pulled off the blindfold I was on the floor of a cinder-block bathroom. My pants were gone and I was surrounded by school girls. My eyes took a moment to fuly adjust to the darkness, and when I could see again I was looking into the face of the little blond leader.

"Nice dick, dick," she said pointing to my exposed penis. I stayed quiet. "But it ain't gonna help you today." Her gang members pulled me to my feet. With two girls on each arm they were able to hold me in place facing their leader. The little blond continued, "James, have you ever heard the screams of a man having his testicles crushed." Standing behind the blond leader was the muscle of the group, the one who had tit-smothered me on the bus. She was a good six inches taller than me, had the face of a horse, and the legs of a weight lifter. She had her left hand in the crotch of her panties fingering herself. With the other hand she was squeezing a tennis ball.

"Can't say as I have ever heard screams like that," I answered. My questioner let out a high pitched school girl laugh that sent chills down my spine and reminded me of Mrs. Mohammad. "Well today is your chance," she said. She turned to the big girl behind her. "Bruna, crush them."

"But Serenity," Bruna said, "his thing is so big. I like it." I could see her finger going back and forth inside her panties.

"Do what you are told, Bruna," she yelled. "Crush his balls." The blond moved out of the way and Bruna stepped forward. She gave the tennis ball a last squeeze, it broke in her hand, and she dropped the husk of the ball on the floor. She took her left hand out her panties and reached for my dick. Gently lifting my cock to give herself access she cupped my testicles in the hand that had just finished off the tennis ball.

"Bruna like your cock very much," she said. "Looking at it make Bruna feel warm and nice. Bruna sorry she has to crush your balls." The powerful right hand tightened on my nuts and groin-pain shot up my body. I pulled with all my might trying to escape, but the gang girls held my arms tight. I screamed.

Then there was something black flying in the damp restroom air. It knocked Serenity to the floor. Coming up in an arch it caught Big Bruna hard in the crotch. Her grip relaxed, her eyes widened in pain, and her mouth dropped open. I looked down and there was the end of a cop's nightstick pointing at me from her crotch like a big black dick. Both of her hands went to her pussy and she dropped to her knees. Behind her, now raising the night stick for an attack on the girls holding my arms, was Deshawn-awanda Jones.

Suddenly my arms were free and the girls were

backing away. My balls were throbbing in pain. I fell to the floor and cupped my testicles in my hands.

"Against the wall, motherfuckers," Deshawnawanda yelled with the nightstick in the air. She was in her skin-tight cop uniform complete with belt, mace, and radio. The girls backed up to the bathroom wall. She yanked Bruna, who was still holding her crotch in pain, to her knees and kicked the big woman. Bruna, afraid of more kicks, crawled toward her gang. Deshawnawanda grabbed little blond Serenity by the collar and lifted her to her feet. Forcing her to face her gang, the cop stood behind her and held the nightstick across her throat with both hands. "One move," Deshawnawanda said to the girls against the wall and I will crush this little bitch's throat so she will never give orders or blow jobs again. You understand." They nodded their heads in unison. I struggled to stand. "Are you okay?" Deshawnawanda asked.

"I think so," I whispered still holding my balls.

"Where are your pants?"

"I don't know," I told her. She looked at the girls against the wall.

"Somewhere out there in the trees," one of them said.

"All right," she said to them, "Drop 'em. Skirts and panties. Throw them out in front of you on the floor." The girls looked to their leader who was still held tight against Deshawnawanda by the nightstick to the throat. "Tell 'em, Serenity." Deshawnawanda jerked the stick tight and the girl gagged.

"Do it," Serenity coughed.

Slowly the five girls took off the skirts and threw them into a pile in the middle of the bathroom.

"Now the panties," Deshawnawanda yelled. "Throw

them on top of the rest." The girls removed their identical thongs and threw them onto the pile of plaid skirts. They had identically shaved pussies, each with a little landing strip of hair just above the cracks. "Bruna," Deshawnawanda yelled, "get Serenity's stuff and put it on the pile." Bruna came over and dropped to her knees before her leader. The big woman unbuttoned the skirt at the waistband and pulled down the plaid skirt and panties in one motion. Serenity had the same style of shaved pussy as the rest. "Now Bruna," Deshawnawanda ordered, throw all the clothes in the toilet.

"Oh no," Bruna complained, "I just got that skirt last week."

"Shut up," Deshawnawanda told her, "I want every bit of that pile to be soaking wet with toilet water." Bruna reluctantly gathered up the clothes and put them in the toilet of the nearest stall. "Push it in hard." Bruna leaned over to push the cloth into the water, her big naked ass sticking out of the stall as she worked.

"Okay girls," Deshawnawanda said as Bruna finished the work of getting the skirts and panties wet. "I'm letting you off easy this time. You can either put your toilet water clothes back on or make a run for it bare assed across the park to the school. But if you ever, and I mean ever, bother Mr. James again in any way, I will hunt your nasty little cunts down and make you regret it for the rest of your lives." She pushed Serenity toward her friends, put her arm around my shoulder and helped me out of the building. Her cop car was parked on the grass just outside the door. She steered me into the passenger seat and got behind the wheel. As we drove away the catholic girls stood in the doorway to the building, naked from waist to knee socks, watching us leave and giving us the finger.

"How's your balls," Deshawnawanda asked as we plummeted over the curb that separated the park from the city streets.

"They will be better if you don't do that," I answered, grabbing my crotch as the car bounced.

"Oh sorry," she said. "I will get you to help as soon as I can." She took me into a residential area of modest houses and tree-lined streets. Pulling into the driveway of a small blue house the garage door opened and we parked inside. She came around and helped me out of the car. I still had no pants and was holding my aching balls in my hand. She helped me limp into the house, directed me to a bedroom, and lay me on a large bed covered in a white silk bedspread. She threw a light blanket over my nakedness and left the room.

When Deshawnawanda returned she had a glass of water and pills. "Take these," she said. "It will help with the pain." I did as she ordered.

"Where am I?" I asked.

"At my house," she said.

"Why are we here?"

She reached under the blanket, took my cock and laid it to the side on my leg. Then she reached beneath and held my balls. Her touch was gentle and her hand was warm. "I can make you all better," she said.

She pulled her hand away and left the room. She was gone about twenty minutes during which time the pills began the work. The throbbing stopped and the pain lessened. Deshawnawanda returned naked, smelling freshly showered. She was a solid, well packed black woman. Mrs. Milpy was the color of wheat bread and seemed loosely connected so that if she spun in a circle her arms, legs, and pendulous breasts might come loose and fly away. Vergen Merry was the color of coffee. She was small, curvy, and round. Deshawnawanda was jet black with muscled legs and hard bullet shaped tits. She had short Afro hair and pussy lips like banana slugs.

Deshawnawanda lay down on the bed next to me and slid her hand under the small blanket to fondle my cock. "Are you feeling better?" she asked.

"A little," I said.

"It feels like you are feeling better," she answered, referring to the beginnings of an erection that was forming in her hand. "Did you like seeing all that teen-aged pussy?"

Being reminded of the girls lined up in the park bathroom with their little cracks exposed, my dick made a jump. Deshawnawanda squeezed it and said, "It seems like you liked it. I didn't have to make them drop their panties like that. I did it for you. I never knew a man who didn't like getting a look at some schoolgirl pussy."

"Thank you," I said.

"I should have had them take off their tops and jump up and down so that their little titties bounced. Would you have like that better?"

"Seeing them with their pants down was sufficient revenge," I said.

"A pussy man," she said. "I like that. Do you like porn? I got all the recent issues of *Police Pussy* and *Cops and Cunts*."

"I'm fine."

"I should say you are," she said gripping my now erect cock in her hand. "The pain would go away even faster if you sucked on one of my tits." She climbed up on me and pushed one of her nipples in my mouth.

Her breast was smooth and her nipples erect. I liked the taste and took it in my mouth. She sighed and pushed her tit hard against my face. After a few minutes of tit sucking she straddled my waist dangling her black breasts in my face so that I could nip at her nipples with my front teeth.

"Oh, you nasty boy," she said as I caught a nipple between my teeth and held it. When I let go she pounced on me with a kiss and jammed her tongue inside my mouth. I sucked her tongue like I had sucked her nipples. While we kissed, Deshawnawanda reached behind her and put my cock at the entrance to her cunt. She rocked back and it slid inside. Deshawnawanda had one of the greatest pussies ever put between the legs of a cop. It was hot, it was wet, and it was tight.

"Oh, you really are a pussy man," she said. My balls felt fine again. In fact, they felt great pinned against Deshawnawand's hot asshole. Deshawnawanda proceeded give my cock a wiggle-ass treat like it had never had before. She bounced up and down on it. She did the squat thing. She wiggled: up and back, back and forth, and round and round. I watched her tits bounce as she did the most energetic pogo on a meat stick I had ever seen. She came three or four times in the process. I didn't want it to end, but finally I couldn't hold back any longer. I let fly with a splooge into her black pussy and we left a serious mess on the bed.

Afterward, we lay on the bed sharing an RC. I thought back to how she saved me in the bathroom at the park.

"How did you learn to fight like that?" I asked. And then Deshawnawanda told me her story.

I had just turned fourteen," she said, "when this young woman who lived down the street from Ebenezer and me was raped in the park. The neighborhood was in an uproar and we didn't talk about anything else for weeks. I told Eb that I sure wouldn't let no man ever rape me and he said what did I think I would do about it if somebody tried. I told him that I would punch the bad man in the eye and Eb said that if I was planning to defend myself I better learn how to do it right. Eb was two years older than me and spent a lot of time out in the garage practicing boxing and judo and karate out of the books he got from the reference desk at the library. Our parents let him put together a makeshift gym with wrestling mats, weights, and a chin-up bar. I said that he should teach me how to fight so that I could defend myself against the rapist.

Eb took me out to the garage and put me on an exercise program. He made me do sit ups and push ups. He showed me how to do karate chops and roundhouse kicks. After a week of training he said I was ready for a test. He would play the rapist and I would fight him off. I remember that day like yesterday. I was wearing purple gym shorts and a t-shirt. My young but well-developed tits jiggled underneath my shirt as I hopped around on the mat. He wore a t-shirt and cut off blue jeans. I bent my knees into a wrestling stance as he took to the mat to face me. He looked at me and said in a low grumbly rapist voice, "Hey, little black girl. I'm going to rape you."

"Stop Eb," I said, "I will never learn if we don't do it real. A rapist would have his thing out." I'd seen his cock before in the bathroom and at various times so I knew what it looked like. I didn't know whether real rapists came at you with their things out or not, but I knew the exercise would be a lot more fun if there was a dick involved. He took it out of his pants and let it dangle in front of me.

"Okay, now say it," I said,

"Hey, little girl," he repeated, "I am going to rape you."

"No you are not," I said, and sent a roundhouse kick to his head. He dodged and came after me. I ran around the mat using my quickness to avoid his grasp. When he got close, I turned and aimed a karate chop at his nose, but he caught my hand, flipped me on my back, and in one quick motion my shorts panties we gone. "Ha, ha, ha, little girl," he said in his fake voice, "What are you going to do now?"

"You will never get me, Mr. Rapist?" I squealed. He dropped on top of me so that his cock was at the entrance to my cunt.

"Oh, yes I will," he said, "and if you don't learn your self defense I will come back and rape you every day." He pushed forward forcing his cock inside me and it rocked my world. Eb and I, like any brother and sister, bickered a lot, but in truth I adored him. He was, after all, my big brother. He was adopted and a white man, but my brother nevertheless. I am not proud to say that the first cock I ever took inside me was my own brother's, but I am not sorry either. Never has a dick felt as good on my clit as his.

So there I was on my back with Eb's dick deep inside me. I couldn't tell him what that meant to me so I stayed in character. "Well, you better get to that raping then, because one of these days I will learn my self defense, and then you will be sorry."

Eb switched to his normal brother voice. "You are okay then?" He had yet to move his dick since getting it up inside me.

"I'm fine," I said. "It's just that your nasty hairy balls are making my butt itch." He pulled out and thrust back in. I gasped with pleasure.

"Take that little girl," he said, back to his fake rapist voice.

"Don't bother me none," I said. He pulled out again and as he pushed back in I raised my hips to meet him. My clit rubbed against the place where his cock meets his body and I came right then, although I kept the orgasm quiet, not wanting to show him how much I liked it. Eb proceeded to give me a loving but athletic brotherly fucking. Toward the end I lifted my legs, held my ankles to give him an open shot at my hole, and he pounded it home. I came one more time with my feet in the air and then he came, shooting his stuff inside me. When he had deposited the last of his cum inside me, he rolled off onto the mat.

"Brother," I said, "it looks like I'm not quite ready for a real rapist yet."

"Practice and training, Deshawnawanda," he said, "practice and training."

In the weeks that followed we went to the garage every afternoon to work on my martial arts. We stretched, we lifted weights, we ran laps, and we studied moves. When the study was over we would go to the mat to see if I could fend him off. I really had no chance. He was a boy and he outweighed my by fifty pounds. For the first few weeks he pretty much just flopped me on the mat and fucked me. One day he turned me over and did me doggie style while reaching around with his hands to fondle my titties while he did it. Another day he tied me to the chin-up bar and fucked me standing up. For a week he took to lying on his back and making me squat on his dick while he pinched my nipples with his fingers.

No matter how Eb did me, I came and came. It seemed like all I had to do was think about the garage and I would orgasm. It was like God has sent me an adopted brother with a magic cock.

Soon he took to making me suck his dick. I would fight him off the best I could with the skills I had but he would end up forcing to me knees to lick his balls and suck his white wiener. I loved his cock in my mouth from the first taste. I would suck on the tip. I would lick up the shaft. But I loved best using my mouth like it was a cunt—just going up and down on it until he shot his stuff. I would lay awake at night in my bed, make the 'O' shape with my mouth, and pretend that Eb's boner was giving me the business. Mother would serve dinner and I would imagine my plate covered with penises.

My brother doesn't have the biggest cock I've ever seen. It ain't small, but it ain't big like yours either. But Eb has huge balls. I spent a lot of time with him sitting on my face, so I have licked and sucked his nutsack a lot. At the time I didn't have anything to compare them to, but since then I have tasted a lot of scrotum, and I have never had my tongue on a set of balls like his. They are semen machines. When he cums he shoots more stuff than any man I have ever met. I jerked him off in a measuring cup once. He put out nearly a cup of cum. You can see that those afternoons in the garage were messy affairs. Teen cunts don't hold much. He would hold me down to fuck me and when I finally got off the matt the stuff would be streaming down my legs. When he took to doing me in the mouth I learned to drink it down but couldn't get it down near as fast as he could pump it out. Sometimes even though I was swallowing as fast as I could the stuff would be blowing back out of my mouth onto his balls and belly. I can remember those days like it was yesterday.

His stuff tasted great and it was my love of sucking him off that made me the cocksucker I am today. A lot of women think they better suck their man's dick or some other woman will be sucking it instead, but they really don't enjoy it that much. I adore dick in my mouth. I like black dicks, white dicks, brown dicks, and yellow dicks. I like 'em big and I like 'em small. I like hard dicks, but I also like soft dicks. Sometimes there is nothing more comforting than to curl up with a cock that is fully drained and just hold it in your mouth and suck on it while it is soft. I don't really know if Ebenezer made me a cocksucker, but if I was going to end up a cocksucker anyway, I was damn lucky to have a brother like him to get me started.

Then one day at the end of a lesson he said, "Hey little black girl, I want to stick my cock in your ass." At the time, I had a virgin ass and had no idea what that would be like. I fought him off like a black whirlwind, but at the end of it all I was tits down on the mat with his cock jammed up my round black virgin butt. For a women the thrill in being butt fucked comes from how slutty it is. You know you are a truly nasty girl when you have your buns in the air and a cock pumping your asshole. When Eb took to butt-fucking me, I fought even harder during the foreplay and harder I fought better we liked it during the sex. Then one afternoon, as he was preparing to take me down for a butt-fuck, he lost concentration for a moment. I spun out of his grip, caught him with a roundhouse kick to the head, and dropped him like a rock.

I thought it was funny. I sat down on the mat next to him and waited for him to regain his bearings. In a few minutes he was back to normal. He looked up at me from the mat with a brotherly smile. "My work here," he said, "is done."

He never fucked me after that day. No man has ever forced himself upon me and more than one has tried. Eb taught me to love cock, to embrace my desire to suck, and to defend myself at all times. He was the best brother a girl could ever have wished for. The fighting served me well. It made me a cop and being a cop gave me the opportunity to save you from those little cunts in the park bathroom.

"And I appreciate that you did," I said. She sat up and was wiping her crotch with a small towel she had taken from the nightstand.

"I hope this little romp makes up for my throwing you against the bars of that cell when you were in jail."

"Forget it," I said.

"Next time we get together, I will blow you. You will really like that, but right now I am on duty and need to get back to the precinct." She found me a pair of pants in a closet that was filled with mens clothes. There were a lot of pants in a lot of different sizes in there. I didn't ask where they came from.

Deshawnawanda dropped me off in front of Otto's and I went up the stairs to the office. Teena was at her desk.

"What happened to you?" she said.

"What do you mean?" I asked.

"That look on your face. You look like you just fucked your best friend's sister. . . . . And your pants don't fit."

"Is it that obvious?"

"What? That your pants don't fit or that you fucked your best friend's sister?"

"Well he wasn't really my best friend, but I did sort of promise I wouldn't fuck her."

"Oh, William," Teena said, "how could you? I thought you were a better man than that . . .Was it Bjorn?"

"No," I said, "Ebenezer."

"Not Ebenezer," she said. "He is such a nice man and he looks up to you so much."

"I know, I know," I said. "I feel terrible."

"Something like that can have long term psychological consequences," Teena said in her most solemn voice. "It happened to me, you know. The memory still haunts me."

"I didn't know that," I told her.

"Yes, it did. I had this great boyfriend named Richard, Richard Long. I was a senior in high school and he was taking me to the prom. I was all dressed up in my hottest high school dress. I expected we would go to dinner, then to the prom, and then go parking up on Boner Hill overlooking the city. It all was going just as planned until the dinner. He told me he had something that was eating him up, and that if we were to ever be true to each other he had to get it out in the open. Then he told me he had fucked my sister. He'd done it twice, both times in the little gardening shed behind our house.

"I was devastated. I ran from the restaurant. He followed and the waiters followed us both yelling because we hadn't paid. When one of the waiters tackled him, I escaped. I walked the streets in tears, unable to cry away the vision of him boning my sister next to the potting soil.

"I made my way to the Tasty Lick, a drive-in burger joint where all the kids went after games. I sat at one of the tables outside crying in my prom dress. Then these three college boys came by. They saw me crying and sat down. One of them bought me a cherry Tasty Lick and I told them about wanting to go to dinner and the prom and up to Boner hill with Richard and that he had fucked my sister in the potting shed. They thought he was a terrible man and offered to go kick his butt. I told them no, so then one of them said that they could take me up on Boner Hill in their van and we could have a lot more fun than those dumb high school kids at that prom.

"So I got in the van with them and we drove up on Boner Hill to see the lights of the city. It was hot in the van so the guys started taking off their shirts and pants and they were all three really buffed with big muscles and hard pecs and tight butts. All that manliness made me want to use my little girl Minnie Mouse voice and I said, 'You big boys wouldn't want me to take off my prom dress, would you?' But they did and underneath I had my new lace stockings and my nicest garters and my cutest panties and my best push-up bra. And the sight of all that pretty underwear drove them crazy. The bra went and panties didn't last much longer. They touched me everywhere and then came the cocks.

"They jumped me big time, fucking me in every position and in every hole. They stuck their meat sticks in my pussy, my mouth, up my ass, between my tits and a couple of places I can't even mention in mixed company. I was so buried in college dick I could hardly breathe. No sooner did one guy shoot his wad and go limp the next one was on me, fresh, hard and ready to go. And could those boys cum? They came and came and came. I had cum on my face, dripping down my tits, and oozing from my twat. Everywhere I turned there was another cock needing to be drained. I sucked 'em off, I jerked 'em off, and I took them up the ass. Eventually I got them all dry and limp. Sweaty and still panting, we broke out a couple of RCs and had a cigarette. Then ten minutes later they started telling me how pretty I was again. Twenty minutes later they were all hard and ready for another round.

"I'm telling you it was a hell of a prom night. It was my own penis party—a cock cotillion—and I was the dick diva. A lot of girls have prom night stories but when it comes to the raw number of cocks involved, mine has got to rank pretty far up there."

"Teena," I said, "what happened with your sister and Richard Long?"

"Oh. They got married. They have two kids and grow marijuana for a living in California."

"Teena," I complained, "does that story have anything at all to do with my having to tell Eb that I promised I wouldn't fuck Deshawnawanda and then I fucked her anyway."

"Deshawnawanda Jones, the cop?"

"Yes. The cop."

"Good job, dude. She is a hot number. Don't worry about it. I will tell Eb for you."

"You will tell him?"

"Yeah," she said, "you don't want to have to look Eb in the eye and tell him what an asshole you are and how as soon as his back was turned you nailed his sister. I will do it for you."

"How would that work?"

Teena pulled out a little steno pad and a pen. "Easy," she said, "give me the details. Did she suck your dick? Did you fuck her in the ass?"

"Teena," I said, "I will tell him myself."

"Are you sure? I really don't mind."

"I will do it."

"Okay, be that way," she said. "Uh, so did you fuck her in the ass?"

"Teena," I said, "get to work." She got up and in a huff and went back to her desk. I would make my confession to Eb when I could but next on the agenda was a trip to find a taxi driver.

The Yellowchecker Taxi Company was not easy to find. Its headquarters were out on the edge of town where all the residents make their living off the automobile. People there buy cars and sell them. They steal cars and strip them. They fix cars, they tow cars, they stow cars, and conceive their children in the back seats of cars. At the Yellowchecker Taxi Company they hired people to drive other people around in cars. The building was a brown shack of a building that tilted slightly to the left. It had a corrugated metal roof and was hidden between a U-Pull-it salvage lot and an auto body repair shop run by Romanians.

The parking area in front of the building was filled with broken Yellowchecker cabs. A couple of them, having no wheels, rested on cinder blocks. The others seemed to be in various states of having their parts removed. I parked my Gremlin next to one of the disabled vehicles. Inside I found a small waiting room well used by drivers. There were overflowing ash trays and magazines featuring naked Romanian women with abnormally large breasts.

Behind a low counter a small round woman was sitting at the dispatch desk. She appeared to be about forty-five years old. She was overweight, but her fat was packed neatly into the round shape that one tends to associate with jolly rather than obese. She had short red hair and wore a bright pink sweat suit.

On seeing me the woman said, "What can I do for you, honey?"

"My name is William James," I said. "I am a private detective." She stood and bounced toward me, her stomach and breasts jiggling with her happy gait.

"A private detective, you say."

"That is correct," I said. I handed her my card. As she examined it a tall thin man wearing mechanic's overalls came through the back door to the office.

"My name is Mrs. Yellowchecker," the woman said.

"But most people call her 'the ugly fat whore,'" the man in the back said.

"That is my husband, Mr. Yellowchecker," she said, indicating with a flip of her red hair that she was talking about the thin man behind her. "He married me for my money. I fucked him stupid on our wedding night and he never recovered. What can I do for you, Mr. James?"

"You can suck his cock," the man in the back said, "just like you do every other man who walks through the door." Mrs. Yellowchecker picked up a stapler from the desk, turned and hurled it at her husband. She was quick for her size and a good aim. The stapler nailed him hard in the right shoulder, but he shrugged off the hit. Mrs. Yellowchecker returned her attention to me.

"I am looking for a missing woman," I said. "Her name is Candace Pantz and I think that one of your drivers may have picked her up last Saturday night after her shift at Totally Naked Women Here."

"So you want me to check the dispatch slips?"

"Of course he wants you to check the dispatch slips, you dumb cunt," the thin man said. "You think licking

his balls is going to tell him who made that pickup."
As he spoke he was approaching Mrs. Yellowchecker
from behind.

"Pay Mr. Yellowchecker no mind," she said to me.
"He has a little tiny cock. Barely visible to the human
eye, and he tries to make up for it with a big mouth."
She reached under the counter and took out a small
plastic box. It contained blue slips separated by date.
She was putting her index finger to the records just as
her husband closed in on her from behind with his
hands out as if preparing to strangle her. As he was
about to grab her neck she spun around and nailed
him with an uppercut to the chin. He dropped like a
rock.

"Dumb bastard," she said and turned back to the
records. "Saturday night you say. I assume you mean
early Sunday morning."

"Probably about two A.M." I said. Mr.
Yellowchecker, shaken by the punch, was struggling
to his knees behind her.

"Ah," she said, "pickup at Totally Naked Women
Here; two A.M. on Sunday morning." Mr. Yellowchecker had gotten to his knees behind her. As she
examined the blue slip, he grabbed her pink sweats on
either side of the elastic waist band and pulled her
pants to her ankles. The pantsing of Mrs. Yellowchecker exposed a round pink stomach with a tuft of
red pubic hair at the bottom. Her husband threw a
shoulder at her bare ass and knocked her forward
onto the counter. In a moment he had the sweat pants
off her ankles and was backing away holding the pink
pants aloft. She lifted her chest from the counter and
turned to face him. That left me looking at her wide
ass, which jiggled like jelly. The blue pickup slip was
still in her hand.

"Hey fatass," he said, "you lost your pants again." She turned to look at me and said, "Excuse me a minute, Mr. James, while I take care of this asshole." She rushed him like a defensive tackle on a football team knocking him down on the floor next to the dispatch desk. She had no trouble manipulating the thin man. Holding him to the floor, she climbed up his body and trapped his head beneath her ample thighs.

"Eat it," she said while pushing her hips into face. Muffled sounds of struggle came from the place between her legs where his head had disappeared. "I better feel some goddamn tongue." He must have complied because she stopped yelling and began a rhythmic back and forth motion with her hips. With her right hand she reached behind her and grabbed him by the balls. She turned to me and said, "When you got no dick, you got to eat a lot of pussy."

"About that pickup?" I said.

"Oh yeah," she said. She looked at the blue slip again continuing to force her vagina into her husband's face. She seemed about to give me the information I needed when Mr. Yellowchecker managed to pull himself free out her back side. From my vantage point the escape move made it look like his head had come out of the crack of her ass. As soon as he was out, he knocked her forward to her hands and knees and threw himself on top of her. With one hand he got the long front zipper of his overalls down.

With Mrs. Yellowchecker on her hands and knees and her husband with his dick out of his overalls he said, "Well look what I found, a big red-haired cunt. I think I'll fuck it." Holding the base of his cock with one hand he pushed his meat inside his wife.

"Is it in yet? Is it in yet?" his wife yelled gleefully as

he pounded her. "I don't feel a thing." He leaned over her back and pulled up the top part of her pink outfit exposing her round tits. He grabbed them with both hands and squeezed hard.

"Do you feel that, whore?"

"I think a fly landed on my tit?" she said. Her body belied her words. She was moving forward and back to meet the thrusts he was making with his hips. "And I think a little tiny worm crawled up my cunt." He pulled his cock out of her and pushed her sideways onto her back. In a flash he was sitting on her tits and had his dick into her mouth. She took it in without protest and sucked.

"Mr. Yellowchecker," I said, "about that pickup on Saturday?"

"Gimme that slip," he said to his wife, "and suck like you mean it." She handed him the slip and took big gulp of cock. "Let's see," he said, "That pickup was by James King. He is one of our best drivers."

"Do you know where I could find him?" I said. He had Mrs. Yellowchecker's head in his hands and was fucking her in the mouth.

"His address is there in the rolodex." He pointed to the card file on the counter. I looked up James King and wrote down his address in my notebook.

"Phone number?" I asked.

"James can't afford a phone," he said. "Anything else we can do for you today."

"I don't think so," I said. He pulled his cock out of his wife's mouth, pumped it a couple of times with his hand and shot semen into her face. She opened her mouth to catch what she could.

"You can fuck Mrs. Yellowchecker," he said. "Do her in the asshole if you want. She's a stupid cunt and don't care none who fucks her or where they stick it."

His wife turned to me with semen on her face and said, "If your cock is more than half an inch long, Mr. James, I'll divorce this son-of-a-bitch and marry you. Then you will have a good woman and a cab company to boot."

"You two seem very happy," I said. "I think I will go look for Mr. King."

"Good enough," Mr. Yellowchecker said, "but if you ever think to yourself I sure would like to fuck a woman who is fat, ugly, and stupid, you just come on back and I'll let you pork the missus."

"And good luck finding that stripper," his wife said.

The address Mr. and Mrs. Yellowchecker gave me was in a trailer park about a mile from the cab company. It was one of those almost invisible little trailer parks you find tucked in the smelly cracks of the city, a place where rats go to die, a place where the women give birth to serial killers, and the men drink whiskey straight from the can. The sign at the entrance said, End of the Road Estates. Underneath there was a smaller sign saying, "single-wide for rent. Inquire at 3B."

I drove down the single road that divided the park. The homes showed both the eccentricities of people outside the mainstream of city life and the drab uniformity of poverty. The houses sported pink flamingos, American flags, lawn gnomes and all manner of decoration and statuary. Every resident seemed to have a home based business. Hand lettered signs in the windows announced "home made soap," "palms read," "therapeutic massage," and "cocks sucked."

I stopped the Gremlin in front of a pink single-wide attached to a small car port. Under the sagging corrugated metal roof of the carport sat a small thin man about fifty years old. He wore a sleeveless t-shirt and gray sweat pants. He was reading a book while keeping an eye on the charcoal in a small pot-style barbecue. He had a brown goatee but hadn't shaved in a week or so.

"Are you James King?" I asked the man.

"I don't know you," he said, barely raising his eyes from his book.

"My name is William James—"

"William James is dead," he announced.

"I am a private detective," I continued, deciding to ignore his comment about my being dead.

"So you are not the philosopher, the father of American pragmatism, come back from the dead to haunt me?"

"No, I am a detective," I said. "Why would William James, the philosopher, want to come back from the dead and haunt you?"

"Oh, he has his reasons, trust me." The man's eyes returned to a book called *Dianetics*.

"I am looking for a cab driver named James King?"

"That's me," he said, laying the book on the table beside him. The table was covered with books, all of them on religious subjects. "Take a seat there." He pointed to a lawn chair of woven plastic strips, most of which were broken or about to break. It didn't look safe.

"I would like to ask you—."

"I don't answer questions from a guy named William James unless he is sitting down. Take that seat." I sat gingerly in the fragile chair. "I'm making bratwurst," he said nodding toward the charcoal which was slowly turning gray with ash.

"I am trying to find Candy Pantz," I said.

"Do you want them for yourself or a loved one?" he

asked. I didn't understand the question and didn't want to get distracted. A detective needs to work with a single purpose.

"I work for Patty Pantz, Candy's sister," I explained. "I understand that you may have picked her up in your cab last Saturday night after her shift at Totally Naked Women Here."

Mr. James seemed about to answer when a woman stumbled into the carport making exaggerated retching noises and spitting onto the gravel driveway. She pulled another lawn chair close to the barbecue and sat down. Looking at Mr. King she said, "I went to borrow an egg from old Mr. Dicklerick and he wouldn't give it to me unless I sucked him off. I swear he has the nastiest tasting cock in the whole trailer park."

"Mr. James," James King said, "this is Miss Lolita Lottas." The woman smiled at me. She appeared to be about thirty. She wore a very short pink dress with a flared petticoat beneath. She was carrying an egg and a naked Barbie doll.

"I am pleased to meet you, Mr. James," she said. She stood in front of her seat, curtsied, and sat back down. "Are you a friend of Jim's?"

"I am a detective," I told her.

"A detective," she exclaimed clapping her hands. "Like Nancy Drew and Sherlock Holmes. That is so exciting."

"I hope I am not like Nancy Drew," I said.

"Oh, why not? I love Nancy Drew. Do you know what else is exciting?"

"What's that Miss Lottas?"

"Call me 'Lo," she said.

"All right, Lo. What else is exciting?"

"That if you were to fuck me it would be a felony?"

She caught me off guard. I looked at James. He smiled back and explained, "Lolita is a retard."

She stood and jumped up and down causing her large braless breasts to bounce violently under her pink little-girl dress. "My case worker, Janice, says that I have the mind of a fourteen year old. That means I can't consent to sex and that anybody who fucks me or feels my tits or asks me to blow them is committing a felony."

"I will be careful then," I told her.

"Janice says I have the body of a woman." Lolita pulled up the stained pink dress and petticoat. She was not wearing underwear. "See," she said, pointing to her crack. "I got the pussy of a woman even though I only have the mind of a fourteen year old. Look at my tits." She leaned over and pulled the straps of the dress down her arms. Big pink breasts tumbled out of the dress. "Mine are bigger than a lot of the girls around here and those girls aren't even retards. Janice likes to hold my tits when she teaches me about all the different evil tricks that men use to get retarded women to fuck them. She says when I get the urge down there I should use my fingers. Janice showed me how and then had me practice on her. Janice likes it better that way, but I like it better with the boys. I guess that's why I'm a retard."

"I don't care what Janice says," I told her. "I don't think you are a retard."

"You are very nice to say that," she said. "I like you. You can fuck me. Retard pussy is the best pussy in the world. Isn't that right, Mr. King?"

"That's right, Lo," he said winking at me.

"Mr. King fucks me when we do my Bibble lessons. He has the friendliest cock in the whole trailer park."

"You take Bibble lessons?" I asked.

"I take them from Mr. King every Sunday. He teaches me about the Holy Chris while I hold his penis. Sometimes he gives me Bibble lessons on other days if he has any beer to drink. When his penis gets big it is just as long as my Barbie."

A light came on in my head. I remembered the black holy book in Patty Pantz's bedroom. I looked at the cab driver.

"You are James King?"

"Good work, detective," he said. "I think I already said that."

"I mean, you are the James King who wrote the Holy Bibble."

"That's right," Lolita said. "He is a genius. Everybody here at the park says that."

"I didn't write it," he said. "I translated it from the word of God into English."

"Your book, Mr. King," I said, "keeps coming up in my investigation. Would you tell me how you came to write it?" He leaned back in his chair and put his hands behind his head.

"Go home, Lolita," he said. "Come back over tonight. I'll give you a Bibble Lesson then."

"Can we read the part where the Holy Chris rides the ass?"

"If you are good," he told her. She clapped her hands and skipped down the gravel road of the trailer park with her egg and her naked Barbie in hand. Mr. King turned to me. "I haven't always been a cabbie," he said. "I had promise. I got a degree in English from the University of Southeastern Idaho at Potato Canyon. After graduation I flailed about looking for a job, but a thorough study of Huckleberry Finn doesn't really qualify a person for a lot of jobs in the private sector. So, like most English majors, I decided that the best thing to do was to get some more education. I applied and was accepted to an advanced writing program at the Massachusetts Institute of Literary Freedom.

In those days the MILF was one of the most prestigious writing programs in the country. The director of the MILF was Mona Anne Skreemer, one of the best fiction writers in the world. She had published a nine hundred page novel in which every single sentence had an allusion to *Finnegan's Wake*. The novel was so brilliant that only three people in the world had been capable of reading it, all of whom are reclusive artists in residence connected to ivy league universities. It was a great honor to be asked to study under her. I dusted off my folio of limericks and got ready for a literary career.

There was only one drawback to being accepted at the MILF. They only allowed one person at a time in each literary discipline. I was mostly a limerick guy, but the only slot they had open was in scripture writing. They had a novelist, a playwright, a poet, a short story writer, and a bunch of others. They wanted somebody who could hear, translate, and transcribe the word of God. It wasn't my specialty but I wasn't going to turn down a chance to study under Mona Skreemer just because I lacked qualifications.

I packed up my bags, jumped a Greyhound in Potato Canyon, and headed for Massachusetts. The MILF was located out in the county about forty miles north of the little town of Blooball in a fenced compound designed to keep out the Massachusetts masses. I got off the bus in Blooball where I was approached by a large bald headed man who handed me a note saying he was there to bring me to the

MILF. We arrived at the compound in late afternoon where he dropped me at one of several small cabins built around a large industrial looking building. He left me in the cabin to unpack. My new home consisted of a single room with a bed, a dresser, a writing desk, a chair, and a bathroom. Before I had completely unpacked my few clothes Mona Anne Skreemer arrived.

Mona was a small woman. At the time she must have been about forty years old. She had short blond hair, small tits, and huge blue eyes. When I first saw her that day she was wearing a light print dress and sneakers. She introduced herself, walked up to me and shoved her hand down my pants. The first words she said to me were, "Nice cock, King."

Mona undid my fly and sat me on the bed in the cabin. Sitting next to me she put one arm around my shoulder and gently fondled my dick and balls with the other hand. She explained to me that she was the mother in this backwoods family of writers and I was to be one of her children. She said she would be like my real mother in the sense that she would love me, teach me, and even discipline me in a way that would allow my natural talents to bloom. She would be even better than my real mother because she would suck my dick and tongue me in the ass. Mona then took my face in her hands and gave me a deep kiss. With our lips clamped together she took hold of my hand and placed it on her cunt.

I rolled her over, lifted her dress, and spread her legs on the cot. She had a great looking pussy for a woman of her age and I gave it a good Idaho boning. When we were done she wiped the cum from her cunt and explained to me how things worked at MILF. Meals were prepared in the main building and eaten family style. When not eating the writers were expected to be in their cabins writing. We got one hour after dinner and all day Sunday for socializing and recreation. Mona would come by every afternoon to talk about my writing and drain my cock. If I got tired of her, she explained, I could fuck any of the other writers, man or woman, but under no circumstances could I fuck her daughter, Zoe. I assured her that would not be a problem. But of course, it was.

I started writing The Holy Bibble. It was tough at first, me not having any experience with writing gospels, but if you seek hard enough God will talk to you. I sought. He started talking, and my fingers hit the keyboard. Mona was very helpful. She came in every afternoon to review my progress and fuck me. She was very talented in both departments. Mona was an accomplished writer and a patient teacher. She taught me how to make my characters come alive on a page and how to make a woman cum in six minutes with just my tongue. I met the other writers and slowly the Holy Bibble began to take shape.

The only problem was Zoe. Zoe was seventeen years old, beautiful, and the only person at MILF with nothing to do. She had short dark hair, a round face, and enormous doe eyes. Her skin was so white that it seemed transparent. While the writers wrote, Zoe cavorted about the camp enjoying the lush natural landscape and life itself. She did all this in shortest shorts and the tiniest bikini tops I had ever seen. Every man at MILF had a boner for her and most of the women did too. In the evenings after dinner when the writers would meet to talk about their progress Zoe would sit in the room listening and doing Yoga exercises that seemed specifically designed to show her hard young breasts and the outline of her labia beneath her panties.

Mona absolutely doted on Zoe. Many afternoons Mona would sit on me with my cock up her ass while we talked about my evolving Holy Bibble. Mona had a great ass and loved talking literature with a dick jammed up it. Many times when she was on top of me like that she would tell me about her hopes and dreams for Zoe. Like most of the writers, I had grown to love Mona and the last thing in the world I wanted to do was hurt her. But my cock had other ideas.

Zoe started visiting me in the mornings. The first visit was truly accidental. I was taking a break from the writing, standing on the small front porch of my cabin. Zoe came by with a butterfly net looking to add to her collection. She was wearing a short pink skirt. When she bent over in front of me to look at some bug she had spotted on the ground I could see the cotton panties beneath her skirt stretched over a smooth teen-aged ass. We talked about the beautiful morning and the butterflies, after which she went on her way and I went back to the keyboard. But I couldn't work. Zoe was on my mind, and when her mother came to fuck me later in the day I pretended Mona was Zoe.

Zoe came by more and more often and our discussions became more intimate. One day she said, "My mother sucks your penis, doesn't she?" I wouldn't and answer and Zoe continued, "I think she sucks all the men's penises here and she lets them put their erections in her anus." I told Zoe those things were none of her business but every day she had another question about her mother's sex life, each one more lurid than the one before. One day I was out on the little front porch and Zoe was showing me, with her rear pointed my direction, how she could put the palms of her hands flat on the ground without bending her knees. The cotton panties stretched across her young labia left nothing to the imagination.

I pulled off my shirt, dropped my pants and yelled, "That is enough." My cock was hard a rock. "Zoe, prepare to get fucked." Zoe let out the cutest little scream of protest I have ever heard and took off running. Stark naked I was off after her.

Zoe was a strong runner. She led me down the path by the cabin where Jeb, the short story writer, worked on his twist endings. Zoe's cries for hep brought him out the door of his cabin.

"What's going on?" Jeb demanded, as Zoe ran by.

"I am going to fuck Zoe," I said.

"I'll have some of that," he said. He dropped his pants and took up the chase with me.

Still yelling for help, Zoe led me by the cabin where Janice the poet did her writing. Hearing the noise Janice came out on the front porch holding hands with Big Denise, the dyke who wrote lesbian erotica. Denise was a true lesbian. Janice was just friendly. Both were topless."

"What are you doing?" Big Denise demanded of Jeb and me.

"We are going to fuck Zoe," Jeb said. "If you want some, you better come along." Both women dropped their pants and joined us. Around another corner we picked up Jon the dramatist. In the end there were five of us, two women and three men, all stark naked running though the woods after Zoe. The women's tits were bouncing and the men's hard cocks were pointing the way. The little imp circled around to the main building, slipped through the door, and locked it behind her. Big Denise, her big lesbian tits swinging in the fresh spring air, hefted Janice up and through a bathroom window. Janice opened the back door and the five of us cornered Zoe in the big living room where we had our nightly talks.

"Mother will be very angry," Zoe yelled. "You all promised to leave me alone." Big Denise got her by the arms. I pulled down the little pink skirt and the cotton panties all in one motion. Seeing her pussy for the first time, the five of us stared in stunned silence. It was the smoothest prettiest little seventeen year old cunt I had ever seem. We were in awe. Zoe squeezed her legs together, embarrassed at the rapt attention she was getting and whimpered, "It's just a pussy."

"She's right," Jeb said. "It's just a pussy. Let's fuck it." Big Denise, still holding Zoe with one arm, pulled off the half t-shirt the girl was wearing, exposing her pouty tits. Both nipples were hard and pointing to the sky. Big Denise grabbed one of the nipples between her thumb and forefinger and squeezed.

"Denise," Zoe said, "You need to kiss me first." The big lesbian leaned over and gave the girl a deep kiss that I thought might smoother her. Janice had my dick in her hand and was jerking me off.

"James should go first," Janice declared. "It was his idea. We have all wanted to do this for months but he is the only one who had the nerve to make it happen."

Big Denise let Zoe out of the lip lock and said to the girl, "James is going first. Is that okay with you?"

"You are raping me," Zoe said, "you can't ask permission."

We started out fairly organized. The big dyke pushed Zoe to the floor in front of the fireplace. Then the two women spread and lifted her legs so that that her cunt faced the ceiling. I jumped on and proceeded to fuck her. Jon and Jeb dropped to their kees on either side of her so Zoe could reach their dicks with her hands. Zoe reached out to them, jerking their cocks gently to prepare them while I pounded her with my cock. I had waited so long to get a piece of that little pie that I came almost immediately. Jeb jumped on next and then Jon. Zoe took the triple play with grace and vigor. Once the three men were done, Denise sat on her face while Janice got down on hands and knees and ate Zoe's cum covered pussy. After that it turned into a free for all. Jon started fucking Janice from behind as she finished eating Zoe. Jeb pushed Denise off and got his cock in Zoe's mouth and from then on all I can remember is undulating flesh, hard cocks, and wet holes. I remember at one point seeing an opening for a second shot at Zoe's cunt, but I wasn't fast enough, and ended up fucking the big dyke, Denise. Denise threatened to cut off my balls but didn't make be pull out until I had delivered a load in her hairy lesbian snatch. I then did Zoe in the ass while Janice licked my balls and had Janice suck my cock while the big dyke finger-fucked me in the butt.

At one point Zoe screamed, "Everybody stop." We did. The young girl sat up and said, "I need an RC. I am not doing anything more until I get an RC." Jon got her a cola and one for the rest of us. Zoe downed hers in two long draughts and declared, "Nothing cuts the taste of cum in your mouth like a cold RC. Now finish up and let's get to it" We drained our colas and jumped on her again. After the break Janice sat on me with my dick up her ass and ate out Denise. Jon and Jeb had rolled Zoe over so she was on her hands and knees and were doing her pussy and face in rhythm. Jeb came in her mouth and fell back exhausted. I got out from beneath Janice and took his place. What Zoe lacked in skill and experience she made up for with youthful enthusiasm. She was honking on my cock like an Idaho farmer's wife and taking it doggie style from Jon when we heard the booming voice of Mona Anne Skreemer.

"Get your goddamn cocks out of my daughter." My cock fell out of Zoe's mouth and we all turned our heads to see Mona standing in the doorway. Mona pulled her daughter out from beneath the pile of writers. "You little slut," she admonished her daughter. "I told you over and over not to fuck the writers."

"But mom," she began.

"No excuses young lady," Mona interrupted. "Go to your room immediately." "Zoe left and Mona turned to us. We writers were standing in a row with our dicks and pussies in our hands. "You could have anything you wanted here," she said to us. "There was just one rule. Don't fuck Zoe. You couldn't do it. I want you all out of here by morning."

The Holy Bibble was close to finished by then. Janice, Denise and I left together and headed to Texas where we settled into a cheap motel. A few days later the dyke ran off with an oil rigger named Jane. Janice gave poetry readings at the local library and sold her pussy on the rodeo circuit. She was a lousy poet but a dedicated and hard working whore. Janice kept my dick happy and paid the bills while I finished the Bibble. When it was done I sent Janice to work for a cowboy pimp named Jethro and took a bus to the city.

After kicking us out of MILF, Mona Anne Skreemer wrote again. She did a mother-daughter coming-of-age, conflict-and-reconcilation novel that got her on all the talk shows, sold a million copies, and ruined her reputation as a serious writer.

I found out quickly that publishers were not all that

interested in new gospels. I figured the established religious publishers would jump on it, but that was not the case. I had to wonder whether people like Joseph Smith, L. Ron Hubbard and Mary Baker Eddy went through the same hardships. After a hundred or so rejections, I self-published. I had two thousand copies printed and sold them out of the trunk of my car and at flea markets. I was making the rounds of book stores trying to get them to stock my gospels when I met Diana Babylon.

"Reverend Diana Babylon," I interrupted, thinking to myself that James King's story was finally getting me somewhere.

"She wasn't reverend then," King said. "She was one of those little sluts with a masters degree in some useless liberal art who has ended up in a book shop peddling best sellers and her cute ass to pay the rent. She read the Holy Bibble. It happened that she was at a down point in her life and she had lost the will to fuck. After a few chapters of the Bibble she went out in the stacks of the bookshop, grabbed some poor schlep and fucked him there on the floor. She told me she came like a virgin again—not a real virgin but that good kind of virgin who knows what she is doing without being so burnt out on the whole sex thing that she can't get a good orgasm anymore.

"That was the start of the Holy Dereamer Gnostic Church of the Tribulation?" I intejected.

"Sort of," he continued. "She had the idea for the church. I had the book, but we couldn't come to a deal on the money. Besides that, I was completely in love with her. She has an ass that can drive a man crazy and I couldn't get enough of it. She didn't feel the same about me. She didn't mind my jumping her now and then, but I wanted her as all mine and that got in the way of making a deal on rights to the book.

"One day we were drinking hard and playing Scrabble for money. Things got out of hand with the bragging. It all came down to one last game. I bet rights to my book against a year's unlimited rights to her ass, to use or pimp out as I saw fit. The game came down to the last tile and she beat me by one point. The rest is history. She is rich with a church congregation that fills the plate every night. I drive a cab, live in a trailer house, and fuck a retard."

"I'd like to ask you about your cab driving," I said.

"Are you sure you wouldn't rather talk about fucking the retarded girl. She is really very good. I could ask her to come over and we could double up on her."

"Maybe later," I said. "Do you pick up the girls after their shifts at Totally Naked Women Here?"

"I do," he said.

"Did you pick up Candy Pantz last Saturday night?"

"I did," he said.

"Where did you take her?"

"Are you asking me to violate the confidentiality of a cab driver and his passenger?"

"Yes."

"Okay, then. As long as you are asking."

"I took her where I always took her: 1414 Betsy Ross Avenue up on Snob Hill."

"You took her there a lot?"

"Yeah, most every night after her shift. I took her there, then came back at five o'clock on the dot to take her back to her apartment. But Saturday it was different."

"How is that?" I asked

"This time she told me to wait. She was in the

house for about ninety minutes, me just sitting there smoking cigarettes and letting the meter run. Then she comes out and wants me to drive her to the little town of Fumbuck. It is a little shit-hole town a ways from here with nothing in it but a disgusting lesbian bar run by a woman named Sow—a womanso ugly no man in his right mind would fuck her even if she were straight."

"I am familiar with the town," I said, remembering in the feel of Sow's giant wet cunt wrapped around my dick.

"Anyway we get there just before dawn. The only thing open is a hardware store. She goes in to buy some batteries and tells me to wait. Candy Pantz had always been one of my nicest customers; always with a smile and something pleasant to say. She was a stripper with the heart of gold."

"They all are. It is too bad the whole world can't follow their examples," I said.

"Then she comes out of the hardware store, the sun is just coming up, and it is like she is a different person. She jumps into the cab and says, 'Get me back to the city,' and gives me the address on Snob Hill. I told her I knew where it was and she answered 'I bet you do,' in a voice dripping with disdain. Then she started talking to herself about the goddamn fishnet stockings she was wearing and how much she hated stripper clothes. I tried to calm her by reminding her that she was, after all, a stripper, and she went off on me about she wasn't a stripper and could never be stripper, and she had disappointed everybody, but that a person just can't be a stripper if that is not what they are destined to be. I took the standard cab driver strategy for dealing with an angry customer and shut up. I delivered her to her apartment as usual and haven't gotten a call to pick her up again. If I did something to piss her off I sure didn't mean it. I like the girl. I liked being her cabbie."

"You haven't seen or heard from her since," I said.

"Not a thing," he said.

"How about Diana Babylon? Do you ever hear from her?"

"She comes to see me now and then. We play a little penny ante Scrabble and she gives me a sympathy fuck. That's about it."

"You don't go to her church?"

"I can't. Not with her having the right to the Bibble?"

"Are you still writing?"

"Yeah. Still hard at it. I am working on a new gospel called The Core Anne. It is the kind of work capable of bringing peace on earth."

"When you finish, I'll buy a copy."

"I will hold you to that," he said. "Do you want me to call the retard back for a fuck before you go?"

"No thanks, James," I said. "I better stay on the case."

"There is a Romanian mother daughter team down the road a little. The mother has tits like bowling balls. We could go down and bone the two of them."

"Rain check," I said. "Got to get going." I left James King tending his bratwurst, turned the Gremlin around, and headed back home. As I drove out of the trailer park I saw two Romanian women sitting on the steps of a pastel pink single wide. The older one had tits like bowling balls and I regretted not taking James up on his offer to fuck them.

I drove to Totally Naked Women Here and parked the Gremlin next to Bjorn's truck. Inside, Bjorn, Eb and Teena were sitting a table just off the stage.

Vagina Smooth was at the pole bent over and showing the small crowd her pink asshole. I took a chair at the table.

"What are you doing here," I demanded of Teena. "Aren't you supposed to be at the office?"

Teena glared at me. "It is seven o'clock, William. The office closes at five." I checked my watch. She was right. Time had gotten away from me.

Bjorn spoke, "Teena is nervous about dancing tomorrow at Otto's. Vagina is showing her some moves. Eb and I are trying to build her confidence."

"They are going to hate me," Teena pouted. "Nobody wants to look at my old saggy tits."

"You have beautiful tits," Bjorn said, putting his arm around her. "You will be the hit of the party."

Teena looked at me. "Do you think so William? Will they like my tits?"

"They will love your tits," I told her. Vagina came over and squatted at the edge of the stage by our table.

"You will be wonderful," Vagina said.

"And you will all come and support me?" Teena asked. We nodded in unison. "You are the best friends and the best boss a girl could ever have."

I noticed that Ebenezer had been quiet the whole time and was staring at me.

"You'll be there, won't you Eb?" I asked.

He leaned across the table toward me and said, "You fucked my sister."

"Did Teena tell you that?" I demanded.

"What difference does it make who told me. You said you wouldn't fuck my sister and then you went and did it."

"Teena," I said, "I told you I wanted to tell him in myself."

"I couldn't help myself," Teena said.

I turned to Eb. "I wanted to tell you myself, Eb. I didn't mean for it to happen. She took me to her house after this giant school girl named Bruna tried to crush my balls and it just happened."

"You fucked her in the ass," Eb said.

"That is not true," I protested, "You can call Deshawnawanda right this moment and ask her. She didn't suck my dick and I didn't fuck her in the ass."

"But Teena said—"

"I made that part up," Teena admitted, "the part about fucking her in the ass."

"Why did you say that?" Eb demanded of Teena.

"I don't know, Eb," she said. "It was a better story if it had some butt fucking in it."

Eb looked at me. "So you just fucked her straight? Pussy fucking with no cock sucking or butt fucking."

"That's right," I assured him.

"Well, that's okay then. I forgive you."

"Thanks, Eb," I said. "And I promise not to do it again."

"Okay," he said. "And if you was to fuck her maybe just once or twice more that would probably be all right too. Just so you aren't like fucking her every day and throwing it in my face. She is, after all, my little sister."

"I won't. I won't," I said. I thought Eb was being a little hard on me considering the number of times and places he had fucked her himself, but I decided not to make an issue of it.

Vagina's set was over. She climbed down off the stage and took the chair next to me at the table. Chesty Tits-a-lot took over on the stage. Vagina's arrival was a good excuse for a change of subject.

"I may have a lead on Candy Pantz," I announced.

Vagina snuggled up to me and the folks at the table leaned forward to hear my story. As Chesty bounced her boobs on stage, I told the people at the table about the conversation with James King.

"I fucked a retarded girl once," Teena said when I was finished.

"The story was about finding Candy," Vagina told her, "not about the retarded girl."

"Sorry," Teena said. "So what is that place on Betsy Ross Avenue?"

"I don't know yet," I admitted, "but you can be sure that will be my next stop."

"And we know now," Bjorn said, "that Candy made it back to her apartment Sunday morning."

"But her sister said she didn't," Vagina continued. "I think you are getting close to something, William."

"So do I," I said.

"It is so exciting," Vagina giggled. "My heart is racing." She took my hand and put it on her naked left breast. "Feel it William."

"Your tit," I said.

"No, William, not my tit. My beating heart."

"You can feel my beating heart too," Teena yelled, pulling her left breast out of her blouse.

Vagina scowled at her. "He is feeling my beating heart, Teena. He doesn't need to feel two beating hearts." Teena stuck out her tongue at Vagina and covered herself.

I stayed around to see Finger Mi and Iwanna Blackcock dance. We all ordered clam chowder and played Scrabble there at the table. About ten I went back to the apartment, showered, and fell to sleep.

Chapter 5

I made breakfast in my apartment out of a pot of coffee and a box of strawberry Pop Tarts. It was a cold morning in the city, weather for solving crimes. I went to the office early to study my notes in the presence of Spade and Marlow. I put the picture of Candy Pantz on my desk and stared at it. Once again, I had the strange feeling that I had seen that vagina before somewhere—somewhere other than on Candy Pantz.

Teena came in about nine. She was wearing a cheerleader outfit and carried a small suitcase. She bounced into my office and shook her chest to show that there was no bra beneath the red top. "Tonight is the night," she announced. "Just little ole me, a pool table, and a bar full of bikers."

"You will be great," I told her.

"Do you like the cheerleader thing?" she said, spinning around to expose the red panties beneath the pleated skirt. "Every guy wants to fuck a cheerleader. I also brought a nurse outfit." She held up the suitcase. "Guys like to fuck nurses too."

"That they do," I observed. "Teena, come here. Look at this picture." Teen leaned over and looked at the picture of Candy.

"Nice pussy," Teena said. "If I had a wiener, I'd fuck it."

"Have you ever seen it before?" I asked.

"Sure," she said, "Five nights a week, seven to one shift, Totally Naked Women Here. Everybody knows that."

"I mean have you ever seen that pussy on anyone else."

"Now you are talking crazy, William. No, I have never seen Candy Pantz's pussy on anybody else." Teena took her suitcase into the outer office and closed the door. I stared at the picture but nothing came to me. Hearing noise in the outer office I took the picture and went to investigate. Teena had changed to the nurse outfit and was standing on her desk doing dance moves. I figured I wasn't going to get any work done in the office with Teena making a racket on the desk, so I went downstairs to Otto's.

Bret was at the bar nursing an early morning RC. She was wearing her biker's spandex. I took the seat next to her and put the picture of Candy on the bar. "I have a strange question for you," I said to her.

"Yes, you can do me doggie style while I lick your secretary's pussy," she said.

"That is not the question."

"I can hope, can't I?"

"Look at this picture," I said. "Have you ever seen that pussy before, other than on Candy Pantz?" She stared at the picture and then said.

"I am reasonably sure that I have never seen Candy's pussy anywhere other than between Candy's legs. What are you getting at?"

"I have the strangest feeling that I have seen this pussy somewhere other than in this picture."

"Like up the skirt of a librarian?"

"Why would you say that?" I demanded.

"No reason. Just that when you are the kind of person who hangs around with librarians, there is no telling what strange things you might see." The mention of librarians reminded me that I had to update Patty on what I had learned from James King. "I got nothing to do this morning," Bret continued,

"How about I give you a blow job?"

"Thanks but no thanks, Bret. I got to work."

"Then how about I come along," she said, "as someone to hold your dick if you get into danger."

"Yeah, come on," I said.

We walked down to the garage and started up the Gremlin. I pulled out onto the streets of the city. The cold morning air came through the still missing driver and passenger side windows. Brett shivered in her riding spandex and hugged herself to keep warm. I was starting to enjoy having her around.

"Can I hold your dick now?" Brett asked.

"I am not in danger, Brett," I told her.

"It is a safety issue. This car doesn't have seat belts. Having me hold your dick could prevent it from being severed in an accident. It is required by the vehicle code." In all those years in parking division, I had never heard of such a law but figured it couldn't hurt any.

"All right," I said, "hold my dick for me."

"Thanks boss." She plunged her hand into my pants and grabbed my cock. She had a firm gentle touch. As I drove, she worked her hand silently up and down the length of it, occasionally sliding her fingers down to cup my balls.

"You didn't say it," I said to her.

"Didn't say what?" she asked.

"That I have the biggest cock you ever saw on a white man."

"Why would I say that? It is rude and demeaning. Besides it is a myth. I know this guy named Bjorn . . ."

"It has been said to me before."

"I'm sorry," she said, "The Holy Bibble tells me I should honor thy cocks and thy cunts for the cock is the staff of the Lord and the cunt is the holy of holies. . . . Besides, yours is not the biggest cock I have ever seen on a white man."

"Really,"

"There is one bigger. But for me it is not size that matters. For me sexual acts are expressions of love between a man and a woman, or several men and a woman, or two women, or several women and a man, and then there are farm animals to think of. The thing is that it is the love in your heart that counts and not the size of your tits and just because a woman doesn't have a set of water balloons hanging off her chest does not mean that her heart is not filled with love for men and women and the Holy Chris."

"That is beautiful," I said.

"If you had some clothespins, I could put them on my nipples."

"I don't have any clothespins," I told her. "Besides, we are here." I pulled the Gremlin up in front of the Mulberry Street branch of the public library. Brett realized where we were as I buttoned my pants.

"I am not going in a library," she announced.

"You wait here."

"This is a bad neighborhood, William. What if some large black men come by and try to rape me?"

"Keep the doors locked," I said and headed toward the stairs of the library.

"But there are no windows," I heard her protest.

Morning clouds still hung over the city and the streets were quiet. The library building squatted in the run down neighborhood like a whore taking a piss in a back alley. As I went up the steps, the oak doors to the building opened. A small Hispanic man flew out and crumpled at my feet. Behind him came

Ebenezer Jones in his library security coat.

"Get out and never come back," he yelled at the little brown man. The Mexican struggled to his feet and staggered down the stairs.

"That's what I said to your seester after I fucked her in the ass last night," he yelled.

I approached my friend. His eyes were downcast. "Eb, I don't think he really fucked Deshawnawanda in the ass last night. He was saying that to hurt you because you threw him out of the library."

"You think so?" Eb said.

"I'm sure of it," I told him. "I came to see Patty. Is she on duty?"

"She isn't here," he said, "and she didn't come in yesterday either. She hasn't called and we are all worried."

"I will find her," I told him.

"Thank you William," he said, "we here at the library would be forever grateful if you would." Eb looked down the street to the Gremlin. "Who is that in your car?" he asked.

"Brett, the skinny girl with no tits from Otto's."

"Is she your partner now?" he pouted.

"She is not my partner,"

"I thought I was your partner."

"You and Bjorn are my helpers. I don't have a partner."

"I bet it is because she holds your dick, isn't it?"

"No, it is not because she holds my dick. She is not my partner."

"I would hold your dick," Eb said. "I'm not gay if that is what you are thinking, but I could still hold your dick."

"I don't need you to hold my dick," I said.

"I fucked my own sister, you know."

"I know that Eb. Deshawnawanda told me."

"A man who has fucked his sister could hold another man's dick."

"I am leaving now," I said. "You are still my friend and assistant. I don't have a partner and I don't want you to hold my dick."

I walked back to the Gremlin and climbed in next to Brett. She was masturbating. As I slid into the car she pulled her hand out of her spandex pants and sniffed her fingers.

"Welcome back, partner," she said. "Short visit."

"Patty has not been in and hasn't called in sick. And don't call me partner." The engine of the Gremlin roared to life and I pointed it in the direction of Patty Pantz's apartment. Brett put her hand back in my pants and held my cock as I drove. When we arrived Brett got out with me. The street was empty except for three Romanian housewives waiting for the flashlight repair shop to open. Bret and I took the stairs to Patty and Candy's apartment.

The door to Candy and Patty's apartment was unlocked, so we prowled the apartment. Everything was as I remembered—clean and orderly. Both bedrooms looked the same as the day I sat on the bed looking up Patty's tweed skirt while she read from the Holy Bibble.

"No sign of them," Brett said. "Let's try the bed."

"Try what with the bed?"

"Try having me take off my pants, and lay on the bed with my legs spread while you pound me with your cock until we both orgasm. It is called sexual intercourse."

"Not now," I said, "we have a case to solve." We

inspected the bathroom. Among the normal toiletries and cosmetics of a bathroom shared by a stripper and a librarian were several wig stands. Two of the wigs were missing.

"Why would Patty and Candy need so many wigs?" I asked Brett. She was standing in the doorway with her hand down her pants again.

"One reason might be that Candy is a stripper and needs to change her look now and again to keep her customers happy—as if her customers ever noticed the hair on her head anyway."

"That seems reasonable," I said.

"And then there is another possibility."

"What is that?"

"Did Patty and Candy look alike?"

"Not at all," I told her. "Candy had bond hair. Patty was a brunette."

"Oh, well that blows that theory. You want to fuck now?"

"We are trying to solve a case here," I told her. "We can't stop and fuck every time you see a bed."

She pulled her hand out of her hands and licked her fingers. "All right already." We finished searching the apartment and went back out to the street. Out on the sidewalk we heard the sounds of Romanian grunting and groaning coming from the flashlight repair shop. Bret and I hurried back to the Gremlin. Once in the car I turned the key and Brett put her hand in my pants to hold my cock. "Where are we going?" she asked.

"Fourteen fourteen Besty Ross Avenue."

"Up on Snob Hill?" She squeezed my dick.

"That's right," I told her.

"Why there?"

"That is where James King took Candy Pantz after her shifts at the strip club and where he let her off the morning she disappeared." Brett leaned over to me, cupped my balls in her hand and kissed me on the neck.

"Oh, William," she said, "this is so exciting. Thanks for taking me along."

"My pleasure?"

We drove toward Snob Hill and onto the curved streets of the residential area that housed the movers and shakers of the city. The people who lived there owned big houses and expensive cars. They sent their children to private schools. The women had pool boys. The men had Hispanic maids who wore push up bras and lots of bright red lipstick.

Fourteen fourteen Betsy Ross Avenue was the address of a large white house with roman style columns. It looked like the kind of house you might see on currency. I drove the Gremlin into the circular driveway and parked. Brett put my cock away and buttoned my pants. We got out together and walked to the front door. I knocked. Brett was sniffing her fingers. After a substantial wait an Hispanic maid opened the door. She had big tits strapped in a push up bra and bright red lipstick. Her white blouse and green skirt were two sizes too small.

"May I help you?" she asked, showing no hint of an accent.

"My name is William James, private detective," I said, showing her the wallet copy of my license. "I would like to speak to the owner of this house."

"Are you on television?" she asked.

"I am not on television."

"The only private detective I ever saw was on

television."

"I am a real private detective, not a TV detective," I told her.

"And he has a huge cock," Brett interrupted.

The maid looked at Brett. "Who are you?" she asked.

"I am his sidekick," Brett said, "I help him solve cases and hold his dick when he drives."

"That is a good job," she said to Brett. "Does he fuck you too?"

"Not when he is on a case, but after he solves one the boning goes for hours," Brett lied.

"My name is Juaneeda," she said to Brett. "I been thinking about giving up this whole maid thing and getting a gig as a sidekick, something where I can ride around helping a guy solve crimes, showing off my tits, and holding his cock while he drives. Do you suppose you could talk to me sometime about what it takes to land that kind of job?"

"Sure," Bret said, "I hang at Otto's."

"The biker bar?"

"Yeah, Come down any morning—"

"Hey," I interrupted, "are you going to get the owner of this house for me or not?"

"Sorry, Mr. James. Commissioner Philopad is not home."

"This is the home of Commissioner Philopad?"

"The one and only. But ever since last Sunday he's had to work long hours down at the warehouse? I haven't hardly seen a hair on his balls for close to a week." Down the hall, over Juaneeda's shoulder, appeared a young woman wearing a plaid Catholic schoolgirl's skirt. I shifted my head so Juandeeda's ample body hid my face.

"Who is it Juaneeda?" the young woman said.

"Just some private detective looking for your father, Miss Serenity," the maid answered.

"A private detective with a big cock?" the young woman demanded.

"That's what his sidekick says, Miss Serenity, but I ain't seen it myself." Serenity had reached the doorway. She pushed Juaneeda out of the way and stared me in the face.

"William James," she growled, "last time I seen you, you were screaming in pain as Big Bruna crushed your balls."

"Last time I seen you and your gang, Serenity, they were bare assed trying to figure out what to do with plaid skirts soaked in toilet water."

"Close the door, Juaneeda," Serenity ordered, "Mr. James and his whore are not welcome here." Juaneeda obeyed, making the 'I'll call you' hand sign to Brett as she did. The two of us were left standing on the porch of the house staring at the big white door.

Brett stared at her feet and touched one toe with the other. "That Mexican woman thought I was your whore," she said.

"Yep. That's what she said." The two of us walked together back to the Gremlin.

"I could be your whore," Brett said.

"What do you mean by that?" I asked.

"I mean I could be your sex slave and do disgusting sexual acts with other men—or women—for pay and then bring the money to you."

"I appreciate the offer, Brett, but no thanks."

"If you ever change your mind."

"I know who to call." We got back into the Gremlin and hit the streets.

"Where are we going now," Brett asked as she dug in my pants to resume her dick holding duties. We headed back toward the city.

"We are going to the warehouse. But first I have to stop at Totally Naked Women Here and then back at my office to get my gun." At the word gun, Brett squeezed my cock hard.

"Your gun," she said, jerking on my dick with renewed vigor.

"My gun," I said.

"Are you going to shoot somebody in the face with it?"

"Just for protection, Brett. Just for protection." She snuggled at my neck jerking my dick as we drove to the strip joint. We pulled up to the strip club as the lunch crowd was just thinning out. Inside Brett and I took a table. I ordered a patty melt. Brett had a bratwurst. Up on the stage Finger Mi was masturbating with a big green leek. Bjorn Fro joined us at the table. He stared hard at Brett.

"Are you traveling with her now?" he demanded of me.

"We will talk about it later Bjorn," I said, "Right now I need your help."

"What's up?"

"I got a new lead on the Pantz case. I told Teena that I would work the Milpy case this afternoon, but I can't. I need you to take over."

"Okay, William," he said. "Consider it handled."

"Take Miji if you want." Bjorn stared at his hands and said nothing. After an awkward silence I said. "Tell me, Bjorn. What's wrong?"

"Miji left me," he said. "She left me for a man with a smaller dick."

"I'm sorry," I said. "It isn't fair."

"I'm sorry too, Bjorn," Brett said. "I hate women who will leave a guy just because of the size of his dick. They are as bad as men who won't look at a woman because she doesn't have any tits to speak of. She might be able to suck the chrome off a trailer hitch, but it don't matter 'cause she doesn't have the melons to hang down while she does it."

"I have to go back to the office," I told him.

"To get his gun," Brett said.

Bjorn's eyes opened wide. "You are taking a gun?"

"I am."

We hadn't finished eating before Vagina Smooth and Chesty Tits-a-lot joined us. I filled them in on my progress in the Pantz case. I told them about my plan to go to the Acme parking meter pole warehouse in search of further clues, but made each of them swear on their mother's vagina that they wouldn't tell a soul. After a lively game of scrabble, Bjorn headed out to meet with Mrs. Milpy while Brett and I drove back to the office.

I parked the Gremlin the in the garage and we walked to Otto's. Outside the twenty speeds were lined up so thick we could hardly get to the door. The bikers were putting up crepe paper and blowing up balloons for the evening fund raiser. Otto waved to us as we walked through the bar to the stairs.

Half way up the steps to my office Bret and I heard screaming. It was Teena. We dashed up the remaining steps and I threw my shoulder at the door. It sprang open and I fell into the office with Brett behind me. Teena was on her back on the floor of the waiting room with her feet in the air. In between those long legs I saw a naked male butt bouncing up and down on her. The man was wearing a green sweater vest and penny loafers. They were fucking so energetically that Brett's and my noisy entrance made no impact. The white male butt kept pounding and Teena kept screaming.

I grabbed the man by the shoulders and threw him off my secretary just, it seems, as she orgasmed. I couldn't help but stare at her shaved pussy, now smeared with semen, as she spasmed on the floor. Then I looked to her attacker. There, sitting against the wall of my office, was Gerald Milpy. He had the green vest and loafers that he always wore. What I had never seen before was the huge cock he carried between his legs. It was as big or bigger than my own.

"Milpy," I yelled, "What the hell are you doing?" He said nothing. Teena struggled to sit up and grabbing a piece of typing paper, covered her cunt.

She looked to Milpy and said, "Gerald, it's over. We are caught." He nodded in agreement. "I'm sorry William," Teena said. "Gerald and I are in love. We have been using your office to meet. I know it was wrong, but we didn't know where else to go."

"Did you consider a motel?" I demanded.

"I mean," she said, "we didn't know any other place where a man could experience the thrill fucking the hell out of the secretary of a private detective while paying that same detective to fuck his own secretary."

Brett shook her head in sympathy with Teena and said, "That kind of sex is the best, William. You got to admit it."

"His secretary?" I said. "What do you mean his secretary?"

"Mrs. Milpy isn't Mrs. Milpy," Teena said, "She is Gerald's secretary. Gerald and I met at Bibble study. "

"You study the Bibble?"

"Yes, I do William. Some day I may become a bride of Chris. Gerald is my stock broker."

"You have a stock broker?"

"Yes, I do William. Gerald wanted to be able to slip away during the day so we could have time together. He sent his secretary to his house where she pretended to be his cheating wife. While you were taking pictures of Deshawnaneequa, he has been coming here to see me here at the office."

"Deshawnaneequa Jones?"

"That's right," Mr. Milpy said, "the older sister of Deshawnawanda."

"So Teena," I said sternly, "when you were all atitty because I had fucked Eb's sister, Deshawanawanda, you knew that I had also fucked his other sister, Deshawnaneequa."

"I did," Teena said.

"And you didn't say anything to me?"

"I couldn't, William. It would have meant exposing my afternoons with Gerald. I was blinded by love."

"What about Otto?" I felt a slap across the side of the head from Brett.

"Who is Otto?" Mr. Milpy asked.

"There is no Otto," Brett said to him. "William said we *ought to* get cleaned up if Teena is still planning to strip tonight." Teena gave me a shush with her finger.

"Yeah, that's what I said. I didn't mention any Otto." Milpy didn't pursue the matter.

I was in shock. Teena had deceived me. Not only was she a Bibble reader, she had tricked me into leaving the office so she could be with Gerald Milpy. Mr. Milpy had deceived me, and Mrs. Milpy wasn't Mrs. Milpy at all. Nothing it seemed, was as it seemed. I thought about poor Eb in the kitchen that day when Mrs. Milpy was dressed up like Aunt Jemima. There he was having to fuck his other sister while watching her suck my cock. Yet he did it all with the hope of becoming my sidekick. And what did I do? I kicked him aside for Brett, letting her hold my dick in the car. I couldn't count the ways in which I had violated the detective's code. I could hear Sam Spade and Philip Marlowe turning in their graves. Falling into Teena's chair I tried to make sense of it all.

Mr. Milpy pulled up his pants and lit a cigarette. Brett lifted naked Teena to her feet insisting that Teena had to start preparations for the show at Otto's. She got a pan of hot soapy water from the bar downstairs, dragged Teena into my office, and closed the door. Mr. Milpy and I were silent in the waiting room—he smoking, me thinking that the city had finally done its job on me. The task of getting Teena cleaned up turned out to be a noisy affair. At one point Brett came out of the office and got some K-Y jelly from Teena's desk announcing to us that it was better to be safe than sorry. The moaning, grunting, and obscenities coming from behind the door eventually drove Mr. Milpy and me down to the bar at Otto's where he spent two hours trying to sell me fixed annuities.

As Milpy and I nursed our RC's, Otto's began to fill with partiers. A man at the door held out a basket for donations to help end needless parking meter deaths, but most of the customers were more interested in the party than the cause. The women were decked out in their skimpiest riding clothes and the men wore spandex so tight you could tell whether they were circumcised. The liquor flowed and the bowls of granola were kept full. Milpy had seen enough and went home. I watched as a little biker chick started out the night by jumping up on the pool table and shaking her tiny titties for an appreciative crowd. She was soon replaced by another young woman in a miniskirt and purple thong. While she was wiggling her ass at the men around the pool table Brett and Teena came down from the office.

I figured Teena would be in the cheerleader outfit or the nurse uniform. I was shocked to see her dressed as a perfect replica of Velda, Mike Hammer's bombshell secretary. She wore a skin tight red dress with a plunging neckline that left no doubt as the fullness of the flesh beneath. Her legs were painted in dark nylon with seams up the back. Her feet were crammed in heels so high they gave me vertigo just looking at them. Every eye watched as she crossed the room and sat next to me.

"Doesn't she look great?" Brett said.

"Wonderful," I said. "What happened to the nurse and the cheerleader?"

"We meditated on the Holy Bibble," Brett said, "and decided that there was no reason to go to the nurse or the cheerleader when, in truth, nobody is hotter than the secretary for a private detective. We found those magazines in the bottom drawer of your desk and used the pictures as a guide."

"I just buy those magazines for the articles," I said.

"Do I look okay?" Teena asked, squeezing a handkerchief between in her hands.

"You look great," I told her.

"I have to remember everything that Brett taught me. I will get on the table trying to show just a little of the thigh above my stockings as I climb up. I dance slowly, turning around so that everybody gets to see my dress and stockings. Then I will carefully lower the zipper on the back of the dress, holding the front over my breasts to build suspense. I act embarrassed and try to blush while leaning over and giving the crowd a look at my cleavage. Then I let one tittie out and play with it. Then the other tittie, still holding the dress up around my waste. I need to dance and let my breasts bounce for a good ten minutes, remembering to bend over occasionally so that they hang down and sway. Brett says the men love that. Once I have fully shown what my tits can do, I let the dress fall to my ankles so everyone can see my garters and my thong. I then dance again for a while and when I sense the crowd wanting more I start pulling the crotch of the thong aside to give glimpses of my pussy. Eventually, I pull down the panties and, naked except for the stockings, I dance again, showing all my stuff in all directions so that no one gets cheated. It is all so much to remember. I don't know if I can do it."

"You will do fine," I assured her.

The assurances were not successful. Otto brought her another RC, but it did no good. She was getting more and more nervous as the night progressed and the time for her performance got closer. Brett comforted her, but I didn't feel good about it.

Finally Otto stood on the bar and yelled above the din of the crowd, "And now for our finale. Direct from the offices of Detective William James, our very own, and dearly beloved, Teena Tigbits." The crowed quieted. Teena slid off the bar stool and staggered toward the pool table through a path made by the bikers. At the edge of the green table she took a deep breath. She climbed up on the table giving a glimpse of white thigh as she did and the crowd gave a gasp. She stood on the table while both men and women bikers pushed toward her jostling for a better view. Teena looked out over the crowd and froze.

Dance, I thought. *Teena please dance.* But she was like a deer in headlights. The crowd was absolutely silent, and in that frightened silence there was an eroticism more intense than any I had ever experienced. Then Teena began to shake. It wasn't a dance, but rather a kind of palsy that ran up and down her body. Trembling, she violently pulled up her dress to reveal the red thong beneath. Holding the hem of the dress high, she pulled aside the crotch of the underwear to expose her shaved cunt. Looking out to the crowd she screamed, "FUCK ME. FUCK ME NOW."

The effect on the crowd was electric; men and women alike pulled off their clothes and clambered toward the table, crawling naked over one another to get to Teena. Bras, panties, boxers, spandex. Clothes were flying everywhere. Teena disappeared under a heap of writhing arms, legs, dicks and pussies. I saw the red dress fly away from the teeming pile of human flesh that had devoured not only Teena but the pool table itself. Otto, tearing off his clothes, climbed over the bar and leaped into the heap of flesh. Brett and I were left alone at the bar to watch in amazement.

"Aren't you jumping in?" I asked Brett.

"Been there, done that. Bought the t-shirt," she said.

"Come with me then. Let's go solve a kidnapping." We went up to the office. I took the Plinker from my desk and put it in my belt. When we came back downstairs the sweating, swearing, and groaning coming from the pile of humanity where the pool table used to be was even louder and smellier than when we had left. I said a quick prayer to the Holy Chris that Teena would get through it all right and we headed out the door.

A few minutes later we were in the Gremlin traveling the dark city streets with Brett holding my cock. The metal of the gun was as cold against my skin as Brett's fingers were warm along my cock. The chilly night air blew through the broken windows of the Gremlin and Brett snuggled against me for warmth. We drove to the warehouse district where men drive forklifts and women grow beards. There, behind a Romanian paprika outlet, I found what I was looking for. The small sign out front read, "Acme Industries, a division of Hydamony, Inc." I pulled into the parking lot and killed the engine.

"You have to stay here," I said to Brett.

"But why?" she protested. "I can help you."

"This is no job for a sidekick."

"You could be killed," she protested. "You owe it to me to let me at least blow you before you go in there."

She could tell by the look on my face that I couldn't say no. She threw her face into my crotch and sucked like it was that last cock she would ever suck. I leaned back in the car seat and stared at the Acme warehouse as her head went up and down on my dick. There was a light on in an upstairs window. As I watched and Brett sucked I saw a shadow in the room. Someone was up there. I shot my load into Brett's mouth. She swallowed like it was cold RC on a hot summer day. I picked up an old fast food napkin from the floor, wiped the cum off her lips and gave her a deep passionate kiss. We had come a long way since that

Monday morning, now almost a week ago, when she had me poke her bicep and asked me to feel her pussy. It is funny how things work in the city. What is crazy scary on Monday is a sidekick blowjob on Friday and you don't understand how it happened.

I got out of the Gremlin and started looking for a way into the warehouse. The front door was locked so I worked my way around the building. A side door was also locked but calling upon my detective experience I lifted the brown welcome mat in front of the door and found the cleverly hidden key. Inside the warehouse ambient light from large windows let me see well enough to make my way among the pallets of parking meter poles. I worked my way toward a stairs that led to offices on the second floor and I ascended slowly and silently, ever aware that I was not alone in the building.

At the top of the stair I faced a long hall with doors on either side. At the far end, light shown from beneath one of them. When I reached the light I found the door ajar. With my back against the wall I stood outside and craned my neck to look inside.

In the room I saw the vagina that had been haunting my dreams since I took the Pantz case—the vagina in the picture that Patty had given me—the vagina that had gotten me beaten up by Mrs. Mohammad—the vagina that had been the star attraction at Totally Naked Women Here—the vagina of Candace Pantz. The woman was naked, back to the wall, with her arms held up and apart by leather straps. She was facing a plump bald man wearing no pants and a naked woman with a huge dimpled ass.

"Bring back Patty," the man yelled at his captive. I knew the voice.

"I cannot," the woman pleaded. "Patty is gone forever."

The man waved his dick at the woman. "I know how to bring Patty back," he said, moving toward her.

"Do it if you must," the prisoner cried, "Patty is gone forever. Banished from this body by the power of the Holy Chris."

"Give her the bone," the fat woman said. "That will do it."

I stepped into the room and drew my weapon. "Stop right there, Filopad," I ordered. Filopad and the woman turned to face me. I now knew woman too. "Captain Natron?" I said.

"That's right, James," Filopad said. "Your beloved Captain Natron."

"What you doing here?" I asked her.

She shook her huge tits and scoffed. "I've been in on it the whole time. There never were any break-a-way poles. It was all a scam. While you were in there fucking the meter maids, Filopad and I were getting rich."

I turned my attention to the imprisoned woman. "Are you Candy Pantz?" I asked.

"Yes, sir," she said, "please help me."

I pointed the gun at the Captain. "Untie her," I ordered.

"You wouldn't shoot me," Natron said. "You've licked my clit and had your finger in my asshole."

"Try me," I said. Natron decided not to risk it and reached up to unbuckle the leather strap that held one of Candy's hands. The first strap was undone when my gun was knocked from my hand and clattered across the floor. Testicular pain shot up my body as I felt my balls being crushed. I pulled away from my attacker and fell to the floor. Above me stood Serenity and Big Bruna.

Serenity looked at Filopad. "Was this man bothering you, Daddy?"

"Thank you dear," Filopad said.

"Daddy," Serenity responded, "please cover up your cock. A daughter shouldn't see her father's big cock hanging out getting ready to fuck that Pantz whore."

"She is right, Commissioner," Natron said. Filopad picked up a small towel and held it over his cock. I lay on the floor in the fetal position holding my balls.

Serenity continued, "We will take Mr. James away if you are done with him. Bruna, I believe, has a couple of things she would like to do to him. When she is done, we will take him out to that farmer's outhouse pit he likes so much."

"Thank you dear," Filopad said. The two school girls began lifting me to my feet by the arms. As they lifted I closed my eyes to block out the pain shooting down my legs. The schoolgirls got me almost to my feet and dropped me. Pain shot up my spine as I fell and my eyes clamped shut. When I opened them I saw the Jones sisters, Deshawnawanda and Deshwananeequa, slamming the schoolgirls against the wall.

"I told you," Deshawnawanda screamed in Serenity's face, "never touch this man." The two black women held the girls against the wall. I crawled toward the Plinker while Natron and Filopad looked on in astonishment from the far wall. I was reaching for the pistol when I heard a gunshot. I rolled over to see Officer Buno with his service pistol aimed at my head.

"Don't touch the gun," he ordered. I pulled my hand back. "Bitches," he yelled at the Jones sisters, "up against the wall." The two sisters backed away from his gun. "Are you okay, Commissioner?"

"I am fine, Bruno," Filopad said. "Thank you."

"Just doing my job," Bruno said. Bruno forced me and the Jones sisters to stand against the wall while he stood in the open door with his gun aimed at us. He was quickly flanked by Serenity and Big Bruna. "What should I do with them?" Bruno demanded.

"The outhouse pit," Serenity suggested.

"Shoot them," Natron said. Everyone looked to Filopad for the answer. There was silence in the room as we awaited his decision.

He turned to Bruno and said, "Shoot them."

"No," cried Candy from her bondage. Bruno lifted his gun to fire. I closed my eyes and prepared to meet my maker. I heard the shot. Realizing I wasn't hit I opened my eyes to see Bruno's big cop body being buried in pile of soft stripper flesh. Vagina Smooth, Chesty Tits-a-Lot, and Finger me were on him wrestling the gun out of his hand. Up and to my left I saw a bullet hole in the warehouse window. Deshawanawanda dashed toward the mass of wrestling strippers and wrenched the gun from Bruno's hand.

"Vagina, Chesty," Patty cried from her bondage on the wall. "You saved me." Deshawnawanda held the gun on Bruno as he crawled out from beneath the pile of tits, tassels, and thongs.

"Against the wall, motherfucker," Deshawnawanda said to Bruno. He joined the pantless Filopad, the naked Capatain Natron, and the two catholic girls against the wall. The three strippers untangled themselves and worked on the straps that held Patty. When she was loose the four of them had a group hug that involved a lot tits being pressed against each other. I stood up and approached the four women while Deshawnawanda and Deshwananeequa watched over the bad guys.

"Are you Candy Pantz?" I asked the naked woman standing among the scantily clad strippers.

"I am," she said, "and you must be William James, private detective. I am so happy to finally meet you."

"But if you are Candy, where is Patty?"

Everyone in the room turned looked at me and said in unison, "Patty and Candy are the same person."

And there in the warehouse it all became clear to me. Candy Pantz and Patty Pantz were the same person. The similarity between the two pussies was no coincidence. The wigs in the apartment said a lot. And then there was the fact that Candy and Patty were never seen together.

"Aha," I exclaimed. I pointed at Candy. "By day a reference librarian with a thousand different sexual acts at her disposal—at night a kindly stripper with a heart of gold. The Patty I knew was the dark side in a psychological death match between your good self and your evil self. Turning to the Holy Bibble you, Candy, found a path by which you could exorcise Patty forever. You left your work and went to the convent at Fumbuck hoping to engage in a regimen of study that would leave Patty in the past, but when the sun came up and it neared time for the library to open, Patty asserted herself and made James King drive her to Filopad's house."

"You Filopad," I said, pointing to the commissioner, "you knew all of this. Candy came to you each night for counsel, but you had no intention of letting Candy exorcise Patty. You needed the librarian, not just for your own sexual perversions, but because she was one of the best reference librarians on the city payroll. You decided you would keep Candy a prisoner here, fuck her, and prevent her from carrying out her plan to become a Bride of Chris."

"You Serenity, with the help of your gang, tried to scare me off the case with the notes and by shooting out the windows in my car."

"And you, Captain Natron," I said, "you and Bruno were in on it. There were no break-a-way meter poles and you knew it from the beginning."

"I am very sorry, William," she said, putting her hand over her hairy pussy. "I got carried away by greed. I should have stood up for you and little Wilsha Dewit, but I didn't. I will carry the shame of it to my grave."

Bruno finally spoke up and said, "Well, I'm not sorry, James. You deserved everything you got, especially the dunk in the outhouse pit."

"Shut up, Hampster Dick," the Jones sisters said in unison.

Vagina Smooth, Finger Mi and Chesty Tits-a-lot covered Candy's nakedness and took her back to Totally Naked Women Here so she could recover from her ordeal and do a set or two before the place closed. Serenity and Bruna left because it was past their bed time and the two of them had school in the morning.

"What should we do with the commissioner and Bruno?" I asked the Jones sisters.

"They need to be punished," Deshawnawanda said.

"Make Filopad eat the old lady's pussy?" Deshawnaneequa said.

"While Bruno licks her asshole," interjected Brett who had suddenly appeared in the doorway.

"Hi Brett," I said, "I solved the case of the missing

Pantz."

"With a cock like yours," she said, "I knew you would."

"Okay boys," I said, "On your knees." Captain took her hand off her hairy crotch and giggled like a school girl.

"You boys be gentle now," she said. Filopad dropped and Natron flopped her big belly over his head. I could hear a gentle slurping coming from her crotch. Bruno kneeled behind her and pushed his face between her big mottled buns. Natron moved her hips back and forth pushing her pussy first into Filopad's face and then her asshole against Officer Bruno's mouth. Brett, who was now standing beside me, put her hand on my cock.

"This is very entertaining," she said. She took a small camera from her purse and took a couple of pictures of the three of them sucking, panting, and sweating. "A few of these pictures sent to the newspapers ought to put an end to these three stealing from the public." On Deshawnawanda's suggestion we rearranged the three of them so that Natron was on her hands and knees while the two men fucked her doggie style and in the face. Brett got some good pictures, one of which was on the front page of the city newspaper the next morning. In the weeks that followed, Commissioner Filopad, Captain Natron and Officer Bruno were driven out of government.

That night I took Brett home to my apartment and let her have her way with me until we were both exhausted.

The next morning Tena was at her desk when I got to work. Her face was flushed and she was sniffing her fingers.

"For God's sake, Teena, give it a break," I said.

"Someone called," she told me. "A woman. She says her cousin in missing. She was referred to you by Candy Pantz."

"Did she make an appointment?"

"She is coming in an hour."

"When she gets here, send her in."